Blossom
and
Bone

MARY E JUNG

<u>Books by Mary E Jung</u>

The Etrucian Royals Series

Queen of Light and Ashes
Queen of Light and Valor

The Libra Witch Series

Blossom and Bone

Standalones

The Socrates
Sanctuary Anthology (NYT #1 Bestselling Author
Sherrilyn Kenyon Fan Publication)
For the Love of Gettysburg Anthology

For My Sister,
courageous scientist and true believer in magic.

Author Note

As you journey through this book, please note that Xephriel, the main male character, has bouts of anxiety and panic attacks. They are not extreme but should be noted for those who have experience with these symptoms. He has a degree of neurodivergence that causes his magic to back fire. You will discover more about this in the book. Out of respect for Xephriel and his story, I've developed this book in a way that will make him feel comfortable while exploring the possibility of a happily ever after. After all, love is more powerful than anything. Amé is very nurturing, but she's a people pleaser. I note this for people who struggle with this personality type and need a heads-up. I take her on a journey to find self-confidence and learn how to fight for what is truly right. She's highly intellectual and loveable. I believe her story is one worth rooting for.

Chapter 1

The Kingdom of Libra
on the Island of Khaos

5,023 Years After the Creation of the World Egg

Amé Floreo, an erudite vegetation witch, lived in Aequitas, the capital of Libra. Her rose-pink shop on Soul Street was nestled between an apothecary and a bone consultation establishment. "Seeds of Love," the name of her store, was painted across the azure signboard in stunning gold calligraphy. White gingerbread trim gave the three-story architecture a beguiling ambiance. The sun dispersed rainbow streams of light that refracted off the crystal hearts embedded in the window frames.

Inside the welcoming plant shop, Amé bent over a wooden worktable in her research lab. She squinted at the magic flower mate doing its damndest to evade her scalpel. "Hold still, please. I need to collect your seeds."

In rebellion, the head of the mutated orchid jerked to the right. The crimson salverform petals fanned outward like a shepherdess bonnet, and the stamens wiggled in protestation. The stem swiveled as if it were dancing, and she watched the leaves bend inward. Amé planted her hands on her hips, mimicking the obvious gesture, and glared at the cheeky Rogue of Fire flower mate.

Witch-made plants had a degree of cognizance and communicated through intuition or telepathy. Amé's flower mates were unique, the only species to exist on the Island of Khaos. Magic and non-magic blossoms had been cross-bred to produce humanoid plants that walked, talked, and interacted with mortals and witches. The plants that housed the flower mates grew to be the size of a horse, but Amé harvested the seeds when they were still juvenile and fit in a pot.

She braced her hands on the edge of the table and narrowed her earthen-brown gaze. The Rogue of Fire orchid, a type of flower mate designed to bring out carnal appetites and a blatant disregard for rules, bobbed from its buried roots to its stigma. It receded a fraction, deceptively showing deference, but without warning, it shot forward and dispensed pollen into Amé's face.

Amé coughed as she sucked in a mouthful of yellow dust and waved her hand in front of her face. "Now that was uncalled for," she admonished the flower mate.

She was rewarded by the petals curling inward, covering the ovary, and refusing to part with its seeds. Unreasonable, that was the characteristic the client had asked her to replicate. It was clear she succeeded. Amé challenged nature, and now she was arguing with a stubborn orchid that wanted to drive her into a frenzy.

Annoyed by the adverse opinions of the Rogue of Fire flower mate, Amé grumbled, "Your powers of seduction and sass will not work on me, my friend. Cease this display of protestation. I'm getting those seeds, and I'd like to gather them with your cooperation if you don't mind."

With a flare of her aura, green magic infused the plant, and her instructions were infused into the plant. Resigned to its seed-collecting fate, the Rogue of Fire flower mate opened its blood-red petals and remained still. She raised her brows, waiting for the orchid to start its banter again, but it kept its inferred promise and behaved.

Under normal circumstances, Amé would have handed the seed to the customer to plant and nourish, but this was a new species. She wanted to be sure no botanical issues arose as it grew. The seeds would also be valuable research material and additional merchandise she could stock.

Angling the scalpel toward the ovary, she made a cut, then held the hole open to collect the seeds with tweezers. "I know it isn't comfortable, but it will feel better in a couple of hours. Your cells regenerate at a rapid rate. You'll be as large as a melon by nightfall, and the cut will be completely forgotten. I'm going to send you on to your mortal mate now that I've collected the seeds. Safe journey. Try not to be too rakish. I know she asked for a challenge, but you are a devil of the finest caliber."

The petals swayed, and a warm red glow radiated through the veins of the flower mate. Despite the exasperating personality of the Rogue Fire orchid, Amé knew a gregarious characteristic balanced the overall effect. Amé added a cup of plant food, a dash of bone powder, and two cups of water to the pot to help speed up the healing process. She wiped her hands on a rag and departed the room to begin her day of selling.

Her flower mates began as a curiosity, a way to solve the questions of 'what is true love and how is it obtained?' The project transformed into her greatest achievement.

Amé had various premade seeds for convenience, but most of her orders were for a unique flower mate. The most popular was the black dahlia. When it bloomed, the black dahlia produced petals the color of the night sky. The flower mate caused sweet heartbreak like a good book that purged the heart through consuming catharsis. Though the black dahlia evoked profound emotions, it also gave the sower a perception of rebirth. Like a phoenix rising from the ashes, the person felt renewed after their excruciating love match.

Amé was strict when communicating that her services did not deliver real love. Clients had to sign a contract to purchase a flower mate. One seed per person. No refunds, no resales, and no coming back in six months for a different seed personality or species. Amé cautioned her customers about becoming obsessed with fantasy. Live in the moment and seek the truth; it was her steadfast moto. Real, binding emotions occurred in the world with people. She was selling a way to learn about the heart's desires, a way to access the deepest secrets of love and explore unknown possibilities. She was not custom-designing a life partner.

Amé parted the curtains of her display window. Soul Street's pastel buildings lined one-next-to-the-other in a hodgepodge of architecture. She watched a few pedestrians stroll by her shop. Their gait was lethargic as they enjoyed the start of the day. Bookshops, cafés, and nick-nack boutiques opened their doors for business. Out of the corner of her eye, she noticed a customer enter the building to her right. The Humerus, the bone consultation establishment, was as conspicuous on Soul Street as the full moon against the night sky.

The Humerus was a charcoal-black two-story structure with exquisite crimson plate tracery. An intricate system of skeleton parts decorated the architraves and in between the painted bricks. As mysterious as the morbid beauty of the Humerus was, it did not compare to the bone witch proprietor, Xephriel Maxis.

Every time Amé glanced next door, a ferocious curiosity overtook her mind. She felt compelled by Xephriel's enigmatic nature. His esoteric persona was pronounced by his distinctive midnight black hooded coat. Xephriel was a reticent witch but always offered a small wave by way of greeting when their paths crossed. She caught a few murmured salutations over the years, but his conversations did not last beyond brief social politeness. He was a bit weird, but she liked Xephriel and made a point to encourage their acquaintanceship.

Her mind shifted from the curiosities of her neighbor and returned to the preparation of her business.

She fussed with a cluster of daffodils and took a whiff of a wine-hued lily on the tiered display pedestal. Languid tendrils of baby ferns brushed her cheek as she turned away from the window. She flipped the sign hanging on the door to show her store had opened and proceeded toward a corner to grab a broom to sweep.

The bells above Amé's door chimed. A mortal woman, for she emitted no signature magic aura of a witch, strolled through the doorway in a pale yellow silk gown. Decorative ties interlaced at her bust, and the lines of the chemise dress draped to her ankles.

Amé came over to assist the woman with her browsing. "Good morning! What brings you into Seeds of Love today?"

The woman turned in her direction and blinked as she responded. "Good morning! I was admiring the beautiful crystal hearts along the window frames of your shop and thought I'd look inside."

"I'm glad you joined me this morning. The crystals were a gift from my grandmother when I decided to enter the world of retail. She said they would bring me luck, devotion, and clarity."

"Wow, what a lovely story. How long have you been a florist?"

Amé let the memories of Seeds of Love color her tone as she replied, "Seven years. It's been an absolute joy."

The woman gazed at a morning glory on a nearby shelf. "That's wonderful! You know, I've never bought a plant before. I've received them as gifts, of course, but I thought I'd choose one for myself."

Amé listened to the woman articulate her purpose for visiting her shop, then gave a decisive nod. "Yes! I think I may be able to find a companion for you. May I ask for your name?"

"Companion?" The woman straightened from her examination of the flower. "What do you mean?"

"Oh! Flowers are like people. They desire friendship, loyalty, and love. Caring for a plant reveals a whole new piece of the heart. Just like a friend, don't you think?"

The woman's eyelashes batted, and a small "o" shaped her mouth. "That is a beautiful sentiment. I love how you describe plants. My name is Martha, and I'd be happy for your assistance as I choose a plant companion to take home."

"Martha, it's a pleasure to meet you. I am, Amé. This shop carries magic and non-magic plants. We can browse whichever you like. I'd like to know a little about your lifestyle so I can discover which plant will suit you best."

Martha untied her straw hat and let the ribbons fall around her shoulders but did not remove it from her head. "Well, let's see. I have three lovely children: one girl and two boys. So, I like to have sturdy and enduring things in my house in case one of them gets too rowdy. My husband and I have known each other since we were adolescents. He's still as charming today as he was when he asked to court me. We have a cat who loves to play with mice and brings them to me as presents. I love to sew clothes, and I'm learning how to make shoes from a friend who owns a shop on Fashion Street."

"Sounds like your family has given you many happy memories. Shoe-making is impressive, and perhaps you will show me a pair when you have perfected your craft. Let me see what plants I can offer you. A companion that will be forgiving if you do not water it right away and will survive if the cat or children knock it over. Let me think about that a minute."

Martha's eyes crinkled with mirth at the edges as she said, "I'm in no rush. I look forward to whichever plant you think will be a good fit. Although, I request it is a non-magic selection."

Amé moved about the room, listening to the whispers of various plants. She stopped by a shelf of exotic mings she had received in shipment from the kingdom of Aurum. A Dwarf Ming Aralia tree chattered to a mini Han Orange tree as Amé debated which plant would suit Martha best. She stroked a leaf of the Dwarf Ming Aralia, and it made a whimsical sound in response.

"Do you wish to go home with the lovely Martha?" She asked the Dwarf Ming Aralia and picked up the potted tree.

"Are you speaking to the plant?" Martha's sea-foam-green gaze widened.

Amé explained, "Plants have a unique language, even if they are not witch-made. Vegetation witches can interpret messages that other people may not hear. Plants respond to me differently than other people."

"I would never have guessed so much went into plant purchases."

Amé leaned her ear toward the small tree, and a few leaves reacted to her magic by brushing against the side of her neck. "Oh, good. We have a match. Your Dwarf Ming Aralia tree would very much like to go home with you and would appreciate it if you found a windowsill that allowed for the most light in the house."

"Will I—Will I have to speak with it?"

"No need to worry. Plants are resilient and intuitive. You will know what to do even without hearing what it says. Now, you should water it once a week. It can go longer, but don't let the soil get unbearably dry. Keep it in sunlight. It will be fine in the winter so long as it can access a lot of light. It won't grow fast, so you will not have to prune it regularly."

Martha inched forward and reached for the plant. "How wonderful!"

"Yes, I believe it is a great match." Amé placed the Dwarf Ming Aralia tree between Martha's hands.

"How much is it?"

"Four gold libras, please." It was an expensive plant, but it did come from halfway around the world.

"I'll have to be careful with it."

"No need to worry," Amé assured Martha, who was looking hesitant now that the price was involved. "It is an enduring plant. You will have it for a long time, and your lifestyle will not daunt it. I think it will embrace the excitement."

Martha's shoulders relaxed, and she shuffled to the front counter to set down her plant. She opened her purse and selected four gold coins. "Thank you for all your help. I am so happy I decided to come into your shop."

"It was wonderful to meet you, Martha. I have cosmetics and skin products, too, if you wish to come another day and look around." She indicated a display shelf full of her signature lavender collection.

Martha tapped her index finger against her lips. "Yes. Let me look at those, too."

A few minutes later, Martha departed Seeds of Love with one Dwarf Ming Aralia tree, a box of lavender skincare products, and one tonic for her hair. Amé counted five gold libras and two silver libras, totaling one hundred and ten libras. She did a little happy dance with her feet and plopped the money into her cash register. Looking at the clock on the wall behind her counter, she saw it was still three and a half hours until lunch.

She strolled over to a fountain, where she kept a watering can. Dipping the small container into the basin, she filled it with water and turned to hydrate her plants. Amé listened to their murmur of pleasure as moisture soaked into the soil. Blossoms and leaves leaned toward the sunshine to suffuse their chlorophyll with light.

Grabbing a bucket containing plant food from behind her counter, she measured half a cup full and poured it into the first pot. Once she was finished feeding her saplings, flowers, and shrubs, she swept the floor and dusted her counter surface. Another chime from the bells above her door signaled a visitor.

Sylvia, her best friend of twenty years, marched through the doorway in a flourish of cheer. Her pink witch aura glowed over her café au lait skin, and a sweet harmonious chord struck against Amé's senses. Amé thought she noticed a flicker of orange, but it didn't signify more than a passing glance.

Sylvia greeted her from the middle of the storefront. "Amé! How is my favorite person on the world egg?"

"Am I ranked above your husband?" Amé teased and leaned the broom against the wall so she could hug her friend.

Sylvia wrapped her arms around Amé's shoulders and gave a tremendous squeeze. "You and Beaux are equal in my heart. It's lovely to see you. Just like yesterday, and the day before that, and every morning since our mothers had tea for the first time."

Amé leaned her head against Sylvia's shoulder. "It was the best day of our lives."

Sylvia pulled away and delivered a wink before she said, "I look forward to seeing you at Witch's Brew for lunch. I have a surprise for you."

"Oh? What is it?"

"It wouldn't be a surprise if I told you!"

"Can't you tell me now?"

Sylvia crossed her arms and buzzed her lips once. "I want you to try to guess. You love puzzles."

"True," She conceded and gripped her chin as she mused, "I like mysteries, and nothing excites me more than riddles and games."

"Don't forget the little wooden pieces designed to drive a person mad!"

Amé chuckled at Sylvia's description of a jigsaw puzzle. "Those too! I like geometry and organization. What can I say? The pictures turn out so beautiful once you get everything in the right spot." She pointed to a wall where a framed picture of a cactus hung. "I did that one last week."

Sylvia feigned a headache and rubbed her temples as if she were in a dramatic play. "Imagining all those little oddly shaped bits frustrates me."

"Well, good thing I'm the puzzler then."

"Yes, and I love that part of your personality. I must be off! I have to open the restaurant with Beaux."

Amé gave Sylvia another hug then peeked around her shoulder as another customer entered Seeds of Love. "I'll see you later."

Sylvia broke away. "Have a great morning! I'll see you at lunch."

As the new witch looked about her storefront, a magenta aura radiated around his body like a second skin, signaling he was a witch. Like animals sensing intent, witch magic behaved in a similar fashion.

A slight vibration tuned to Amé's magic and her witch sight sensitized to the etheric field. As she adjusted to the other witch's aura, a discordant screech transpired. A pleasant monotone settled between them, and there was once again harmony resonating between their magics. Amé's witch instincts recognized the customer was approachable, and she proceeded to engage him in conversation.

"How can I help you today?" Amé asked the witch, and he turned to her with equal affability.

His lips spread into a smile. "I am here to find plants to enhance my studio space. I was told you are the best at matching the appropriate plant to the desire of a customer."

Amé felt pride at hearing her skills were appreciated. "Thank you. I would also like to thank whoever expressed their sentiments to you."

"Dorothia Thackary, my younger sister, has a lovely greenhouse filled with flowers and shrubs from your store."

Sudden recognition elucidated the witch's identity. "Oh! Mr. Thackary, it's a pleasure to meet you. Dorothia has spoken highly of you every time she comes here."

"She does enjoy your company." Mr. Thackary took off his gloves and put them in his pocket as he perused a shelf of potted roses.

"She mentioned you were a painter. I would love to see your work," Amé enthused and watched as Mr. Thackary made a turn about her shop.

Amé noted he had similar features to Dorothia. They both had sandy blond hair that was fine and soft. Rosy cheeks added a youthful quality to their countenances, and cheery blue eyes mimicked a tropical lagoon.

Mr. Thackary faced her as he said, "Maybe we can help each other today. You can find me beautiful flowers, and I will bring you a picture that will take your breath away the next time I visit Seeds of Love."

"You're very kind, Mr. Thackary. Let's see what I have in the greenhouse." She turned on her heel and padded toward a bright bubble-gum pink door that led to a back courtyard.

Mr. Thackary followed, and a peaceful mood settled over their conversation. They entered her greenhouse. She had to pay a little extra rent to have more space behind her building, but it was worth every silver libra. She held out her hand and waved to encompass her collection.

Mr. Thackary took in the plethora of vegetation encased in the glass area. "I can see why my sister is so envious of your shop. Most of the plant selections I have not seen before."

Amé pointed to her latest investment. "I'm waiting to install the newest solar technology on the roof panels. I won't have to hoist the delicate plants up to the second floor during the winter months anymore."

"It's lucky we don't have much of a winter here, and it rarely snows. We're lucky when it gets to forty degrees. I imagine the conditions of the island are ideal for growing flowers." Mr. Thackary brought his interest to her again and strolled farther into the greenhouse.

"My plants aren't complaining, and neither will I once I get the panels in place."

He remarked, "Indeed, I would think it's convenient to have all the plants in one spot year-round."

She ran a hand over the leaves of a tiger lily and looked up to meet Mr. Thackary's gaze. "Without a doubt.

Let's resume your shopping. I have a lot of vibrant and inspiring choices, but some of the plants can require a lot of care and delicate handling."

"That will not be a problem. I would like to take time away from my work to rejuvenate my ideas. I think caring for a few flowers may help stimulate my artwork."

"How about Bleeding Hearts, then?" Amé swished between the rows of plants, not minding the hem of her pink gown getting muddy and wet from the damp ground.

Mr. Thackary's lips turned down a smidge, and he scrunched his eyebrows at her preference of flower. "I do not have the expertise you do, Miss Floreo, but why did you suggest such a melancholy name?"

"Oh, but they are not a despondent flower in the least! Bleeding Hearts are a vivid pink and beat with a steady rhythm from their style. They are one of my favorite magic flowers, and when they wilt, their petals secrete red nectar that can be used for dyes. Or, if I'm being bold, paint for your masterpieces. They can be very finicky. Do not disturb them, and make sure to pay close attention if they need to be repotted. You will need to pair them with other flowers because they do not bloom long, but when they do, you will surely be inspired." She indicated the

Bleeding Hearts hidden among hydrangeas and magic canary flowers.

Mr. Thackary peered over her shoulder. "Wow, they are extraordinary. I see that the other pot has a few flowers dripping with the nectar. The color will make an exquisite dye. I will take a couple of clusters of these."

"Let me get a cart for your choices. I'll be right back." She paused at the end of the greenhouse and rolled a wooden wagon back toward Mr. Thackary.

After settling the flower pots, Amé turned down a row to show Mr. Thackary the Verbena. "I love the variety of colors Verbenas produce. I cross the species to get as many shades as possible in a pot. Verbena adds a lot of artistry to a room. They attract butterflies and need full sun. You can water them once every couple of weeks, but make sure there is a way for the pot to drain. You will also have to cut off the dead blossoms regularly." She drew a pair of shears from her apron pocket and snipped off a flower at the base of the pistil to demonstrate.

Mr. Thackary placed two Verbena clusters next to the Bleeding Hearts. "I like these as well. One more, I think. How about a flower that calls to my witch soul?"

Amé wheeled the cart, counting four aisles across from her position, and directed her path toward her witch-made plants. She came to a flower that mimicked the sun. Strands of orange light flowed through saucer-shaped petals, and the center stigma blinked like a firefly. Long, lanceolate leaves bowed outward, and a thick, sturdy stem, about twelve inches high, held the blossom head in place. Citrus and sugar nectar combined to give the flower its unique perfume.

"This is called a Sol flower. It emits the light it soaks up. The more sun it gets, the stronger its scent and magic. It will get more yellow or more orange depending on the season."

Mr. Thackary leaned forward and sniffed at the anther of the Sol Flower. "How do I care for it?"

"I will send a list of instructions home with you. This one will need to be sprayed with water instead of the soil being drenched. It needs constant sunlight year-round. Because it is a magic flower, you will need to feed it the special nutrients I mix up here in my shop. I'll give you an extra sample today with your purchase. It is a delicate flower, so do not repot it. Let it do its thing."

"Excellent. I love all the selections we've made today, and I'm ready to conclude my purchase." Mr. Thackary helped her roll the cart to the front of the store while Amé carried the Sol flower.

They entered the shop again, and Amé calculated the price of each plant, filled a bag with nutrients, a bag with the soil she made for magic plants, and then waited while Mr. Thackary placed his purchases inside his carriage. Mr. Thackary handed her a total of three hundred and fifteen libras. Amé deposited the coins into her cash drawer before waving farewell. As Mr. Thackary trotted off down the street, Hennley, her apprentice, entered Seeds of Love.

Hennley Redding was a rosaceae witch, though she was marvelous with all plants. She attended classes at the witch academy in the morning and then apprenticed in Amé's shop until four in the afternoon. Amé adored Hennley and was grateful for the extra help.

Hennley had a deep red cotton gown on that heightened her freckled complexion. Slipping an ivory-crocheted satchel off her shoulder, Hennley plopped it on the counter as she greeted Amé. "Good morning, Amé!"

"Good Morning, Hennley! How were classes?"

Hennley scrunched her nose. "Professor Nettle is strict and stuffy. He makes foreign language class boring. I did learn about Bittersweet Nightshade in my botany lesson!"

"Oh, do tell! I love to hear about the academy." Amé selected a glass cup from the shelf under her counter and handed it to Hennley to fill at the fountain.

Hennley sent her a grateful smile and grasped the glass. Meandering over to the fountain, she tipped the lip of the cup into the trickling water. After taking a sip, she recounted her day. "Professor Berkley showed us a beautiful diagram she hand-painted on one of her expeditions to the southern coast of Libra. I love star-shaped blossoms the best, and Bittersweet Nightshades have a brilliant violet tone. So beautiful, and yet in the wrong dose, it's instant death."

Amé drummed her fingers on her arms as she recalled her poison lessons. "Yes, do not get on the wrong side of a deadly nightshade witch. They are the most fierce of poison witches. Although witches who study poisons and venoms aren't usually evil, it's a good idea to proceed with caution."

Hennley took a long gulp of water before saying, "There are a few witches who concentrate on poison in my school. I've only spoken to them during study sessions for botany class. They gossip about Blood Street. It sounds like a horrible place to live or work."

"Blood Street is one of those necessary evils the kings and queens ignore. They allow a witch like the Taxidermist to oversee the entire street. His vile magic is the reason the insanity wing in the hospital is overrun."

Hennley's shoulders twitched in repulsion, and she set down her empty glass on a nearby table. "My parents have whispered about what happens on Blood Street. Necromancers, blood potions, and poison are a few professions they mentioned. I know about the Taxidermist by reputation and rumor in Aequitas."

"Most people are aware of his magic. He is a despicable witch. He sells enchanted suits made of witch and mortal skin on the black market. The magic hide sticks to a person like their real skin, transforming the living person into the image of the dead one. That's only one of his horrible talents."

"I'm going to be sick," Hennley placed a hand over her mouth and worked her throat muscles as she swallowed.

"Aye." Amé brushed her fingers through her long mahogany tresses. "He is evil. Imagine walking around in someone else's skin. The scary part is, you could be speaking to a person and have no idea they were an entirely different visage."

"How do you know so much about the Taxidermist? You're a vegetation witch living on Soul Street. Blood Street is on the other side of the city." Her lips turned down, souring her expression as if she tasted filth.

Amé drummed her fingernails against the marble of her counter. "Before I developed flower mates, I was an herb consultant on Healing Street. I would dispense medicine in the incurable disease department at the hospital when they were understaffed. I haven't renewed my witch potion license since I opened Seeds of Love. You can only work or volunteer at the hospital if you have a certificate from the witch council saying you are cleared to develop, mix, and dispense medicine to patients. I can't go into details about the patients I cared for, but I can inform you that the Taxidermist's magic put those people in the hospital."

Hennley grabbed Amé's hand, giving it a light squeeze. "Your experience as a vegetation witch always inspires me. Those poor people! It must be terrifying to live with an incurable disease brought on by a maniac. I'll be sure to stay far away from Blood Street."

"Not all blood, poison, and witches dealing with death work on Blood Street. I have a witch acquaintance who owns a blood dispensary on Healing Street called Ichor.

She helps people who need transfusions or witches who have rare diseases from magic disorders. Be careful what rumors you listen to."

"Yes, Amé."

Amé waved her hand as if to clear the air of the bitter topic. "I'll be in the greenhouse until lunch. Holler if you need assistance."

"Will do," Hennley trotted around the counter and slid out a ledger that had a checklist of things to do for the shop. "See you after lunch, boss."

Chapter 2

Xephriel Maxis rested his chin on his clasped fingers as he listened to a vexed mortal. Mrs. Rendell had come to his bone consulting business, the Humerus, to inquire about a finger bone. She suspected the phalanx might have belonged to her missing husband. Mrs. Rendell fidgeted with the leather strap of her purse as she stared at him in mournful silence. Dim orange candlelight cast shadows on her pitiful features, and he felt her distress as if it were his own.

Xephriel's magic created an overwhelming empathic dissonance with people, and it caused him physical pain. The layer of epidermis that conducted magic was sensitive, and his mind was potent with activity. As a result, he was untouchable and absorbed magic, auras, and emotions in excess. He was a sponge for other people's feelings and a magnet for all things supernatural.

A tingle of nerves through his being signaled that the power of the bones was easing the empathic condition that manifested from the proximity to Mrs. Rendell's grief. Before her emotions could be sucked into his body, the bone magic dissipated and scattered her projections into the etheric field. He watched as the bones embedded into his building glowed to match his indigo aura, indicating that it was safe for him to proceed with the consultation.

He watched as Mrs. Rendell drew a black velvet box from her silver embroidered handbag and pushed it across the table surface. Xephriel noted the crow bones in his divination table glowed red in reaction to the box's contents. The bone inside the velvet box produced a terrifying energy that clashed against his aura and produced screeching turbulence. His neck stiffened as he cringed against the facsimile of nails clawing down a chalkboard.

Xephriel's indigo aura radiated off his body and veiled the room. A dull wobble of sound waves echoed as his psychic senses merged with the bones fixed in the maroon-tinged table. He felt his magic activate and stared at the bones that would help decipher the message from the dead.

Crow claws and beaks had been arranged in a complex pattern of bone language. The symbols read death, transformation, destiny, and reciprocity. Crows were carrion birds that consumed death and transferred the power of the spirit world into their blood and marrow. He traced the intricate scripture with his pointer finger and summoned his spirit guides.

Static made the hair on his arms rise as the dead souls of the crows responded. The messenger spirits fluttered through the veil between the spirit world and the physical plane. They perched on the table, his shoulders, and fluttered in the air to protect him from malevolence. The air became denser, the crows using their magic to seal Xephriel and Mrs. Rendell in an invisible shield of protection.

Satisfied they were guarded against malicious magic, Xephriel picked up the black velvet box and lifted the lid. Inside was an adult middle phalanx for a ring finger. He watched a faint lime green aura glow around the bone, and a steady sensation like a heartbeat pulsed against his palm.

Xephriel rolled the phalanx bone forward, then backward, between his index finger and thumb. Most mortals did not radiate a visible aura when they were alive. When they died, their souls were imprinted on the bones, and that created enough residual energy for a bone witch to divine.

"Is it his bone?" Mrs. Rendell inched closer and twisted her fingers.

"Maybe." Xephriel acknowledged Mrs. Rendell's question, but he did not remove his gaze from the phalanx bone. "Mr. Rendell," He addressed the bone in his hand, his tone authoritative and resonating with a baritone.

Mrs. Rendell jumped with a bit of a whimper and wrung the front of her dress. "Is he here?"

"Mr. Rendell." Xephriel ignored her question and continued to communicate with the spirit world. His magic was a command to souls, and they usually flocked to the power of his words.

"I'm here." A soft tenor voice echoed from the bone, and the green light flickered as each word was enunciated.

"Khaos, save me. That's his voice!" Mrs. Rendell leaned over the table, and moisture glistened from her astonished stare.

"Mr. Rendell, where are you?" Xephriel listened for a reply. The spirit crows settled on the table and pecked at the black box.

Mrs. Rendell scurried back, trembling as she pointed. "Who is moving the box?" Her voice hitched on a squeak.

"Crow spirits. They won't harm you." Xephriel informed Mrs. Rendell. His tone was even as he concentrated on establishing a connection to the spirit world.

"I'm here." Mr. Rendell's soul resonated louder as the link to the etheric plane became stronger with the assistance of Xephriel's magic. The bone became a beacon of green against the black of his gloved hand.

"Where do your bones lay?" Xephriel could get souls to lead him to their bodies, but the channel between the dead and the living was more accessible with the recently departed. As the body decayed, the soul drifted farther from its physical presence. Mr. Rendell had been missing for eight months, according to his wife. It took more magical effort to bring Mr. Rendell's soul through the veil separating the physical plane.

"It is dark and cold. It has been painful. So, so painful."

Xephriel heard a rustle of trees in the ether. His magic was picking up on the environment around Mr. Rendell's bones. "Are you in a forest or garden?"

"I am deep. Deep down."

"Mr. Rendell, I hear trees. Are you buried in a forest?" On occasion, spirits needed questions repeated because the message they received through the etheric field got distorted. Bone magic bridged the gaps, but the soul required time to articulate the same way it could when inside its body.

"I am underground, but I wasn't meant to be."

"He was a landscaper. He built parks throughout the city," Mrs. Rendell supplied. She was pressed against a wall toward the front of the consultation room. She swallowed. Her throat muscles were clenched as she spoke around her ebbing fear. "I didn't know what to do when I got that box this morning, but it was the right decision to bring it here."

"We'll find him. Let's let him talk to us, so we don't lose the connection." He gentled his voice. Xephriel tried again to glean more information from Mr. Rendell's soul. "Do you know where you are, Mr. Rendell?"

"I am trapped. I am down. Deep down. It is cold. There is pain. So much pain. Trees. I love trees. I hear them now."

Xephriel became silent like death and closed his eyes. He listened to the crow spirits guiding him into the etheric field and tracked a gold metaphysical thread from the bone to Mr. Rendell's spirit. Ancestral magic could take Xephriel's mind and part of his soul beyond the physical plane. Witches called realm walking, or temporary separation of the body, "astral projection."

Mr. Rendell's silhouette floated out of the black etheric field, an amaranthine haze overlaying the world around them. Xephriel followed Mr. Rendell through the realm of spirits and unfading memories. Xephriel searched for the location of the body by tugging on the metaphysical thread that was bound to Mr. Rendell's soul.

He watched as Mr. Rendell stretched his hand as if feeling for a presence, and a shadow door appeared. Physics didn't operate the same way in the spirit world, and like a dream, things could materialize or disappear at the whim of the one controlling the subconscious. Xephriel's magic was guiding them, but Mr. Rendell was the one making decisions.

Mr. Rendell pushed the door open, and a brilliant light shone across the threshold. The light crept upward, filling the space beyond. Xephriel drifted through the white interdimensional passageway, and on the other side was an illusionary garden.

Wistful purple clematis wove around an iron trellis. A winding slate stone path led to an opulent gazebo decorated with hanging multicolored glass beads. As Xephriel glided along the path, Mr. Rendell's spirit jerked to the left. The mystic thread pulled Xephriel's astral projection around a bed of thyme, sage, and lavender. Pumpkins and lush hydrangea bushes filled the picturesque view. Pastel colors mixed with burgundy celosia complemented the artistic composition of the garden.

"There." Mr. Rendell pointed to a large circular stone structure.

Xephriel shifted to the edge and looked down. "A well?"

"Yes. A well I built. This is one of my gardens." Mr. Rendell exhaled as if his soul felt relief.

"Mr. Rendell. I have your finger bone. Did you have an accident? Is that how you passed on?"

Mr. Rendell shook his head no and stared at his palms. In his soul form, Mr. Rendell was not missing any digits, and the confusion was clear as he elucidated on his death. "My finger was collected."

"Collected?" Xephriel wanted to be sure he understood Mr. Rendell. Bone collectors were not dangerous, but a few became obsessed with their possessions. Some harvested their specimens from living mortals and witches.

"Yes," Mr. Rendell confirmed and hovered over the well. "It was cut off and taken. I cannot know peace until all my bones are together and I am found."

"We will take your body out of the well. I can promise you that. Do you know how your body ended up in the well?"

"No. I cannot remember. None of us can remember."

Xephriel looked around as souls began to fill the memory. He counted three total, not including Mr. Rendell. "I'm so sorry you are all trapped."

"Remove us from the well, find our bones, and we will rest in peace."

Xephriel linked his psyche to his body and faded out of the etheric realm. His astral projection glided through dimensions, a kaleidoscope of colors and shapes morphed around his vision. He was dizzy, turned upside down, backward, and shot forward like an arrow until he found the shadow door. A white light blinded his sight, and he was once more a cohesive unit.

Xephriel closed his magical sight and blinked. Time didn't move the same way in the spirit realm as it did in the physical world. He was gone about twenty minutes, according to the grandfather clock across the room, but it felt like the meeting with Mr. Rendell was shorter. Mrs.

Rendell moved back to the table and stared as Xephriel became aware of his surroundings.

"He is in a well in one of the gardens he built. There were archways and a gazebo with lights and beads strung on it. Do you know which one that might be?" His voice rang like a thunderclap in his ears.

Mrs. Rendell shivered as he addressed her, but she picked up the bone and wept. Through her sorrow, she whispered, "It might be the garden near the Kaleidoscope Art Gallery. He loved that design the most. Thank you for finding him, Mr. Maxis."

"Of course, but how did you come by this bone?" He asked Mrs. Rendell and lit a bundle of dried sage.

He waved the smoking herbs over the table, then let them rest in a glass dish to cleanse the room of any unwanted energy. Anything could stalk him from the etheric field, but sage contained a natural compound that redirected rogue spirits to where they belonged. It did not banish Mr. Rendell, who was flickering behind his wife, his soul refusing to detach from the finger bone.

"The box came to my house, but I didn't see the messenger."

"Why did you not go to Justice Street and seek one of the imperial law enforcement officers?"

"Honestly, I didn't know what to do. I was so scared. I searched for the first bone witch in the directory near my house. Did–did something bad happen to him?"

"I think Mr. Rendell and a few others may be victims of an unpleasant affair."

"Oh," Mrs. Rendell clutched the neckline of her dress. "My poor Eric. Will you come with me, Mr. Maxis? I'd feel more comfortable if you helped me explain all this to the officers."

"I will go with you. I know a bone witch who works as a private investigator on Justice Street. He is very kind and will help you find your husband."

"I brought my horse. I was in such a rush I didn't think to have the carriage prepared."

Xephriel wanted to offer her comfort, but her emotions were so distraught it was starting to affect his empathic nature. He let the sage cleanse his psychic senses, ignoring the dull pain around his skull, and said, "That is all right. If you meet me by the Rowdy Racecourse stable, a few buildings from here, I can ride my horse. I need to close up the Humerus, and then I'll join you."

Mrs. Rendell agreed and departed his store. The crow spirits drifted into the spirit world, their charge over Xephriel's protection complete. When his shop was once more silent, except for his boots clicking against the black marble floor, he reached into his jacket pocket and pulled out a brass key ring.

He chose a large bone sculpted like a shop skeleton key. The clavicle bone had belonged to his grandfather and had been imbued with ancestral magic. Most bone witches did not travel from their family's mausoleum because their magic amplified in proximity to their lineage. Xephriel's empathic discord extended past the living, and the bone key was the only piece of his heritage that did not cause him harm.

He ran the pad of his gloved thumb over the smooth bar of the key and felt the signature magic of his ancestors vibrate through his system. He slipped out of the Humerus and held up a hand to shade against the piercing rays of the sun. He kept the inside of his building dark because he was sensitive to light when a migraine took hold of his senses. That happened frequently enough that the gloom became a permanent part of his lifestyle. Shutting the door behind him, Xephriel inserted the bone key into the lock. He heard a click both from the spirit plane and inside the lock mechanism as magic and metal combined to protect what he cherished most.

As he took his first stride toward the center of Aequitas, he spotted Amé coming out of her shop. She paused on the half-moon-shaped landing before her entrance and waved. Xephriel kept his head down so his face was hidden and murmured a greeting.

Amé, his vivacious and persistent neighbor, skipped down her cement stairs. She stopped beside him and inhaled the city air, a fragrance he always found had a hint of horse manure, humidity, and gas from the lamps lining the streets.

Amé looked about his same age. He would be thirty-four, two weeks before the winter solstice. She stood at the height of his chest, her posture dignified. A pastel-pink cotton gown flowed over her figure. Burgundy shimmered through her long brown hair that hung like strands of straw. Her aura was a vibrant green, like grass, and glowed a welcoming beacon. Maybe it was her wide eyes that left him speechless, but he often found himself struck silent when they met. Amé had a convivial gaze the color of fertile soil and framed with sweeping lashes. His indigo aura flared, and his inherent witch magic buzzed in response to her presence.

Most witches gave him a headache or created such discord that he wanted to flee. With Amé, Xephriel always felt tethered, like she was a rock in the stormy sea of his life. Odd, because he barely interacted with her, but the fact remained.

For all her robust energy, Xephriel was too afraid to close the distance of their acquaintanceship. Emotions were his bane, and it was hard to have any kind of relationship when he was always on the cusp of physical torment outside of the Humerus. Still, her delightful personality maintained an open and pleasant channel of conversation. Try as he might, he didn't want to refuse that glimmer of a connection.

"Good afternoon, Xephriel!" She tried to peer under his hood. Her eyes squinted as if that would help her view his features.

His lips twitched in amusement at her efforts to glimpse his face. "Good afternoon, Amé."

She edged back after a minute and clasped her hands behind her back. "Off to lunch?"

"I'm headed to Justice Street with a client." It seemed to be their routine. He would leave, or she would arrive, and they didn't have enough time to pass more than a few words between them.

"I hope you didn't have trouble during your consultation."

"Just a bone reading that needs clarification from a friend." He didn't want to disclose client information, nor did he wish to frighten Amé with the details of what Mr. Rendell's bone revealed.

"Ah, well. I'd better let you get on with it then. Be safe on your way to Justice Street." She waved to him again and ambled in the opposite direction.

"Thank you. Have a good day, too." Xephriel called after her and proceeded to the stables.

Today was warm, the perfect end-of-summer weather, and the breeze had a cooling effect. Xephriel stuck his hands in his pockets and admired the azure sky. A few puffy clouds drifted across the endless expanse. He felt exposed in the light, as if all his secrets were on full display. No one could hide from the sun; even in the shade, the world was still visible. Only night could conceal everything, and it was the time of day Xephriel liked best. People slumbered, and auras were quiet, so he could remove his hood and feel the intensity of supernatural existence slip away.

The sidewalk leveled out as he approached the stables, where Mrs. Rendell waited with her chestnut bay thoroughbred. He gave her a polite nod of acknowledgment before sliding open the barn door.

Xephriel greeted the manager, Mr. Quinn, and the instantaneous onslaught of the man's emotions permeated his system. Backing up a few paces, he put a hand to his forehead and gritted his teeth. Pain, like a stab wound through his skull, ached as images scuttled across his internal vision. Xephriel noticed Mr. Quinn tending to the horses, riding across the fields of his ranch with his grandchildren, watched his wife swinging on a tire, and the moment he held his newborn son in his arms. All the past memories, the hope for his future, and the complex web of feelings that wove together in Mr. Quinn's mind were revealed to Xephriel.

Gripping the bone key in his pocket, Xephriel waited for the enchanted conduit to absorb the overflow of his magic. After a minute, his breathing deepened, and his headache diminished. Xephriel settled from the visions and heard Mr. Quinn address him from across the room.

"Everything all right, Xephriel?"

Xephriel angled his head to the side so he could better view Mr. Quinn. "I'm fine. Just a headache."

"This time of year gets my head blocked up. All the pollen from the autumn weeds and the dampness from the rainfall settles in my sinuses."

"Yes, allergies." Xephriel didn't like to talk about his empathic affliction outside his family and close friends, so he went along with Mr. Quinn's assumption.

"Honey will clear that right up. Want the name of my apothecary?"

"I think there's an apothecary near my consultation shop. Thank you for your offer. I'll try the honey."

Mr. Quinn tipped his cap and went back to work. "If you need anything before you take Carrion out, let me know. He's the best horse I have in the stables. Never makes a sound and will do anything for carrots."

Xephriel felt pride in his horse's good behavior and said, "He's counted among my best friends. Thank you for taking care of him."

"You're welcome. Safe travels."

"Thank you." Xephriel loped to the back of the stable and stopped at the second to last stall on the right.

Carrion stuck his nose through the window of his pen as Xephriel approached. He stroked the black stallion's mane before inspecting the living conditions. Carrion nuzzled his shoulder and whinnied, ready to be let out of his confinement.

Xephriel entered the stall and hoisted the saddle and reins down from the wall. After securing the straps, he hooked his boot into the stirrup and swung his leg over the horse's back. Riding Carrion out of the stables, he trotted toward Justice Street.

As he took in the city, Xephriel considered his life and the intricacies of what brought about his sensitivity to emotions. Every one of Xephriel's family members was a bone witch, as far back as his generational records dated. Xephriel, like all bone witches, was proud of his history.

The problem Xephriel encountered, that other bone witches did not, was that the magic controlling the empathy overwhelmed and attacked him. The transmission of magic came in too strong, and his body absorbed too much emotion at once. Instead of his system transferring the empathic current into usable energy, it created destruction. It was like living with a storm that would never be appeased. No amount of medical treatment had cured him of the ailment. The only thing that worked to ease the intensity of his magic disruption was witch spider silk.

The silk was found in the Arachnid Mountains and came from an evolutionary species of spider witch. The combination of the thread patterns and magic from the spiders' silk made the fabric resistant to the supernatural world. One tailor on Fashion Street was able to weave the silk into enchanted fabric and sew in the magic that allowed Xephriel to interact with people. The silk muted the empathic dissonance, but it did not eliminate the problem altogether.

He gripped the reins as he watched people go about their lives. They lived in blissful ignorance of what their inner feelings revealed to him. The world was full of auras and visible lights. Xephriel tracked the overlaying strings of the universe with his psychic vision as if everything was veiled by a multicolored net. Mystical sound waves bounced off passing witches and ricocheted inside his body. He was an aura magnet, and he fought the annoyance of his condition.

He glanced over at Mrs. Rendell and watched her husband's spirit hovering by her, following his bone. He longed for that kind of devotion, but to open himself up to any connection was fatal. His life was a study of the impossible, and every day he was reminded of his differences.

Unable to get close to anyone, forbidden to love and have a soul-binding relationship, Xephriel resigned himself to the fate of walking the world egg alone. Although, he supposed he wasn't quite forlorn with lost souls dogging his heels. He found his purpose in bone consulting and resolved his immediate empathic issues by building the Humerus to be a safe haven. There was no need to torture himself by wanting more.

Yet every time he met with Amé, he yearned. His heart cried out from the depth of his misery and demanded that he not push her away. He didn't know why, but for some reason, her candor made him feel hopeful. She emitted peace and love.

The inconvenience of that exquisite emotion is why Xephriel stayed away from her. What was the point in having hope when he was doomed to be a captive of his magic forever?

Chapter 3

Witch's Brew, a restaurant on Soul Street, belonged to Amé's best friend, Sylvia Matherson. It was a two-story brick building with heart shapes cut out of its stained veneer trim. The window frames and door were painted an aloe green, and the bubble gum pink signboard had apple blossoms bordering the red letters of the restaurant's name. A yellow awning shaded a rectangular porch, where tables and chairs were arranged for outdoor seating.

Amé inhaled a rich aroma of butter, garlic, and roasted duck. The luxurious scent coaxed a growl from her stomach. Gripping the brass spoon handle, she pushed open the arch-top door. Inside, layers of delicious smells permeated the air. Onion soup, crab and scallop pasta, roasted carrots, and fresh-baked bread were mixed in sumptuous harmony.

Greta, one of the servers at Witch's Brew, waved to Amé and glided to the front of the restaurant. "Afternoon, Amé!"

Amé bounced a little on her heels in anticipation of her meal. "Afternoon Greta! My usual window seat if you have it, please."

Greta flourished a menu and walked toward the back of Witch's Brew, where a small two-person table was arranged so patrons could gaze out the window. "It's a beautiful day. The weather is perfect. The sun is shining. After the rain all last week, it's a welcome reprieve."

Sitting down and receiving the menu, Amé said, "I love the rain, but it's nice to feel the sun when I'm outside. At least we are past the rainy season."

Greta pulled out a notepad from her apron pocket and slipped a pen from her bun. She twisted the barrel so the ink tip was prepped for scribing. "How's the new heating system for the greenhouse coming?"

"Oh, it's coming, but I can't lift the solar panels. I'll need to call the construction workers who set up the greenhouse."

Greta's face brightened with interest. "I'll have to stop in later and get more rose bushes. I have serious garden goals this year."

"I'll have a selection set out for you. Hennley cultivated a beautiful purple species you will love!"

"They sound divine. Oh, speaking of roses! I've been considering a flower mate as well." Greta's tone lowered in volume at the end of her thought.

Amé angled her head to consider the young waitress. "Did something happen between you and Drekson?"

The long exhalation was enough to pick up on Greta's frustration and disappointment. "He ended our courtship for another woman."

"I'm sorry to hear that, Greta. I'd be happy to design a flower mate for you. Do you have any particular characteristic in mind?"

"The thing is, I'm not sure I can afford one." Greta's fingers whitened around the notebook, and her head drooped to her chest in defeat.

Amé bobbed her head as she debated her answer. She was fair, but she didn't want to share prices in public in case a potential client was in earshot. "How about you come by the shop when you get off work, and I will see what I can do for you?"

Greta's demeanor transformed at the prospect. Her eyes brightened as she smiled wide. "I'll be by in the evening. I have an appointment on Fashion Street, so it won't be until sevenish."

"That's perfectly fine." Amé didn't have plans for her evening. Well, she amended her mental note. Her plans involved reading a book and drinking tea. She had no problem moving said schedule around for her friend. "Come around seven and a half, and we'll talk about a flower mate purchase." She turned back to the menu and made a flash decision for her lunch. "I think I'll have the dandelion tea and onion soup to start, Greta."

Greta jotted the order down for the kitchen ticket and inserted the pen into her hair. "I'll be right back with your order."

"Thank you. I'm sure she knows, but could you inform Sylvia I'm here?"

"Sure thing, Amé."

Amé wiggled in her chair until she was reclined into a comfortable position and peeked out the window. She watched pedestrians stroll down the street, their leisure creating a peaceful mood. A small boy ran around a gaslight pole, chasing his puppy while his mother hurried to catch up. Amé smiled at the scene and settled her arms across her lap. She loved observing children. Their infectious laughter caused a flutter in her chest. They were ready for adventure and camaraderie at a moment's notice.

She was in no hurry to have children; witches evolved to live about three hundred years or longer. Amé had plenty of time to fall in love, build a relationship with her partner, and later bring babies into their lives. She imagined a world where she had balance in life and love. There was no need to rush.

Her business thrived. She had a small fortune and a comfortable lifestyle. All her immediate needs were met and satisfied. Seeds of Love filled her happiness. Including a love connection in the mix was an added bonus but not a priority.

Amé had courtship offers before, but every time a man wanted to move beyond café meetings and late dinner outings, she ended the relationship. She didn't like how she felt as a person or as a couple when she was courted by those men. There was an element that didn't feel right. Amé felt like a seed lying dormant beneath the soil, waiting for sunlight to coax her to grow.

She believed love happened on a molecular level, a process so minute, so intrinsic to the universe that a person was caught up in it without realization. When two people recognized each other as soulmates, it was a profound awakening. Inside her heart, she knew her epiphany with another witch or mortal had yet to occur. Mere attraction was not enough to ignite her passion.

An unexpected image of Xephriel eclipsed her musings. Her neighbor was a curiosity, but a deeper desire drew her to his reclusive nature. She wanted to understand why he hid inside his mysterious house of bones. Why did he cover himself so completely?

She had been a little afraid of Xephriel when she had first opened her shop next to the Humerus. A dark blue aura surrounded him like a cape of midnight, so opaque that it took two years before she realized it wasn't black. Strange magic blocked her from viewing the full scope of his witch signature. Her aura didn't resonate against his when they closed proximity. He was an enigma, and perhaps, since she loved riddles and fitting pieces together in the places they belonged, he was an irresistible distraction.

Despite the stand-offish behavior and cryptic personality, Amé knew that if an opportunity presented itself for her to get past his barriers, she would take it. Xephriel was interesting and rooted in her soul. She sensed there was more to him than what he presented to the world.

That slice of intelligence and mysticism lured her with its profound uniqueness.

Greta returned with her tea and onion soup, then shifted toward the front of the restaurant to engage another customer. Bringing her nose to her soup, Amé breathed all the way to her ravenous stomach. She watched cheesy bread float on top of the beef broth soup. The caramelized onion slices beckoned her to partake in the sumptuous cuisine.

While she waited for the soup to cool, Amé ran a nail down the list of items available for lunch again and decided on a vegetable and pasta salad to add to her appetizer. With an exclamation of eagerness, she picked up her spoon and dipped the end around the floating cheese crouton, bringing up the broth to sample first. A hint of brandy tickled her sense of smell as Amé opened her lips and tipped the broth over her tongue.

She let the liquid spread and linger over her tastebuds before swallowing. Closing her eyes, she inhaled through her nose to get the full effect of the flavor. It was marvelous. The onions were cooked, so they caramelized and infused the broth. The beef was a perfect complement to the sweet and spicy flavor. The brandy heightened the fragrance but cut the thick, rich quality that might have overindulged her appetite. Aged cheese made the soup creamy and smooth. Everything she tasted was balanced and delightful. She took another bite, this time with the onions. The food melted inside her mouth, and soon her hunger was replaced with euphoria.

Amé was about to pick up the bread when Sylvia burst through the kitchen doors and greeted her as if they hadn't seen each other that morning. "My favorite diner!"

Amé lifted her arms and hugged her friend. "You look even more radiant than you did a few hours ago. What's your secret?"

"Oh, there's a secret, but I want to leave you in suspense for a few minutes."

Amé crooked both brows upward, but she decided to let her friend have her fun. Sylvia was the mistress of big surprises. Instead, Amé asked, "How is Beaux?"

"My husband is hard at work being head chef and loving it! Even after five years of marriage, he can't get enough of the kitchen or me." She winked and plopped into the opposite chair.

"I'm still in awe of the cake he made for my birthday."

"Best thing he ever did was quit his job as a financial adviser, marry me, and help me open Witch's Brew. Speaking of cooking, I must tell you something!"

Amé wiggled forward and crossed her arms on the table. "Yes! What's with all the mystery?"

Sylvia's black spiral curls bounced with her enthusiasm. "Beaux and I are going to have a baby!"

Amé squealed with delight and reached for her friend's hands across the table. "That's wonderful news! I'm so happy for you both. Congratulations! Ah! I'm going to be an aunty."

Sylvia let go of one of her hands and brushed at a stray tear. "I'm so happy, but gosh, these hormones turn me into a weepy sap in seconds. We finished the first trimester."

"Well, no wonder you are glowing. Now I understand why I glimpsed an orange aura mixed with your pink." Amé peered across the table and met Sylvia's hazel-green eyes. She watched as happiness overtook her friend's expression.

"Yes! Like my grandmother's aura color. Beaux is nervous about having a witch baby, but I said they are exactly like mortal babies."

"I'm sure he'll be fine once he holds the baby in his arms."

"True! How are you? How's the shop?" Sylvia pulled back her hands and waited for Amé to respond.

"It's still going well. Still as happy today as I am every day."

Sylvia narrowed her gaze and leaned forward a little. "Your tone suggests otherwise."

Amé held up her hands to diffuse any confusion. "No, no. I am happy. Undeniably so. The problem is, I wonder if this is it. I've achieved everything I want, and this is it for the rest of my life."

"Hmmm." Sylvia drummed her red fingernails on the table and popped her lips. "Perhaps."

Amé crossed her arms and angled her head to the right. "You know how devoted I am to my plants."

"That's true, but you've also had amazing adventures."

Amé's lips curled into a wicked smile. "Who could forget my trip to the Valencia Mountains to gather Titan Lily seeds?"

Sylvia threw her head back and laughed. "Exactly. You have a wild side, too."

Amé sobered and flopped backward, placing her hands on her lap. "Business has taken off, but maybe I need to make time for myself."

"It sounds like you need a harmless distraction. How about a shopping trip? We'll go look at baby clothes on Fashion Street."

Amé perked up at the thought of buying tiny shoes for the new baby-to-be. "Yes! I can close Seeds of Love for a few hours. We haven't been shopping in ages."

Sylvia clapped her hands. "Excellent. I'll let Beaux know he will be running the show for a while tomorrow. We'll go in the morning."

"Perfect! I'll give Hennley the day off."

Sylvia hopped up from her seat and rounded the table to hug Amé. "I'm heading back into the kitchen, but I am looking forward to tomorrow. It will be a positive change of pace for both of us. Enjoy lunch."

"Tell Beaux I said hi, and the food is divine."

"Of course!" Sylvia strode behind the swinging kitchen door, waving a hand over her shoulder.

Amé chuckled at her friend's vivacious nature and returned to her soup. Greta checked on her after a few minutes, and Amé relayed the rest of her order. She ate undisturbed and then checked her watch. She had ten minutes before she needed to return to Seeds of Love. Sipping the last dregs of her tea, Amé finished her meal and left two silver libras. Greta bid her farewell as Amé glided out the door and returned to her shop.

Chapter 4

Xephriel steered Carrion across the dirt road of Justice Street and dismounted before a building that looked like it was held together by sorcerous will alone. Pieces of mortar had fallen from the exterior, leaving cracks and rough patches mapping a trail from the ground level to the second floor. The iron railing, chipped and bent to the side, had a pattern of twisted thorns and bones. The dilapidated roof leaked onto the sidewalk, and the windows were boarded shut. An eagle skull hung on the door in place of a knocker.

Mrs. Rendell's audible intake of breath at the conditions of the building caused a sympathetic cringe from Xephriel. His friend was a bizarre concoction of charming and eccentric. Nobeleace Dracaena, or "Noble" as he preferred to be called, belonged in a category of witch all to himself. His father was a bone witch, and his mother was a mortal acrobat in the Phantasmagoria Circus on Entertainment Street. He had three aura colors. Witches did not usually have more than one aura signature, but Noble had an unusual magic mutation.

A mastermind of contradictions, Noble hid behind a negligent atmosphere while dismantling plots of criminal intricacies and seeking justice for the dead. Despite his atrocious architectural circumstances, Noble could solve peculiar cases that baffled even the Court of Harmony detectives. In short, he was an antisocial psychopath with a kind heart and flare for the dramatic.

Xephriel had been his friend since childhood; both of them were isolated because of the gifts they possessed. Both unable to cope with anyone outside their family and the bone witch community. Yet, they found each other in the chaos of discovering how to manage their magic and diversities. Xephriel had to remain distanced from people because of emotions disrupting his life, but Noble inadvertently pushed people away.

"You'll have to ignore the outside," Xephriel reassured Mrs. Rendell and knocked on the puce-painted door.

"I'm trying to imagine how the entire thing won't fall on my head when I walk inside."

Xephriel's lips inched upward in amusement at her reflection of the building. "It's better on the inside. He's a longtime friend and will take good care of your case."

After another hard knock using the eagle skull, the door swung open with sensational force. As if announcing a whirlwind performance, Noble opened his arms by greeting when he spotted Xephriel. "My friend! What a surprise. You normally warn me before you arrive so I can don my bones. One moment while I dress for the occasion."

Xephriel watched as Noble spun on his toes and headed back into the foyer. All the while, he could hear him shouting, "You brought something interesting. That bone you've got tucked away is calling out for help. Phalanx, if I'm not mistaken."

"How does he know about the bone?" Mrs. Rendell's eyes rounded as she patted the box in her skirt pocket.

"He's able to sense any bone, anywhere, with his magic. He might have also gleaned the information from the spirit world."

"Death," Noble announced as he returned wearing a necklace of snake vertebrae, three wrist cuffs made from the pelvis of a tiger, and a hat sewn with crow bones. His auras of sky blue, red, and white danced around his body like enchanted serpents as he continued, "Death has a peculiar scent and one that I am intimate with. I could smell the marrow of the bone, and you can't mistake the difference between mortal and witch. Their biology is unique, even down to the bones. As for recognizing which bone you have brought me—that, my dear, is a secret." He concluded his speech with a bow and gestured for Xephriel and Mrs. Rendell to enter his establishment.

"Thank you for meeting with us." Xephriel entered the gaslit hallway and moved to the side so Mrs. Rendell could join them in the narrow space.

Noble took the lead up the stairs to his consultation office. "I'd never turn away my best friend. Welcome. Welcome. This way."

Mrs. Rendell tip-toed over the threshold and glanced up the rickety wooden stairs, hesitant to proceed. "Is he always so—enthusiastic? Why does he need to wear so many bones?"

Xephriel shuffled at the uncomfortable mention of Noble's attire. Although it wasn't abnormal for a bone witch to wear bones for their occupation or magic, mortals didn't often experience the full effect. "It's to help me."

"Oh, well, that's nice of him." She shifted and shut the front door. She took a tentative step toward the staircase.

After another moment of debate, she proceeded toward the second floor, Xephriel right behind. He entered Noble's office and offered a wicker chair for Mrs. Rendell to rest. She removed the velvet box from her pocket and placed it on the walnut desk. Xephriel leaned on the wall near the back corner, giving Noble space to work.

Flourishing a pocket-size magnifying glass, Noble examined the box. After a moment, in which his face transitioned through several intense expressions, he extracted the phalanx. Xephriel observed his friend fiddle with the bone and hold it to his ear. When he had finished his prognosis, Noble placed the finger bone back in the container and flopped in his seat. Spinning once with the wooden swivel office chair, Noble steepled his fingers and popped his lips.

"Three bodies in the same well. That is interesting."

Xephriel responded from his corner of the room. "Possible serial collector, but I'm not sure."

"The choice of location is remarkable. Slower decomposition because of the water accumulation, and the bodies are buried in a place no one would think to look. I don't like cases involving water. No one thinks about the torture it inflicts on the dead." Noble's demeanor soured as he tapped each finger against the other in an agitated pattern. "Respect for the dead. It's a lost courtesy."

"It seems this person may not have respect for the living either. Thank you for taking on the case," Xephriel spoke up from his place.

Noble waved his thanks away, a gesture that conveyed he was more than willing to assist and act in the name of justice. "I am positive the Court of Harmony will get wind of this situation. Murder always puts a wedge in their hindquarters. I'll have to report it because of protocol. It's going to bring officers to your doorstep. I know how you love visitors, so I'm warning you." Noble dropped his hands, a bit of sarcasm oozing from the last sentence, and leaned over his desk. "For now, I'd like to hear your side of the story, Mrs. Rendell, before I speak with your husband."

Mrs. Rendell cleared her throat and glanced around the room. Her nervousness hit Xephriel like a punch to the gut, but he endured it. She fidgeted in her seat and then said, "Eight months ago, Eric did not come home from work. He was designing a private garden for the Kaleidoscope Art Gallery on Entertainment Street. It was unusual for Eric not to send a message to me if he was late. I inquired about my husband's whereabouts at the front desk, but they said he had already gone home. I returned home, but he hadn't arrived. I sent a message to the Art Gallery owner, trying to discover where the miscommunication broke down. A message returned with the same answer - he'd left for the day. I contacted his family. They had not heard from him, nor had he come to their residence. He would never disappear. Never. I filed a missing person's form with the Court of Harmony law enforcement officials. I hadn't heard anything back and assumed my husband was gone for good. This morning, I got a package in the mail. It was a black box. When I opened it, the bone lay inside. I went to a bone witch, thinking magic could confirm if it was my husband's bone or not."

Noble nodded and slanted his gaze to Xephriel. "What did you find out from Mr. Rendell?"

"You have all the information I gleaned from my encounter."

"Yes, but why? Let us find out what exactly happened to Mr. Rendell. I'm going to give him a moment to settle, and then we'll go about our interview."

"Settle?" Mrs. Rendell squeaked.

Noble picked up his pen and began scribbling over a large notepad. "Yes, he's been here the entire time. Did you think he would float away after contacting you? He's been commenting since I opened my front door. I'm going to jot down everything I've heard so far, and then we will proceed with the investigation."

Mrs. Rendell's mouth opened and closed, unable to form words. "I'm-well-I should have come here eight months ago, I suppose."

"Without a doubt. Have no fear, Mrs. Rendell! We will discover the truth behind this case."

Xephriel watched as the bone on the table flickered with an evergreen light. Mr. Rendell's spirit perched on the end of the table. His shimmering outline matched his bone's aura color. Noble set up a circle of crow and raven bones around Mr. Rendell's phalanx. Xephriel had known Mr. Rendell would monitor his bone once the connection was made. He didn't mention it to Mrs. Rendell because he didn't want to frighten her.

Noble had no shame whatsoever when communicating with souls. Libra needed people like Noble, willing to be bold with their magic in the right ways. He was proud of his magic and boisterous in his demonstration of it. Still, Noble could be overwhelming, and the more excited he got about a case, the less he filtered his idiosyncrasies.

"Mr. Rendell," Noble turned his head so he was staring at the ghost. "Tell us everything you can remember, please."

Mr. Rendell's voice came in fuzzy through the etheric plane. "I was–I was–" His ghostly features gave the impression he was pinched and frustrated.

"Take your time. No rush." Noble's hands lifted in a pacifying manner.

Though Mrs. Rendell couldn't see Mr. Rendell, his voice reverberated through the atmosphere. She leaned toward the desk and said, "I'm here, Eric. We're all here to help you."

The encouragement from his wife seemed to assist in organizing his thoughts because Mr. Rendell launched into his tale. "I was out in the Mosaic garden at the Kaleidoscope Art Gallery. A woman. A woman in a cloak. I couldn't–couldn't view her face."

"What did the woman in the cloak want?" Noble addressed Mr. Rendell's spirit as he took notes.

Mr. Rendell's spirit started to become clearer. His opaque features cringed. "I think. She wanted me to--she-she pulled something out. A seed, I think. It was lime with yellow marbling."

Noble paused his dictation and tapped the end of the pen on his lips. "A seed? Interesting."

"She asked me if I could plant the seed in the Mosaic garden. She said it was crucial."

Noble swiveled in his chair until he was aligned with Xephriel's sight. "What do you make of the seed, my friend?"

Beyond the decomposition of bones and how remains fertilized the world egg, Xephriel had little knowledge about plants. He was confused about why the killer would require help to put a seed in the ground. "I think it's peculiar behavior."

"Yes. Why would the killer want Mr. Rendell to plant a seed? It isn't that hard to dig a hole and drop it in."

Mr. Rendell's aura darkened to a deep emerald as he recalled his death sequence. "She put it in my hand and said I needed to feel the seed. I pushed it away. It felt wrong. I think the seed voiced a message to me."

"What did the seed say to you?" Noble perked up, and his wrist moved in rapid strokes as he inked his thoughts onto the paper.

"The seed said, 'She's not the one. Take me home.' The woman was persistent. She became angry when I refused to plant the seed and drew out a knife. I didn't have time to react. She stabbed me in the neck. Clipped off my finger with gardening shears. I couldn't scream. Couldn't save myself."

Mr. Rendell began to cry as his death resurfaced. Mrs. Rendell reached out as if she could touch her husband and make it better even though she couldn't find him.

Noble jumped up from his chair and swished his knee-length violet coat as he sauntered to a bookshelf. "Say no more, Mr. Rendell. You have exerted yourself enough." Noble stroked his smooth pointy chin and hissed in a breath as he drew his brows to the middle of his forehead. "A conscious seed, a mysterious woman targeting a gardener, a public well. Let me think. Let me think."

The seeds had to be magical. Xephriel interjected, "It sounds like a witch is involved. Mr. Rendell is mortal, and he couldn't have heard anyone's voice besides the woman in the cloak. It suggests a supernatural presence if he heard the seeds speaking. Why would a witch want to kill a mortal gardener? That makes no sense at all."

"Oh, but it must make sense because it occurred. Let's analyze the scenario, shall we? If the killer is a witch, then we have a few suppositions. A witch makes a seed and, when sown, does something phenomenal. We'll discover that in time. She waits, looking for the right candidate. The Mosaic garden is the perfect lookout. She's hidden, there's high traffic, and the potential for people to be knowledgeable about plants is a higher probability than if she were to hide out in a tavern or on the street. Why doesn't she target witches? Interesting thought, since a vegetation witch would know what to do with a magic seed. This seed. This seed is the key. Is the plant a guide? Is the seed poisonous? A love spell? What is the motive? Let us say none of that is correct, and the witch did not make the seed at all. She had to obtain the seed from another person. Where did she acquire it, and why? What was the time frame between each victim? Why collect the finger bone? Why send the bone to Mrs. Rendell? If the killer isn't a witch, then how did a mortal come into possession of a magic seed? So many questions. What do you think, Mortimer?"

At the mention of his name, a new voice entered the conversation. Mrs. Rendell shrieked and pointed at the bookshelf as half of a witch skeleton began to twitch and animate. Xephriel groaned at Noble's theatrics and pinched the bridge of his nose.

"I think," A robust masculine tone boomed through the room. His skull's jaw opened and closed at the hinges. "We will have our answer if we remove the bones from the well. We can follow the thread of their spirits to their bones and then to the killer. The rest of it sounds outrageous. I've never heard of anyone being harmed for a seed."

"Outrageous, and yet those seeds had a significant impact on the killer's psyche. They motivated her to madness. Did the magic in the seeds cause her to become deranged, or was there another factor? Are there other killers out there with the same insanity from the seeds? If there aren't any more killers, then why did this woman turn into one? The Court of Harmony would know if there was a passel of troublemakers planting vicious flowers around Aequitas. I would have heard something from my network. It's all so fascinating. The perfect puzzle! I'm tingling with anticipation."

Mortimer rolled his skull around in a circle, the effect causing Mrs. Rendell to turn away and pick a handkerchief from her purse. Xephriel thought her skin had a green tinge. Mortimer clicked his chipped teeth together and said, "It's possible the seeds were from a poisonous plant. When they come in contact with skin, it can cause madness. A spell on the seeds could induce psychological disturbance. There are plenty of diseases that target magic. Without the actual seed to examine, we can only guess."

Noble jotted down Mortimer's theories. He glanced over his shoulder as he asked, "Do you see how mesmerizing all this is? A more impossible problem could not have fallen into our laps."

Mortimer waved a boney hand. "Yes, yes. It's all very interesting. When are you going to give me legs so I can go on an investigation with you?"

Noble set down the pen and put his hands on his hips as he addressed Mortimer. "I am not a magician. I cannot conjure bones out of thin air."

"Can't you? I thought you were an all-powerful omni-grim?"

"Hah! You flatter me, but I cannot do the impossible. Only Khaos can do that." Noble turned to the rest of the room and announced, "I think we're done here for now. Mr. Rendell, do you wish to speak to your wife before we hand her back your phalanx?"

"Please." The plea was whispered as if his heart broke, and Xephriel felt sorrow and agony from that one word.

"We'll leave you two alone. Mrs. Rendell, we'll be back in a moment."

"That thing isn't going to talk anymore, is it?" She'd gone pale from the encounter with Mortimer, and Xephriel was afraid she might have reached her limit.

"No, No. Mortimer is listening now. Have no fear of him. He cannot come off the shelf, though he protests that I should find a way for him to do so. The lower half of his bones were ground into cinders. Nasty business. He should be grateful I rescued him and gave him a home."

"Oh, god. Please, stop. I'm going to be ill." Mrs. Rendell bent over and panted, exerting all her energy into achieving serenity.

Xephriel rubbed his hands over his face and started to regret his decision to ask Noble for help. "I think Mrs. Rendell has had enough for today. Let her say goodbye."

"Yes, of course. That's what I said. Out we go!" Noble strutted across the room.

Xephriel said to Mrs. Rendell, "I'll be just outside. Find your closure with your husband, and then we can be on our way."

"Thank you," She gave a weak lift of her lips, a sign of kindness, and leaned over to peer at the finger bone.

Outside, Xephriel crossed his arms and glared at Noble. His tone projected the ire Noble couldn't visualize on his features. "Was that necessary?"

"What? Mortimer's expertise is valuable to me. He can detect nuances that do not come through to our physical world. Besides, he's a great sounding board. I do all my best predicting with him." Noble protested and tugged on the lapels of his jacket.

"For Khaos' sake! Couldn't you have done that after we left?"

Noble widened his mossy-green stare and dropped his jaw in shock. "And miss an opportunity to glean more information?"

"You scared her to death!" It was rare for Xephriel to raise his voice, but Noble had a way of provoking his exasperation.

Hand over heart, Noble declared, "Now, who is being dramatic? You knew my methods before arriving, so don't play the gallant knight."

Xephriel conceded to the logic of Noble's statement, but he still felt it prudent to defend Mrs. Rendell. "What you say is true, but you were showing off."

"I was," Noble admitted without remorse and winked with a grin.

Xephriel steered their conversation back to the case. "A vegetation witch might be able to tell us why the killer needed someone else to nurture the seed."

"Without the seed, even a vegetation witch cannot guess. Or they would give us too many guesses. We need more evidence. I'll start poking around the well and get the bones out to interview the victims. Mrs. Rendell can leave me directions to the garden. I'm serious, though. The

Court of Harmony isn't going to like this. They will want it taken care of without much fuss. That means as soon as they catch wind that we're digging up a pile of bones at the back of the famous art gallery on Entertainment Street, the imperial detectives are going to swarm. Since you brought me the bone, they will ask you questions about the reading."

Xephriel leaned against the wall and tugged at his hood for emphasis. "I'll be fine, but I appreciate the warning. Why are you so worried about the imperial detectives anyway? Aren't you all on the same justice team?"

Noble pursed his lips and scratched his curly brown head. "You'd think so, but their methods do not align with mine. We often butt heads."

"You butt heads with everyone." Xephriel meant it in good humor. He cared for his friend and would not truly insult him.

Noble dropped his arms and tucked one hand into his pants pocket. "Except you. We've been outcasts of society since we were children. You and I would make an effective team."

Xephriel couldn't handle interacting with human bones for long periods of time, and his friend knew that.

It was nice to have the offer. He switched the subject to Noble's building.

Xephriel knocked on the bent railing around the landing and said, "Look at the state of this place! I think it's gotten worse since I was here last."

"Hah! I don't have time to worry about glamouring my house. It's functional, and that's all I care about."

"It's a wonder anyone finds this place."

Noble's face turned serious, and a subtle shift in his trifecta of auras showed his darkened mood. "That's the point. I've tangled with terrible people. I don't want their friends looking too closely at where I sleep."

Xephriel pushed off the wall and said, "Thank you for helping."

The lines around Noble's eyes wrinkled with contentment, and his mouth relaxed. "You're welcome here any time, even if it's just to criticize my living conditions."

Xephriel crooked his neck to inspect the ceiling. "Ah well, the chipped paint look is growing on me."

Noble strolled to his office door. "Like mold."

"You might have that, too." Xephriel joked.

Noble leaned so his head and shoulders stuck out the doorway. "I'll fix that for your next visit."

"My lungs thank you."

As he peeked at Mrs. Rendell, Xephriel felt relief glide off her form. Her shoulders were hunched as she cried, but her emotions were less tangled. She had comfort in knowing the truth, and soon she would have full closure when she laid her husband's bones to rest. Xephriel hadn't encountered a murder case before, but he understood death had complexities like life. He hoped they found the killer before more souls needed their stories heard.

Chapter 5

Amé returned to her shop around one in the afternoon
and found Hennley inside the greenhouse whispering to
black and white rose bushes. Haunting lullabies poured
from the black roses, their songs compelling lost souls
trapped on the physical plane. Amé's ear pricked as the
somber tune wove a rich lamentation through the atmosphere. The white roses responded in a romantic aria that
captivated the innocence of youth.

To a mortal ear, the roses would be like any other
flower, but to a vegetation witch, they were magical.
White and black roses belonged together. Their harmony
was unique among all the world egg's flora.

A legend was scribed that, one day, a rosaceae witch
took a couple of tears from Khaos, mixed them with coal,
dipped a white rose in the mixture, and created a new

species the color of black nothingness. The blossoms absorbed the mournful sonnet of Khaos' heart, but the species did not transform like other magic plants.

A mystical chill wind swept under her hair and raised a chill over her flesh. Pollen from her plants glittered under the sun. The magic plants fell into tranquility as they listened to the roses' duet.

She watched the way the thorny stems of the white and black roses wound together. The barbed wire effect seemed to imply that even shears could not separate the two bushes. The black and white petals brushed against each other like a tender kiss.

Her feet inched toward the potted plants. Her mind whirled as bones and blood, water and soil, trees and scythe culminated together inside her mind. Amé became disconnected, like her soul was in one place, and her body existed elsewhere.

Bones wrapped in lilies and creeping vines overwhelmed her spirit vision. Bones scattered like a royal carpet as crocuses sprouted between the white gaps and made a path through the strange divination magic clicked into place from the roses' twining melodies. In the distance, she heard the chorus of life and death, and it plucked at the strings of her soul.

Xephriel consumed her meditation, his midnight blue aura filling her divine sight. His black attire was congruent with the shade of the petals. Her psychic senses took control, and she was left dizzy with magic. Amé couldn't tear her mind from the image of black roses twining up Xephriel's legs, his voice calling to her as he stretched out a hand sprouting with blood-red lilies. Two words flashed, but she couldn't venture to guess what they might have been. Amé was half aware of her greenhouse and Hennley as the entire event transpired.

Hennley looked up, her red tresses falling to the side as she cocked her head in question. "Amé?"

Blinking, she resumed consciousness of her surroundings. All witches had a touch of prophecy, a trait passed down from their god Khaos, but it was rare for vegetation witches. Amé was baffled why it happened to her, why the roses triggered such a profound response from her magic.

Hennley regarded her odd manner and said, "You look like you have uncovered a new species of magical plants."

"I certainly feel that way," Amé murmured the words; her lips moved, but her thoughts were detached. "I'm sensitive to the roses' melody. Help me load these rose bushes into a wagon."

"Where are we moving them?"

"I'm not sure. I suppose the answer will come to me. For now, let's bring them to the storefront."

Hennley hastened to the other end of the greenhouse and brought a wooden wagon. They bent their knees and grunted as they hoisted the black rose bush first, then positioned the white rose bush next. The interlocked stems were challenging to maneuver, their thorns creating a hook that bent the flowers as they shifted. When they had the pots settled, Amé grabbed the wagon handle while Hennley pushed from behind. They wheeled the flowers into the storefront right as a customer in a black cloak strode inside Seeds of Love.

Amé straightened and flipped her dark locks over her shoulder to address the customer. "Hello, my name is Amé! I'm the shop owner of Seeds of Love. How can I help you?"

Even covered in a cloak, Amé noticed the hem of the woman's black dress and brown riding boots. Amé raised her eyebrows as the woman flinched at her greeting. She turned her chin over a shoulder to inform Hennley to move the wagon behind the counter. Hennley grabbed the handle and heaved a load of potted roses out of view. Amé turned her attention back to the woman, who hovered at the entrance as if she needed a speedy escape route.

"What can I help you find today?" Amé tried again to engage the woman, keeping her customer service tone polite and approachable.

A gray haze shrouded the woman, and a double image flickered, making Amé's eyes cross. She blinked, but the illusion was gone, and an imperceptible sound wave bounced off Amé's aura.

Ah, she's a witch.

The witch's shoulders were hunched as she inched toward Amé. It was peculiar behavior. Even more strange, this woman had a faint red signature radiating around her head like a halo. A witch didn't dull their aura in the presence of another witch unless they had to hide their magical identity. Amé didn't feel any malice from the witch, but there was an air of caution niggling at her instincts.

The witch's aura spectrum resonated so faintly that Amé might have mistaken her for a mortal if that one spot of cherry red hadn't been visible. It was disconcerting, but Amé wasn't in the business of denying someone a plant based on her personal perspectives. Still, she felt her shoulders cringe from the cryptic magic.

The witch spoke in a rush. "I am here for a flower mate."

Amé's eyelids fluttered as realization shook her out of her musings, and sensitivity to her client urged her into action. "Yes! Yes, of course. Right, this way."

The witch shadowed Amé to a staircase; the flower mate seeds were stored on the second floor of her shop. Amé scaled the creaky wooden steps. The gas lights illuminated the upstairs hall. She shimmied a skeletal key from a chain around her neck and strode to the right. Inserting the key into the lock of the black door, she twisted the knob and opened the showroom. She shifted aside so the witch could enter first.

Two bay windows, acting as a prism as the light filtered through the glass, cast optical rainbows across the wooden floorboards. Thirty jars were lined along five rows of shelves. An oak worktable was at the far end, with pink and green gift boxes organized on the surface. The pretty containers were no bigger than a ring box, and next to them lay satin ribbons to match the color of the magic seeds.

"What type of seed are you looking for?"

The witch paused in the center of the room and studied the jars but remained silent. Amé's usual approach wasn't working, so she tried a different tactic. "What's your name?"

The witch tugged her hood tighter around her face and said, "I prefer not to give it."

"That's all right. Let me tell you about the contract while you look at the pre-made seeds I have available to purchase. These seeds are designed with a particular set of traits such as tragic love, sweet friendship turned into love, the eternal romantic, the rogue, or the show stopper. You get the idea. You can pick one of these, or I can customize a flower mate. The contract states that you may have one seed. No refunds, no reselling, no asking for more later. This is your only flower mate, so you want to be sure to pick the best personality for you. I will replace your seed if it is damaged before you plant it and it does not grow, or the flower mate does not produce the desired result because of the impairment. You can get a refund on a damaged seed within one year, but no longer. I'll have a copy of the contract, so the date you purchased it will be stated for both of our records. You may recommend my product to anyone, but you cannot sell it to another witch to replicate."

The witch leaned her head near the jars and mumbled behind her cloak. "I understand the terms."

Amé gave the woman space and said, "The jars are labeled by the personality types. I'll let you look for a moment. If you need anything, let me know."

"Thanks."

Amé picked up a bottle of Fire Dragon seeds, the strange pulse of the witch's aura giving her inspiration. The seeds were vermillion in color, with supernatural flames rushing like blood under the skin. The seeds jumped inside the glass, glowing orange and red as passion animated their small oval shapes. Amé slid the jar back on the shelf as she considered the witch browsing her collection. Too much heat could cause combustion in a relationship, and the witch's red aura suggested her passions ran deep. A Seaside Rendezvous or a Made For Romance, cooling flower mates, might be better suited to her character.

Although, the enigmatic concentration of the witch's aura was something to consider. Amé bit a fingernail as she cast a covert glance toward the witch. Was the witch unstable? Should Amé sell her a seed? She wanted to please the customer and give her a chance at true love. There wasn't a clause in the contract that prohibited certain clients from purchasing a seed, nor did Amé believe in biased discrimination. It was merely her opinion of the witch's aura that caused her discomfort. It was too late now, and she had to find a seed for the witch, even if she felt uneasy about the way her aura glowed.

Amé turned her attention to the witch and noticed she had paused at the Cotton Candy seeds. The witch grabbed her selection from the shelf. The seeds quivered in a pile, their whispered voices echoing, 'not her, not her.' Amé frowned at the message. That had never occurred before. She didn't have a plan for clients who were unsuitable for the purchase of a flower mate, and her worry magnified. What if the witch hurt the flower mate when it grew? What if she was being paranoid and the witch was merely termagant? The seeds might be reacting to the incorrect personality type. Amé chastised herself, the debate in her mind a tangible thing. She desperately wanted to be nice to the customer, but her warning bells were ringing.

Before she could diagnose the cause for her seeds' sudden erratic behavior, the witch announced, "I'll take them all."

Amé's eyebrows shot upward in astonishment. "That's not exactly how it works. One seed is usually enough. Did you need me to go over the contract again? You can take a look at it before making a decision."

"I'll take them all." The witch's recalcitrant voice grated down Amé's spine like iron nails.

Amé inhaled deeply and found her inner patience. "I am here to help you make a decision that will give you the best experience possible. The seeds you are holding are resisting and might not be the right fit at this time."

"I'll pay you for them if that's the issue." The witch insisted and tucked the glass bottle under her arm.

Amé didn't argue with people who bought the wrong potted aloe and refused her expertise, but she tended to become more stubborn when it came to magic plants. "I would strongly recommend you reconsider. Flower mates are a guide to finding your true love and heart's desires. It will be more enjoyable with a mate who reciprocates your feelings. Even magic can't alter compatibility, and love should be a two-way street."

"I won't reconsider. Thank you."

Amé clenched her jaw, and her ingrained customer service mentality warred with her personal feelings. "You can take one seed, and I won't budge on that."

"Fine. Fine." The witch conceded and thrust the jar toward Amé. "I will take one seed."

"I'll get you a gift box." She turned so her emotions wouldn't rise in reaction to the termagant witch. Amé was even-tempered, but this witch provoked her to fight for her seeds. As she walked away, a sensation like pins pricking at her skin caused her green aura to flare. The sale wasn't right. She could feel it.

Amé counted to twenty as she crossed the room, taking a breath in through her nose and exhaling through her mouth. Her strides were steady and careful as she came to the worktable and selected a pink box and blue silk ribbon. She picked a contract from a stack on the far end of the table. She found a smile through her escalating irritation so she could deliver a harmonious conclusion to the sale. Inside, she was seething, and it was not a feeling Amé was accustomed to.

"Let's put your seed in the box, and then I'll explain how the development process works. While I'm preparing the gift box, you can sign the contract." Amé instructed the witch as she rejoined her in the center of the room.

She handed a pen and the contract to the witch and set her mind to the task of wrapping the seed in the box. Amé wiggled off the bottle's cork and tipped the glass so one seed tumbled to the opening. The bubblegum pink oval with blue vertical stripes popped against her palm. The little seed jumped in sporadic intervals. Placing the witch's Cotton Candy seed into the gift box, Amé set the lid on top and tied the sky blue ribbon in a tidy bow.

A faint rattling sound came from behind, and Amé peeked over her shoulder to see the other seeds jostling inside their bottles. The seeds never behaved like they were ready to crack their containers and roll away. Alarmed but unsure of what to do without understanding the provocation for their action, Amé ignored the seeds' warning. The witch was odd, to be sure, but other than her acerbic character, there was nothing to prove she was the direct cause of the seeds' distress.

Amé circled back to the witch and handed her the box and instruction booklet. "The seeds are coded to be gender-neutral, so you will have to be clear about what you want when you plant your Cotton Candy plant. The magic will recognize your wishes and will grow according to your desires. You must plant the seed in the ground and water it twice a day until it blooms. It will grow to be about the size of a sapling, so be sure to give it lots of room. Once it blooms, you will need to prepare clothes because the people who come out of the blossoms are naked, like a newborn. The person conjured will live for one day and one night, no more, but if it feels neglected, it will wither and die faster. The more you love, the stronger the magic.

After the time is up, the flower that bloomed, along with the flower mate, will wither and die."

The witch gripped her box and moved to the door, her cloak swishing as she strode across the wooden floor. For a moment, the witch's entire aura lit up and engulfed her body in a crimson burst. The seeds clinked in their glass jars, and Amé listened as incoherent whispers filled the atmosphere. The seeds settled once the witch was gone, and Amé had no choice but to believe she had made a mistake. A horrible, unsettled feeling coiled in her gut.

How could she get the seed back without causing a scene? Amé didn't want to put Hennley in danger, but one of her flower mates might be in the hands of a maniac. The one seed only clause in the contract was all she could fall back on. The witch couldn't come back for more, and although it was heartbreaking that one of her flower mates might go home with a bad person, it wasn't worth Amé or Hennley's safety.

Before she departed the flower mate room, Amé perused the contract until she found the signature. There was no legible name, just a bunch of squiggles. The customer neglected to leave her address as well. Amé marked the edge of the paper to indicate which one was the bad sale. Slipping the contract into her filing cabinet, she hurried from the room. Hennley would be alone with the witch, and Amé wasn't sure something nefarious wouldn't happen at the end of the transaction.

She closed the door and locked it with the skeleton key. She proceeded down the stairs and pivoted left to calculate the purchase at the register till. Hennley was shimmying a few products on the shelves by the fountain. Thankfully, the witch had not bothered her, and that gave Amé a bit of relief.

Setting down her rag to attend to the final sale, Hennley maneuvered around a bamboo cluster. Amé met Hennley's gaze over the cash register and held up a hand for her to stay away. The witch placed a pouch of libras near the register and sped to the store's exit. Amé tried to call out, but all that remained in the store was the air of unease.

Amé opened the leather coin pouch and drew a breath through her clenched teeth. She poured out the gold libras and counted. A total of two hundred gold coins lay in a glittering pile. Four thousand libras! It was way beyond what the seeds cost. Hennley came over and widened her amber gaze as she watched Amé double-check her tally.

"That's not how much a flower mate costs." Hennley placed a hand over her mouth.

Amé shook her head no and replied, "It isn't. I can't imagine why she would give me this much. Should I go after her?"

"I didn't like the way she acted. She gave me the creeps." Hennley glanced at the storefront. "If we go after her, she might cause trouble. Did you see how odd her aura glowed?"

Amé rubbed her eyelids with her fingertips and heaved out her exasperation. "You're probably right. She's bound to be back again anyway to complain or try to purchase more. And yes, her aura was strange. I've never seen anything like it. Our auras concentrate around our hearts, not our heads."

"You know, she seems familiar." Hennley crossed her arms and drifted into a contemplative stare.

"Familiar how?"

"I don't know. Do you remember a few months ago, we had that witch come in for a seed, and she wore a masquerade disguise over her face?"

"Oh, yes! That was a bizarre one, too. But that witch had a yellow aura, and this witch was emitting red."

"Yes, but they were very similar in behavior. The masked witch twitched whenever you spoke to her, and she left with a seed that was completely wrong for her.

Remember you said how difficult it was to convince her to buy a Café Dream seed, but she bought a Tarnished Prince seed instead? And that witch overpaid, too. Not nearly this much, it was only by twenty libras, but it was enough that it stuck in my memory. I think you said a customer overpaid back at the start of the spring season. How many witches can there be looking for a flower mate and tossing money around as if they couldn't care less about their bank account?"

"You're right. That's a lot of coincidences. They weren't as aggressive, but each one acted so odd and paid me more than they should have. Plus, every one of them had a different aura color and attire that concealed their features. There's got to be something to that. But I couldn't possibly guess what the reason would be. I'd normally say it was the same person, but it is impossible to change the color of an aura. Witches are all predestined to certain magic that correlates to color, and that color remains, even after death."

Hennley blew a strand of red-brick hair out of her eyes and opened her arms in a sign of uncertainty. "No idea, but you could buy another greenhouse with that money."

"That's not a bad idea. I'd have to think of where to put it, though."

"True."

Amé opened the register drawer, swiped the libras off the counter, and deposited them. "I'm going to go crazy with some of the customers that come in for a flower mate. I should have taken into consideration that a situation might arise in which I needed to forbid a sale. Without that clause in the contract, I don't have ammunition against bad sales. I'll have to revise that after careful consideration. For now, back to the rose bushes."

Hennley peeked around the corner. "Yes, where are we going with them? Are they part of a display idea? Delivery?"

"No, they are going to be a gift for Xephriel Maxis, our neighbor who runs the Humerus."

Hennley straightened so fast that she almost knocked a sample lotion off the front showcase. "Come again? I didn't expect that answer. He's so mysterious. All those bones around his windows, doors, and even on the roof. How do you think he placed the bones in the building itself? I've always been curious about that. What made you think of him?"

Amé tapped her fingers against the marble surface and angled her head to the side. "I don't know. This entire day has been strange, but I'm sure the roses are meant to go to him. As for the bones all over his building, I think it's kind of fascinating. I love the little fangs and shells."

"It's mostly creepy." But Hennley had a teasing tone that suggested she wasn't entirely put off by it.

"Regardless, I'm giving him a gift. I'm long overdue. Seven years overdue, to be exact." Amé felt a little shame she hadn't extended her hospitality sooner.

"You are usually so attentive to our fellow Soul Street shopkeepers. Wasn't it last week you gave Mrs. Ithica a mandarin orange tree for her twenty-fifth store anniversary?"

Amé peeked over her shoulder at the white and black rose bushes. "I did give her the orange tree. Xephriel was very standoffish when we first met, but after getting to know him, I think he's shy. And by the time I realized he was a perfectly pleasant witch, I'd completely forgotten to give him a gift."

Hennley sauntered to the roses and gripped the edge of the wagon. "What made you think of it today?"

"The roses sang to me."

"You sound like one of those divination witches with their prophecies."

"We all have a little divination in our souls, and even mortals can feel the pull of fate."

Hennley heaved backward on the wagon handle and panted at the weight. "Fate or curiosity, let's go deliver the roses and hope he doesn't give us a bone in exchange."

"I'd like a little shell if he does. The patterns are so pretty, and they always retain the scent of the sea. Don't you think that is romantic?" Amé mused as she bent over and pushed the wagon from behind.

"No! I'm fine not receiving anything at all. But maybe you want a token to admire while thinking of Mr. Maxis?" Hennley teased and helped wheel the roses out of Seeds of Love.

Amé chuckled and bent to take a whiff of a rose anther's fragrance. Life and death intertwined and whispered they belonged together. The romantic gesture between flowers took root in her heart. Maybe, the gift would break through Xephriel's reservations and plant a seed that they could be friends. Or maybe, she reflected, this was a path she had no control over. Maybe, that fear of being stagnant was about to be disrupted.

Chapter 6

Xephriel stabled Carrion, making sure to brush him down and nuzzle his nose. His thoroughbred was patient, amiable, and loved to be doted on. After a pleasant farewell, he paid Mr. Quinn for extra oats and carrots, then strolled back to the Humerus.

He hunched his shoulders as he watched the pavement and placed his hands in his jacket pockets. A headache punctuated the front of his head, and he became desperate to return to the safety of the Humerus. He needed a dose of lavender and chamomile tea to ease the pain. Afterward, he'd lie down with an amethyst on the center of his forehead to purge the residual psychic scum that seeped through the spider silk's magic barrier. He mostly wanted to quiet darkness of his sanctuary and the permanent solitude found in the Humerus.

As he approached his building, he glimpsed Amé with her apprentice, pushing rose bushes out of her shop. They wheeled the wagon down a wooden ramp and onto the sidewalk. He halted when he realized Amé had directed the cart in front of his shop. Xephriel recovered his composure and ran to the Humerus. He arrived as they began to unload the pots.

"What's this?" He queried as they set down a cluster of black roses.

Amé addressed him with a pleasant welcome. "Hello, Xephriel! I have a present for you."

He peered down at the black and white roses, uncertain of how he should respond to her sudden delivery. "Uh, thank you."

Amé swept her hair away from her eyes and motioned to her apprentice. "This is Hennley. She's a rosaceae witch and pruned these two bushes today."

Hennley gave a small wave. "Nice to meet you."

Xephriel bobbed his head in greeting, then returned his attention to Amé. "Thank you. The roses are a very generous gift. Um, to what do I owe this honor?"

"You're welcome. There's no reason. I thought the black and white colors would suit the atmosphere of the

Humerus. Where would you like to put them?" Amé surveyed his area of the street as her voice trailed off.

"I have a bit of land in the courtyard out back."

She tapped a finger against her chin and looked at the sky as she mused. "The buildings are squashed together, and they are too heavy to haul up the stairs. It's too bad you don't have a ramp. Although," She paused her speech and bent over to get a better view of the space in front of the Humerus. "I can build a box in front of your property and make a small garden. It will be in coordination with the city ordinances and add a nice touch to the entryway."

Xephriel looked from Amé to the space beside his stairs. He had no idea if that was true, but he was polite in his response. "Thank you. I'll defer to your expertise in this situation."

Amé's features overspread with pleasure. Her dark gaze glistened, her cheeks rounded like apples, and two dimples creased at the corners of her mouth. The overall effect caused her face to become exquisite. Her tone was as sweet as her expression as she replied, "You're welcome. I'll build the box and bring the soil. It won't take long."

"Is there anything I can do to help?"

Her answer was immediate. "Of course. Let me get the supplies, and then you can help me hammer the planks together."

She turned to Hennley, asking her to watch the shop while they worked. Her apprentice acquiesced and strode back into Seeds of Love. Amé gave Xephriel a brief explanation of what she intended to do, then went to get her toolbox.

Xephriel bent to sniff a black rose, the aroma like frozen earth in winter. The color was so black that it was hard to differentiate each petal. The sun's beams seemed to absorb and disappear into the blossom's folds. He moved his nose to a white bud and appreciated its sweet fragrance. The white rose smelled like cotton bathed in the summer light.

Luminous and dark, warm and frigid, the two variations of flowers complemented each other in their opposites. Like a healing spell, his headache dissipated, and Xephriel was left with a shadow of the day's toils. Strange, he did not require the use of gems or tonics to eliminate the potency of his empathic overload. He squinted at the roses and wondered how they brought him relief.

Amé returned with her tools and rummaged around the box until she discovered a tape measure. "I need to measure the spot where we will build your garden. Hold this end for me, please, next to your stairs, and I'll see if I have wood planks that will fit the space."

Xephriel did as instructed and watched her mark the length down on a notepad. His inquisitive line of ponderings exchanged so that he now became engrossed in the process of building a garden. Amé put her pen horizontally between her teeth and signaled for him to drop the tape measure. She determined the width and then scribed the dimensions. She was gone the next instant to examine the materials in her shop.

Xephriel didn't know what to make of his vivacious neighbor. They hadn't engaged beyond pleasantries in the seven years since Amé opened Seeds of Love. He couldn't fathom what possessed her to engage in a full acquaintanceship that afternoon and build him a garden. Not that he minded, but he was wary of all people.

Amé made him nervous, but it wasn't unpleasant. It was the opposite of what he felt with other people. She filled the space with an abundance of comfort. He was washed in tranquility every time they were in close proximity. The confounding dichotomy of desiring her attention and the fear of his empathic dissonance unraveled his careful state of reticence.

Like a whirlwind, Amé blew into his life, and he couldn't keep his distance. A fateful twine of thread spun him toward the spool that represented Amé, and whether it turned out to be cataclysmic or cathartic, he would have to wait and see.

"I'm going to have to cut a few pieces of plywood to fit the parameters. Want to help?" Amé called from the doorway of Seeds of Love.

Xephriel snapped out of his reverie, and he answered, "Sure, I'll come over."

He entered Seeds of Love, and Amé rotated her hand in a circle to guide him into her greenhouse. Sunlight glowed through the glass structure, and flowers bloomed in magnificent shades, creating a patchwork of multicolored petals intermixed with lush green. The scenery was breathtaking and fresh, and his nose detected a plethora of earthy scents. Magic plants radiated vivid auras. Species he had never seen before sparkled against an assortment of leafy vegetation.

"This is amazing." He followed her down a row of herbs. The distinction of basil, thyme, and sage lingered as he passed by.

Amé peeked over her shoulder. "Thank you. Cultivating unique plants has been my passion since I was a child."

"The colors are spectacular, and I've never seen so many magical flowers."

"It's my greenhouse and soil that makes the colors stand out. I also have an overhead sprinkler system that I have to control manually, but it moistens the plants at the same time. The consistency in light and water is how I manage optimal vegetation development."

Xephriel bent to gander at the solar panels leaning against the side of the glass wall. "I could help put up the panels when you are ready if you would like."

Her cheeks pinkened as she responded, "That would be appreciated."

He liked her answering blush, and it sent prickles over his skin. "I'd be happy to come over any time you need an extra hand." The response was unexpected. The words tumbled out of him without conscious engagement.

Xephriel made himself vulnerable by opening a channel of familiarity. It went against all his reclusive instincts. Baffling, to be sure, but the words were out there now. If he wanted to preserve any of his common sense, he'd do well to hold his tongue and not offer anything else to Amé.

Xephriel paused by a midnight blue flower with dewy speckles on the petals. "What's this one called?"

Amé turned around, and her countenance softened into a nostalgic reflection. "This is one of the magic plants I cultivated. It's called a Khaos lily. The sparkles represent the stars. It's an effect of my magic. The plant releases tiny drops of moisture through the petals, and when the light disperses through the water beads, it makes the flower twinkle. The dark blue color is for Khaos' eyelashes. I always loved that part of the world egg creation story."

"How do you create magic flowers?" He was intrigued by Amé's world of blossoms and greenery.

Amé slid her thumb over a leaf curling out from the Khaos lily's stem. "Let me think a moment about how I should explain it." Her green aura illuminated and intensified as she ruminated. She rubbed her lips together, then answered, "Plants have cells and languages like mortals and witches. Inside the cells, instructions tell the plant what to do. My magic opens a channel between the plants' molecular structure and my consciousness. We communicate, but instead of words, it's with energy and thoughts. They tell me what cell makes color, what cell designs its shape, or how their photosynthesis works, that sort of thing. We form a relationship, a bond. If I want to create a Khaos lily, I first have to study how the original lily is constructed. Then I can communicate with the flower to determine how to change it. Of course, it takes time because altering the biological makeup of a living thing requires patience, respect, and mutual consent. A flower won't become different because I ask. It has to want to evolve. It takes several tries before a new species or a magic plant emerges."

"How many species of magic plants have you created?"

"I'd have to look at my notebook to know for sure. Off the top of my head, I'd say at least thirty."

"Are the roses you brought me a magic species you cultivated?"

"No, but black roses were made by a rosaceae witch before Khaos went to sleep. They have a mournful song that compels lost souls to find their peace in the afterlife. They can extract negative energy from a person, and they have healing properties that can cure a broken heart. Plants have their own kind of magic."

That explained why his headache had dulled. The natural properties of the black roses drew out the negative vibes lingering from his morning's adventures.

Xephriel leaned toward Amé, a motion that shocked him when he registered what he was doing. Her presence felt like a remedy, and he wanted to partake in a dose of her abundant nourishment. It was so out of character for him that he froze on the spot. He couldn't retreat and refused to draw closer.

He managed to ignore his peculiar reaction and expressed, "They suit the Humerus, indeed. I'm glad you thought of me."

She stared up at him with honesty and peacefulness. The moment suspended, gathering their auras together like night and day exchanging in a twilight kiss. Then she blinked, her fingers trembling as she tucked her hair behind her ear. Their connection was lost, and Xephriel leaned on the table of plants and steadied his mind. His shoulders sagged as the short pants of panic changed to deep rehabilitating breaths and soothed his rising anxiety.

Amé resumed her steady gait down the aisles, her voice croaking at the beginning of her next question. "How did your visit to Justice Street go? You said you had a bone reading that led you to that end of town."

"I can't go into details, but a client came to get a bone consultation on her missing husband. He was a land-scaper for the city."

"Were you able to help her find him?"

He pressed his lips together and recalled the tragic morning. "I did, but the situation was complicated."

"Sounds like you had a rough morning. Let's make your rose garden and see if we can turn your day around."

He was grateful for the subject change and appreciated that she didn't pry for information. Witches with green auras resonated at frequencies that understood healing and respected all lifeforms. They dedicated their lives to people and nurtured their relationships. They were helpful, willing to compromise, and cooperated to create harmonious connections.

Green auras had an accepting disposition that made them gentle and patient. As a result, they were attentive to other people's emotions. Xephriel couldn't pinpoint if it was Amé's aura that was compelling him to abandon his reservations or if was Amé herself.

Xephriel didn't allow himself to be romantic or imagine he could find a life partner. The layer of epidermis that conducted magic through all witches was more sensitive for Xephriel. Proximity to that particular organ was potent. Direct contact with anyone when he wore the spider silk caused him to have nosebleeds. If the touch lingered, he would have a migraine. Full skin-to-skin contact for more than a minute would give him a seizure. He was afraid of people, but it was nothing compared to the terror that arose at the notion of intimacy.

What if his partner thought they could cure him but ended up causing more damage? What if they agreed never to touch him but grew to resent it later? The guilt would always be between them. If a handshake gave him a headache, he didn't want to predict what a kiss would do.

The only feasible way he could have a chance at a romantic relationship would be if he found his heart song. Heart songs established total harmony between the couple. Xephriel might have direct contact, and though he detected the spectrum of the other person's emotions, it wouldn't unravel his mind and wreck his body.

He didn't believe a heart song bond would cure him. There was no way to identify why his mind overwhelmed him with empathic dissonance, but he'd have peace with one person. Although, all of that was a hope he developed in order to keep from spiraling into endless depression. He'd grown used to his condition, but that didn't mean it didn't eat away at his sanity.

Connecting with a heart song was rare, and no one knew its origin. Whether Khaos put it in place as part of witch magic and biology or simply made it a part of the universe's mystery, most records of its existence were handed down by word of mouth.

The heart song occurred between witches more than mortals because of magic. Direct skin contact revealed whether the heart song was present. If two people resonated at congruent frequencies, the chords of their souls synthesized into music as they interacted. The sound waves faded when the couple united their auras and magic through the heart song ritual.

He often wondered if the spider silk prevented him from finding his heart song. In muting his surroundings, he may have also cut off any chance of finding the one person whose compatibility would release him from his empathic oppression. The chances were slim since he was untouchable, but he could be wrong. The heart song might form in other ways. If he didn't meet his heart song, it didn't mean he couldn't encounter love. Love and soul frequencies were not synonymous with each other. Many people fell in love without being soul-mates.

All of this flashed through his mind as he strolled after Amé. Xephriel had been drawn to Amé since the moment they met seven years ago. Why? He never guessed. It was certain that this moment was different than the other meetings. This interaction was important. Against his better judgment, he let his intuition guide him.

Amé arrived at the end of her greenhouse, oblivious to his musings, and paused by a worktable scattered with tools. She lifted a wooden board propped against the glass wall and set it down on the surface of the table. Xephriel studied Amé as she grabbed a measuring stick and checked the length against the dimensions written in her notebook. She drew a mark with charcoal on the edge of the wood and set the board aside. Picking up several more pieces, she repeated the process.

"Ready to cut these down to size?" She handed him a saw and slipped on a pair of leather work gloves.

He secured the plywood with a clamp on the end of the worktable and angled the saw's teeth to cut one of the boards. The metal scraping against the wood reminded Xephriel of a zipper. It was soothing and rhythmic.

Xephriel carried the boards when they finished, and Amé grabbed her toolbox. She lined up the boards against the side of the Humerus. Once she was certain the angle was correct, she motioned for Xephriel.

"I'll need you to hold the panels together while I nail them," she said and grabbed the hammer.

He lined up the wood so the corners created a nine-ty-degree angle. "Like this?"

She tied her hair with a leather string and then poised the nail. "Perfect."

Her movements were fluid, like water, graceful and hypnotic. Ingenuity, curiosity, and cooperation glided from her aura, brushing over his psychic senses like a feather. Xephriel watched Amé work, her shoulder muscles tensing under her dress as she hammered nails into the boards.

Once the box was constructed, Amé pushed it flush with the side of the Humerus. Wiping the back of her forearm across her brow, she moved to nail the next plank to the base structure. Once she was finished, she placed her tools inside the box and released her hair from the tie. It tumbled over her shoulders, straight like long needles, and gleamed as the light rippled against the strands.

Amé informed him they were ready to lay the dirt down and plant the rose bushes. They filled a wheel barrel with soil, and Xephriel helped roll it out of the shop. Amé shoveled dirt into the flower box and showed him how to loosen the roots in the pots so they could transfer the roses.

"You have to be careful. Flowers don't like to be disturbed, especially when they've made a comfortable home for their roots. Watch out for the thorns too." She demonstrated with her trowel as she worked on the white roses.

His silk gloves were saturated with dampness as he worked to remove the black rose bush from its pot. Xephriel closed his fist over the dirt and felt it clump, then crumble. It was therapeutic to sift through handfuls of porous soil and nutrients. The fragrance of the roses and the musk from the mixture of composites permeated his nostrils.

"I didn't realize gardening could be so relaxing," Xephriel mused as he ran his hand around the base of the stems.

Amé paused her digging and peeked around the white roses. "I love to sink my fingers into the dirt and feel the connection to the world egg. Quiet moments help me relax, and I can listen to the wind rustle the leaves or birds sing to each other. I like to feel like the world is making an impression on me instead of the other way around."

Her words hit home. He found himself confiding in Amé. "I've struggled with being an empath my whole life. The noise of crowds and the invasion of projected emotions wears me down."

"You are welcome to come to my greenhouse anytime you want a break. Plants have healing power, especially for the mind and soul. Not all magic runs through the veins of witches."

He was silent a moment, letting her offer to hang between them. He didn't often make friends and appreciated having a space outside the Humerus where he could feel safe. "Thank you. That means a lot to me."

"Can I ask a question about your bones?" She paused her digging and sat down, crossing her legs.

"Sure."

"Why do you have them plastered into your building?"

He cleared his throat and shifted so he also sat on the cobblestone sidewalk. "The bones placed throughout my shop protect me from receiving the brunt of emotions people emit when I have consultations. It will even dull witches' auras. It's like being inside a soundproof room, except for magic and emotions."

"Are there particular bones that protect more than others?"

"Cats, birds of prey like hawks and eagles, or spider exoskeletons can be used for protection. Bats are used for clairvoyance, observation, and illusions. I have a lot of their fangs and wing bones placed in the walls and foundation of the building. A combination of animal bones will intensify the bone magic. Of course, the strongest bone magic is ancestral, but even the souls of mortals and witches can cause me discomfort."

"You have cat bones in your walls?" Her tone wasn't judgmental. It sounded more curious. She turned her head toward the Humerus to scrutinize the bones.

"Yes. They are beneficial to psychic awareness. I find bones, or I guess you could say they find me. I go into the woods and look for carcasses, or if I'm traveling, a bone might reveal itself to me. Cat bones are part of that collection."

"It's kind of morbid thinking about picking at a carcass, but I'm also strangely fascinated by this. It's kind of like hunting for truffles or discovering a new species of plant." At this point, she asked, "You mix the bones, brick, and mortar, and then you can interact with people?"

"The Humerus is set up as one big warding system. The bones you see are from specific animals with a spiritual affinity for protection. Unlike the symbols I arrange for divination, the patterns aren't in a particular order. The bone magic activates with my intentions and absorbs emotions and auras. It's a great security system, too. No one is going to break into a place with skulls and fangs embedded around the window sills." He laughed at the last statement, which was meant to be a joke.

Amé's lips twitched in amusement, and she asked, "How did you get all the bones into the building? They have been there ever since I opened Seeds of Love."

Xephriel returned to tending to the roses as he conveyed, "I had the original building knocked down, and I commissioned the Humerus. The workers weren't experienced with bones, so I had to help with the assembly."

Amé's mouth hung open, but she recovered her astonishment and declared, "I think you are quite the resourceful witch. You may not be able to sell it unless, of course, the owner loves bones."

"I don't plan to leave the Humerus, ever. Well, until I die anyway, then my bones will go to the ancestral burial site at the Maxis estate."

"Another bone witch could take over the business, or perhaps one of your children. It'll be your legacy."

She meant it as reassurance, but the comment still stung. Xephriel would never have children. The Humerus would likely be auctioned off, or another family member would take care of it. He fell silent because what else could he say? Xephriel wasn't going to explain how his empathic condition prevented him from sharing himself with a life partner. Children weren't even an option.

"Your clothes protect you as well?" Her voice dropped in tone as she asked her next question, almost as if she sensed he was uncomfortable.

"Touching people is worse than being in their presence. I don't want to chance brushing against someone, so the clothes help when I'm in public," he said and dumped more dirt into the flowerbox.

"I'm so sorry, Xephriel. I can't imagine what it must be like to keep your distance from people."

Xephriel looked down to see the rose bush was ready to move to the garden box. "It is difficult to have any kind of relationship with people, but I have friends who understand. Mostly bone witches because they are also inconvenienced with empathy. They wear bones to dull the effects of their magic, and because of that, I can interact with them. Or they are in a place where their bone magic redirects their emotions, and I don't internalize their feelings. I've tried everything to help dull my empathic condition. I endured more doctors as a child than I bet anyone else has in a lifetime. No one on Healing Street could find a way to dull the impact emotions had on my body. The spider silk is the only thing that's worked."

She stood and clapped her hands together, sending dirt puffing in the air. "The bones in your building, too."

"Yes, and the bones. Although, most people think they are morbid. Most of my clients don't know what to do when they come inside to ask for my services. I suppose it would be strange to see bones in the walls if you didn't grow up with that being your norm."

"I have high respect for bones. I don't find them morbid at all. I get ground rat bones from Lia, our apothecary neighbor. I mix it into the soil to boost calcium levels and phosphor. Not to mention all the zinc and magnesium stored in marrow enriches the soil. Bone meal is essential for fertilizer. My plants get the best food, and that's why they grow so well, especially the magical plants."

Xephriel felt a tug as if an invisible hand wrapped around his aura to get his attention. He retreated, trying to deny the tension urging him to cast aside his fears. He was compelled by the witch before him and didn't know what to make of the feeling.

Amé was offering him friendship and kindness, but all he wanted to do was flee. The Humerus door was mere feet away. All he had to do was get up and rush inside, and he would be safe. An epic war clashed inside his soul, but his body refused to budge from the spot between the potted roses and his sanctuary.

Amé dug around the pot with her trowel, unaware of his turbulence. "Soil helps to decompose bones, and in return, the bones create a fertile environment for things to grow. Your magic and mine are very compatible and necessary to the life and death cycles."

Xephriel reached down to lift the roses at the same time Amé did, and an electrical current zipped up his arm. The static traveled toward his heart and resonated in his chest. He waited for the familiar pounding headache, the nosebleed that came from direct contact, but nothing happened.

Maybe it was the spider silk that blocked her magic from causing him harm. It might have been her inherent nurturing aura. Whatever the reason, all Xephriel could do was stare at his palm.

He looked up at Amé's sharp inhalation, and icy trepidation slithered in his veins. Gone was the warmth, and in its place was a fear so profound it immobilized Xephriel. He was not the only one who felt that charge.

Amé dropped the roots and regarded her gloved palm. She shook her hand as if it stung, but after a minute, she seemed fine and reached for the bush. Xephriel stilled as the implication of what their touch caused rattled through his system.

He trembled at the notion of acknowledging a mysticism that might indeed exist. Was it possible that Amé's aura was able to adapt to his empathic dissonance? Was this magic between them the elusive heart song?

Xephriel allowed Amé to lift out the rose bush and gulped down his anxiety. He needed air and space to contemplate what had happened. If Amé had any inclination that their connection was unique, she didn't show it. Xephriel wasn't sure what hurt most, the fact that he might have found his heart song and she was oblivious, or that she wasn't his heart song and he was so desperate to have that connection he'd made the whole thing up.

The image of her shaking her hand reeled in a loop.

For seven years, he'd lived beside Amé. He was so adamant about staying away from people that Xephriel had a suspicion he might have died without knowing that his possible salvation was a few feet away. At that moment, with hope on the horizon, he crumbled.

Before he touched Amé, the idea of a heart song was just that, a myth, a way to keep him sane in the complete desolation of his life. Now that the legend had a possibility of being real, he retreated from deliverance.

Call it self-preservation or stupidity, but Xephriel rejected his previous notions on heart songs and harmony. He embraced his reticence where he was safe. Fear was his succor. It was better to protect himself and prevent disappointment than to take a leap of faith.

Chapter 1

Amé patted the dirt around the black and white rose bushes, then straightened and plopped her hands on her hips. "Perfect! They look amazing and add to the mystery of the Humerus."

Xephriel's hooded head nodded once. "I would not have picked roses for myself."

"My flower senses are rarely wrong. Except for today." She crossed her arms and exchanged her jovial attitude for a stern contemplation. "The customer I had before I came here gave me the creeps. Every instinct told me not to sell her a flower mate, but I didn't listen. I have a horrible habit of being nice to everyone and expecting them to be nice to me in return. It's ridiculous how I'll convince myself everyone deserves a chance, even when I clearly know they don't deserve it."

Xephriel leaned against the railing on his stairs and mimicked her crossed arms. "Being nice isn't a bad thing. There's a lot of people in the world who need your kindness."

"Yes, but when I need to be a little mean or confident in my feelings, I find it difficult to accomplish the task. I don't know why it would have been so bad for me to shoo the customer out of my store. I persuaded myself not to judge her, but I'm fairly certain she was a psychopath."

"What gave you the impression she was psychotic?"

Amé pulled off her gloves and tossed them in the wagon with the empty flower pots. "My flower mate seeds rattled in their jars. They are sentient, so they pick up on magic signatures like witches. They gave me the impression they were terrified of the customer. At that point, I should have told her to leave without a flower mate, but I didn't. I sold the seed anyway. It's not even about the money. The profit I make from the other plants is enough for a comfortable lifestyle. I don't mind losing a sale. I don't want people to be lonely or miss their chance at love. This felt different. My seeds didn't like her, and I feel I should have listened to them."

"Unless she threatened you, there would be no way to know the exact state of her mind. Don't beat yourself up about the sale. Maybe you were right, and she really needed a seed to feel better about her life."

"She didn't threaten me, but she was unpleasant. The seeds grow from the intention of the sower. If she doesn't nurture her seed, it won't produce a flower mate."

He dropped his arms, the action sudden and surprising as he asked, "What exactly is a flower mate?"

"I developed a magic plant that grows the idea of true love. I made a plant person."

Xephriel's reaction was hidden by the hood, but his manner gave Amé the belief that what she said was significant. "How did you make a person out of a plant?"

She gathered her supplies and placed them in the wagon as she said, "A lot of cross genetics and magic."

Xephriel stroked his stubbled chin. "What gave you the idea to make a sentient plant that could grow into a sower's true love?"

"My best friend wondered why someone couldn't home order their perfect mate. I took that potential and elaborated on it. The flower mate magic activates to the person who cares for it. As it grows, it learns. It will take a certain scent they use for perfume, the way they speak, whatever commands the flower receives, and convert that information to appear as their caregiver's version of true love. It lasts for one day and one night, then withers and dies. That's why there aren't hundreds of giant plants overtaking Aequitas. It's meant as a way to guide people to their heart's desires, to the secrets we are too scared to reveal or those we have not yet unveiled."

Xephriel unfurled his fingers, a gesture indicating he had another question. "Do you get a lot of customers asking for flower mates?"

Amé leaned backward and rested against the Humerus. "I don't advertise that I have them. Friends or previous customers refer most people who come shopping for a flower mate. I have a strict contract and code of conduct that must be signed before selling a seed. Costumers cannot buy more than one, and I don't allow buyers to pick a new personality when they are unsatisfied."

"Are your seeds the only sentient plants that exist?"

"That I can't be sure of, but I know I'm the only one who has invented a plant that can produce the heart's desires."

Xephriel looked down both directions of the street and lowered his voice before saying, "Would you mind coming into the Humerus so we can talk in private?"

She bristled. Her spine went rigid as her suspicion manifested from his sudden change in demeanor. "What's wrong?"

Xephriel made the same jerking movement of his head as he scanned the area. "It's not a good idea for me to follow through with my line of conjecture on a public street. I promise you are safe in the Humerus, but I would like your opinion on one of my bone readings if you do not mind."

Amé watched him fidget, and his tone was so serious it sent a ripple of apprehension over her skin. "Let me go relieve Hennley for the day and close up my shop, and then I will be over."

"I'll wait for you inside. Knock on the door when you arrive."

Amé wheeled her gardening load back to Seeds of Love. Her blood felt as if it had frozen in the last few minutes. Hennley greeted her from the counter as she sorted the skin care products. After rolling the tools and pots back into the greenhouse, Amé returned to let Hennley know she could leave. Amé glanced at the clock. It was three, a little early to close her shop, but Xephriel had a desperation about him.

Amé shut the door behind Hennley and locked it. She drew the curtains across her display window, switched her store sign to closed, and removed her work boots. Amé secured the door to her greenhouse, washed her hands and face with water from the fountain, and proceeded out of her shop again. As she rushed up the stairs to the Humerus, the white and black rose bushes flashed in her peripheral vision.

The roses rustled from a mystic wind, content to have their roots settled in the soil where they could intertwine. Honied soprano tones undulated over a haunting bass, striking a harmonious chord that took her breath away. She was right to bring the roses to Xephriel.

She turned to the curved black door of the Humerus and lifted her hand to the skull and cross-bones knocker. The door and window frames were decorated with small bird skulls, seashells, fangs, and tiny animal claws. The small teeth added a savage beauty to the Humerus' structure.

With deliberation, she raised her hand. Her fingers gripped the crossed femoral bones of a small creature, and she rapped on Xephriel's door. She dropped her arm to her side, waiting for the mysterious owner of the Humerus to grant her entrance. The door cracked open, and Xephriel stood in the doorway like a gatekeeper against the ebony background.

The interior of the Humerus felt like perpetual twilight with its drawn navy blue curtains and orange sunset candlelight. The urgency of Xephriel's summons was forgotten in the enchantment of the Humerus.

Beautiful ivory bones in every shape and size decorated the interior like an enchanted crypt, a secret palace of death. She was mesmerized by the bones scattered over tables, in glass jars, dangling over chairs, and fixed into alabaster columns holding up the structure of the building. Bones even made a segmented spiral path under the surface of the black marble floor. White against black, against his midnight blue aura, it was like a galaxy of fatality.

She stared at the chandelier above her head and placed a hand over her mouth in awe. "What kind of bones are those?" She pointed up as an effusive film blurred her vision.

Xephriel's voice resonated low and rich, her ears responding to its smooth timbre. "The candle cups are screwed into the metacarpals of a fox, the arms of the chandelier are made from wolf rib bones, the bowl is a beaver skull, the chains are snake vertebrae, and the canopy is a stag pelvis. I had it converted to operate gas lighting."

"It's stunning." She looked beyond Xephriel to a wall of small drawers. "What is in the cabinet?"

He pivoted and made a small "ah" sound. "Those are rare bones I collect. Some I use for divination, and others I just like."

"What sort of rare bones?" Her tone came out breathless as she stared across the room.

"Dragon claws. Panther teeth and claws, peacock bones, monkey carpals, python bones, poison frog bones, hippopotamus teeth, and swan bones are in the other drawers. If possible, I like to collect the whole animal, but teeth, talons, and small bones like joints, carpals, or sesamoids might only be available."

"You have dragon claws and scales? That is extraordinary."

He was so reserved outside the Humerus, but his mood changed when Amé engaged him about the bones. Xephriel angled his hooded head, and she guessed he was staring at her when he said, "Do you want to see them?"

She bounced on the balls of her feet in excitement. "Yes! I've never seen a dragon, let alone its bones!"

A quirk of his lips captivated her. He led her to his wall of treasure, pointing at a drawer with a golden dragon painted on the panel. Xephriel dug into his pocket for a set of keys and voiced, "I've never seen one either, just its bones. My father has an entire dragon skeleton in his antique room. He won't tell me how he obtained it."

The drawers at the top of the cabinet were thin and about three inches wide. They were tiered to the larger drawers on the bottom. On each panel, right above the lock, was a gold picture of an animal. At first glance, the cabinet appeared black like the rest of the room, but she realized the structure was purple like eggplant as she drew closer.

Amé watched him insert a tiny gold key into a lock and twist his wrist to the right. He slid open the dark purple drawer. He drew a rectangular box out of the cabinet and brought it to her eye level. The inside was lined in black velvet.

Glimmering blue, silver, and red scales palpitated a rainbow aura even in death. The scales rippled in rhythmic intervals as if they were breathing. Her eyes misted as she turned her interest to the claws. They were black and curved, and the points were dipped in gold. They were massive, and she would need two hands to grasp around the circumference.

"Aren't you afraid of thieves?"

Xephriel tilted his head back and pointed to the ceiling. "I have it protected."

Amé followed the direction of his finger and noticed spikes suspended above the drawers. "What if that falls on you?"

He looked down at her and said, "It might, but it will fall on anyone who tries to break in without a key. It's connected to a mechanism inside the wall, which runs through a back panel in the cabinet. If anyone forces open the drawers, it will fall. If a thief uses a lock-picking device, the lock itself will trigger a failsafe that clicks into place. That causes a secondary slide to fall over the front of the drawers, and the spikes impale the unfortunate thief."

"I pity any thief dumb enough to walk over your threshold."

"Bone collectors will risk death to steal dragon scales. At least the unsavory types. Most bone witches or mortal collectors will trade or search a dragon cave. However, I don't recommend the latter. Dragons live a few millennia and are known to roast first, ask questions never." He replaced the drawer and locked it with the key.

Amé inched away but was aware of the ceiling of skewers. "I'm glad I trade in plants, although there are a few that are carnivorous."

"Such as?"

"Cephalous is an exotic type of pitcher plant. They eat insects and live in swamps. I've seen one at the witch's academy. There's a professor there who trades in rare species and travels the world. He brought one of the Cephalous back to Libra from his adventures. There are mystical plants, like the animals you collect. A hydra vine that grows in the Amazonia forest ensnares elephants, crocodiles, mortals, and witches. Pretty much anything with flesh. The most common carnivorous plant is the Venus Fly Trap. I sold a few pots of those last year. They are small, eat insects, and look like clam shells."

Xephriel wandered away from the drawers and sat on the edge of a square table. "Remind me not to travel anywhere I can get eaten by a plant."

Amé chuckled and turned her attention to the glamor of the Humerus. "I never imagined bones to be so beautiful."

"Well, I never imagined flowers were so deadly."

Amé drew in her breath as she realized she had segued the conversation away from Xephriel's original purpose.

"Oh, I'm so sorry. I got us completely off track. What is it you wished to speak with me about?"

Xephriel crossed his arms and leaned toward her, his voice low and deliberate. "I'd like to know more about your flower mates."

"Okay. Sure. Why all the secrecy?"

He paused as if gathering his thoughts, and she really wished she could view the scope of his features. With tentative measure, he asked, "I think they may be connected to a murder."

"Murder?" She shouted loud enough that the word echoed around the room.

Xephriel flinched and cleared his throat. "A client came with a finger bone today, and I did the reading. I took the client to meet with my friend, a private investigator. The spirit of the bone confided that a woman harassed him into planting a seed. She grew agitated with him, stabbed him in the neck, cut off his finger, and he ended up in a well. The seed is what baffled us. According to your explanation, it seems to me that she had one of your flower mates in her possession."

"Did this spirit say what the seed looked like?"

"Lime with yellow marbling."

"I'm going to be sick." Amé put a hand to her mouth as she gasped out, "That could be one of my Adventure in the Woods seeds. They are predesigned to love the outdoors, especially rock climbing or extreme mountain hiking. It's for people who like to take risks and delve into their primal nature. That's not enough for me to be sure it was one of my seeds. Was there anything else that led you to believe it could be a flower mate?"

Xephriel nodded his head once. "The seed communicated to the mortal. I've never heard of a seed that could speak until you mentioned earlier that your flower mates have that ability."

Fear ran cold and deep in her veins as she whispered, "What did the seed say?"

"'She's not the one. Take me home.'"

Amé bent over, clutching her stomach as dread stole her breath. "Oh god. That's so similar to what my seeds pleaded with the strange customer. I've got to find that witch, but I don't know how."

Xephriel was delicate as he asked, "You believe this witch could be connected to this case?"

"Xephriel," She couldn't get her mouth to work right, but she managed to murmur, "Not only do I believe they might be the same person, but I also think she might very well do it again."

Chapter 8

Xephriel's courtyard was a small space in the back of the Humerus. It was cobbled with hermit crab shells to help ease the psychic tension he experienced when interacting with people. The animal spirits resonating inside the shells mimicked the sound of the ocean, liberating his stress and fear.

A few clam and oyster shells interspersed between the colorful turbos to create a patchwork of pearlescence. Glass filled in the gaps around the sea creature remains to protect their delicate structure while giving the illusion of the sea.

He brought Amé outside after their discussion on flower mates because he needed a safe space to think. Her emotions had slammed into him like a hammer, and it was clouding his judgment. Xephriel didn't know what to make of the whole situation. Part of him was still fighting the mysterious electrical shock that occurred when he touched Amé; the other part was suspicious. He didn't want to believe Amé was capable of harming anyone, but he couldn't deny the facts. The magical seed that the cloaked woman wanted Mr. Rendell to plant came from Seeds of Love.

The strange customer might be the witch responsible for the killings, or Amé could have misled him and been the killer herself. He wasn't inclined to believe the latter as it would expose her as the killer, and that didn't sit right. Amé was involved in the case, but he didn't know how. If he kept Amé talking, maybe he'd uncover more information.

The crab bones had unique magic that brought out truth and clarity. They protected the home and dispelled negative energy. If Amé had secrets, the shells would compel her to reveal them. Xephriel pushed his bone magic into the ether, activating the spirits, and waited for Amé's reaction.

Xephriel gave Amé time to wander while he gathered a teapot and cups from a small kitchen inside the Humerus. He returned with the tea set and watched Amé play with a cluster of tiny bells. He opened the flow of dialogue by asking, "What do you think of the Humerus?"

"Your home is beautiful. It feels like a puzzle as I pass through the rooms. It all fits together and makes this hauntingly beautiful picture."

"Thank you. Most people think my home is creepy. Especially clients. They don't know I'm empathic and do not hide their initial reactions from me."

"Well, I think it's a gem." Amé glided to the table and picked up a teacup. She tipped it upside down and studied the outer shape. "What bones are the tea cups made of?"

"That's porcelain." His voice colored with amusement at her innocent inquiry.

"Oh." She set the cup down and took a seat in one of the wicker chairs.

"I'll be a moment. I'm going to bring the tea." He returned to the courtyard after a moment and poured steaming water into the pot with tea leaves. "I selected a black tea from the southern coast of Khaos Island."

Amé leaned over and sniffed appreciatively. "I love black tea. The stronger, the better. Camellia Sinensis and Jasminum Sambac. Robust and bitter, with a sweet floral overtone. The tea comes from the town of Loridae. The farmers in Loridae are the only ones on the island who add jasmine to their recipe. Their blend is bold and alluring, just the way I like my tea."

"Your nose is correct. There's also a hint of—"

"Rose and chrysanthemum. It's subtle, but if you breathe out through your mouth, you can taste it on the end notes."

His gaze widened at her description of the tea flavor, but he shouldn't be surprised since she was a vegetation witch. "What is your plant expertise, if you don't mind me asking?"

"Not at all. Like all vegetation witches, I can work with any plant, but I prefer to experiment with plant genetics and reproduction. I also have a certificate from the witch academy for agronomics, a fancy word for soil management. My plant food is unique to my plants and flower mates. Before I opened Seeds of Love, I studied Libra's environment and ecosystem, but I haven't been on an expedition in years. I'm the only witch to create flower mates that I'm aware of."

They were back on track, and Xephriel pressed for more information. "How long does it take to make a flower mate? What's the process you go through?"

Her answer was immediate and confident. "It takes six months to a year to develop a custom-made seed. I usually harvest the seeds from flower mates I've already cultivated. If I make a new flower mate for a customer, I'll have to cross-breed a plant I've already made with the new characteristics that were ordered. There's a base flower mate that I use in those cases. If the seeds ever ran out or were stolen, I would have to start from my original formula. That would take a couple of years to perfect again."

Incredulous, Xephriel dropped his jaw and dumped a spoon full of sugar on the table. He swept the sugar onto his palm and dumped it on the saucer. Recovering from his embarrassing miss with the tea cup, he blurted, "Six months to a year? Do people wait that long?"

"They will wait for me to create the perfect flower mate. I have the premade seeds for those who want a companion immediately." Her pride shone through her umber gaze, and her eyelids crinkled around the edges as she smiled.

She was enthralling when she gazed at him with total candor and vibrancy. He drew his brows together in consternation, unsure of what to make of the reaction he had to her smile. He wasn't used to *his* feelings being discordant. Other people lobbed their emotions at him and caused chaos. He didn't have to dissect what was going on inside his mind and heart. As he pieced together the case and Amé's personality, Xephriel found the predominant feelings in his being were his own.

"What if the customer finds true love before they get the seed?" He asked, his mind back on his secret interrogation and the strange captivation scattered into the ether.

"I add the seed to my collection and sell it to another client."

Xephriel took a sip of his tea and collected his thoughts before delivering his next questions. "What is it about your seeds that would drive a person to use them inappropriately? Why would someone need others to plant them?"

Amé swirled the tea in her cup, and confusion marred her features. "I don't understand why someone would kill for a seed if that's what you are hinting at. The magic from my blood is manipulated by the flower mates. It's the ingredient I use to bind all the plant's genetic codes with the magic and make them come alive for a brief time. The flower mates themselves cannot do anything other than walk and talk. They are a reflection of what a person feels. They don't even have sex organs as we do, so they can't become the lover of the sower. The gender is a loose appearance, stemming from the idea of what the customer believes is appealing. As for why a customer couldn't plant the seed, it would have to be because of their intentions. The seed will grow when the magic is triggered by true love. If there's any purpose beyond the code I imprinted, the seed will die."

Xephriel finished the last gulp of tea and set down his cup. He twirled the handle in a circle and stared at Amé. She could not see his expression, but he had a full view of hers, and he did not think she was lying. Nor did his bone magic pick up on any hidden truths. The pulse of his indigo aura around the crab shells remained steady and dull. If a lie formed from her thoughts or speech, the crab shells would have flared with a red glow like the crow bones in his divination table. She was telling the truth, but he wanted to be sure there wasn't any underlying issue from her past.

"Have you ever had any complaints about your flower mates? Is there some sort of flaw in them that perhaps you overlooked?"

Amé folded her hands in her lap and regarded him with candor. "There is no flaw that I'm aware of, other than the fact that they cannot mutate into a real person and give a lasting relationship. I don't view that as a problem, but I've had customers in the past who have complained.

I'll replace a damaged seed, but I won't give a refund for mismatched personalities. I do my best to engage clients when they purchase a seed and give suggestions on the best fit for their idea of true love. Once they purchase a seed and leave my shop, the situation is out of my control. I usually smooth over sales disputes by offering a free magic plant of their choosing. It's calmed people down in the past. There are always people who will complain, but there is no reason for me to believe the seeds would cause a disgruntled customer to murder."

Xephriel had to admit Amé couldn't have anything to do with the case other than selling her seeds to the wrong person. Noble might have a different opinion, but nothing triggered a negative sensation from Xephriel. If anything, the love and pride for her work fed the magic in the crab shells and resonated against his empathy. He had no choice but to drop the interrogation and return to a more pleasant conversation. There was no need to cause her unnecessary uneasiness.

"What does your family think about your flower mates?" Xephriel poured more tea into their cups and sat back to listen.

Amé blew across the surface of her tea. "My mother thinks it's a fantastic idea. She's a hopeless romantic and

their conversation, but the spirits in the shells had picked up another message. He listened to the etheric field, the guiding spirits filtering through the veil and surrounding him with their protection. Hope and trust, they conveyed. Glancing from under his hood, Xephriel studied Amé's welcoming green aura.

What had entwined their lives, and was it for the better or for the worse?

Chapter 9

Amé met Sylvia outside Seeds of Love the next morning.
Sylvia's carriage stopped along the sidewalk. The driver
tipped his chin down in acknowledgment as Amé greeted
him and made her way toward the street. Sylvia swung
open the door and scooted to the end of the bench seat so
Amé could perch on her side of the cushion.

Her friend wore a radiant canary yellow and powder
blue chemise gown that complemented her teak complexion. She greeted Amé with a clap of her lace-gloved hands.
"We haven't been shopping in ages! I'm so excited. Where
should we start?"

"Fashion Street." It was a dry response, but Amé
crooked a smile to show she was teasing.

Sylvia batted her arm with her ivory silk purse and responded to her sarcasm. "You're not funny. Where on Fashion Street?"

"Why don't we start shopping for the baby?"

"Of course, but we need to get you clothes, too! How about a new dress? Or a hat?"

Amé shut the carriage door and settled next to her friend as the horses trotted down the street. "I don't look good in hats."

"That's because you don't get one to fit your cute round head."

"I have no interest in covering my head in feathers and ribbons, let alone dolling myself up when I'll be covered in dirt an hour later."

Sylvia squared her shoulders and wagged her pointer finger in the air. "You are going to buy a new addition to your wardrobe today, and I won't be persuaded otherwise."

"I'll take a look at Harry & Pearls. I'd like a new brooch."

"Now, we're talking! We only have an hour. Beaux doesn't want me exerting myself. I told him I'd be fine, but he worries."

"It's because he loves you."

Sylvia looped her arm around Amé's and leaned her head on her shoulder. "I know. He's wonderful, but I need a little space to be pregnant in peace."

Amé patted her friend's hand and propped her head on top of Sylvia's black curls. "Speaking of needing peace, I had a horrible afternoon yesterday."

Sylvia looked up through the curtain of her lashes. "What happened?"

"I had a weird experience with a customer during their purchase of a flower mate seed. When I delivered roses to Xephriel, it got strange."

Sylvia sat up with such force that Amé was almost knocked out. "I'm intrigued by everything in that last sentence. I'm dying to hear about your neighbor."

Amé didn't think she should tell Sylvia about the murder, but she rattled off the rest of the details. "The customer purchased a Cotton Candy seed, and I tried to persuade her out of it because the seeds inside the jar were trembling and whispering 'not her.' You know I'm not good at rejecting customers. I sold her the seed, despite my reservations, because I didn't think it would do any harm. I've had customers in the past who didn't take my advice well. I figured the worst that would happen was she'd ask for a refund. The rest of the seeds behaved the same way, and I knew the witch was different. All of the flower mate seeds were frightened of her, and that made me really uncomfortable. Did I listen to myself or my seeds? No. I wanted to please her and give her a chance to find true love. This incessant need to believe in the good inside everyone has gotten out of hand. I've decided not to sell any more seeds until I can revise the way I handle the transactions. I have to get a better handle on my business. I can't keep going on like this."

"You know," Sylvia mused, "I have disgruntled customers. People like to complain, even though our food is delicious. I don't give in. I tell customers they have to pay for the food, and if they don't like it, then they don't have to come back. I will compensate for a free meal if something disastrous happens, but not for a petty qualm about taste or presentation. If anyone comes into my restaurant with belligerent intentions, Greta shoves them right back out the door. You have to do the same thing with your flower mates. I know you want to help people and give them their best chance at love, but what you are doing is hurting clients and yourself. You are a vegetation witch; you are powerful and intuitive with your plants. Trust your instincts and tell your customers to believe in you or get out."

"You're right. I'm going to make drastic changes to the way I run my business. I shouldn't let people bully me around, especially in my shop. I definitely have to stop being nice to the point I don't make wise decisions."

Sylvia gave her shoulders a squeeze and said, "That's my girl! I love how you always view the good in people and give anyone a chance to prove their worth. You need to apply it in smaller doses, especially when doing business contracts and sales. Now, tell me all about your neighbor."

"I heard black and white roses singing to each other, and I got this sense that they should be gifted to Xephriel. There was an image of bones and flowers intertwining in my mind."

"You had a prophetic vision?"

Amé leaned her arm against the carriage window and recollected the song she heard. "I'm not sure. The melody was profound, and the image took over my consciousness. It was like having an out-of-body experience, but vegetation witches can't astral project like witches with divination magic. It was really strange, but I was convinced the roses belonged to Xephriel."

Sylvia looked at the corner of the carriage roof and deliberated, "Prophecy is powerful magic. There must be more to the message from the roses. What do you think it means?"

"I have no idea. I like Xephriel, even though he has an elusive nature, and his aura is a little intimidating. He's not a typical witch or man, and his magic is complex and alluring. He's like a puzzle, and none of the pieces I place make the picture I expect."

"You and your puzzles! No wonder you're drawn to him."

Amé flicked at her emerald silk gown as if she noticed a piece of dust. "I'm probably curious about him since he hides behind that hood all the time. The inside of the Humerus is riveting. I want to go back and take a closer look at his consultation room if he lets me."

"Oh, what's it look like inside? Is it creepy?" Sylvia turned on the bench seat so she faced Amé.

"The Humerus isn't creepy at all. There are bones everywhere, but they are polished and placed in intricate patterns throughout the building, like a mural. It's like being in a palace of death."

Sylvia shivered and buzzed her lips. "Sounds creepy to me, but you always had unorthodox taste in men."

"I don't have a romantic interest in Xephriel."

"You never know what will develop over time. I've listened to you talk about men you've courted before, and this is different. You never had a plant guide you to a specific person. His magic interests you. You feel drawn to him even though he's shrouded in mystery. There's a bond between you and Xephriel, and I wouldn't be surprised if he ended up wiggling into your heart."

Amé blew out an exasperated breath. "It's a romantic idea, but I don't think I have the option to enter into a courtship with him."

"Why not?"

"He's got an empathic condition that creates disharmony with other witches' auras. The emotions people project cause chaos with his magic. That's why he wears the hood all the time. The clothing is enchanted to block supernatural vibrations and limit his empathic reception."

"Surely, love wouldn't cause him harm." Sylvia would not let this go now. She had a determined turn to her mouth and was sitting so erect a book could balance on her head. All signs led to her best friend cheering behind her back until true love championed overall.

"He can't touch anyone, or their emotions will hurt him. I'd feel terrible if I was the cause of his pain. It's not meant to be."

"Oh." Sylvia's shoulders slumped, and her bottom lip popped out from her dissatisfaction.

"There's no possible way we could ever be together as anything more than friends. For his safety, I need to keep my distance."

Sylvia crossed her arms and wiggled down so she was leaning on Amé's shoulder again. "Well, that sucks. You two would make the perfect couple."

"You've never met him!"

"I can tell by the way you talk about him. 'Palace of death,'" Sylvia parroted. "Come on, Amé! You're fooling yourself if you think he's your friendly neighbor."

"What are we buying for the baby?" Amé changed the topic because examining a way to get around Xephriel's magic condition seemed like a dangerous path to tread. She didn't want to fall in love with him, only for it to lead to a dead end. A warning bell clanged in her mind that if she gave her heart to Xephriel, she would never get it back. Amé didn't know where the conviction came from, but it settled in her soul.

At the mention of the baby, Sylvia left all interest in Xephriel behind and lapsed into a baby list a mile long. Amé listened to Sylvia talk about pram brands, the style of baby outfits, and a nursing blanket. The only nursery term Amé understood involved plants. She jotted a few must-haves down to gift Sylvia later, but it was all foreign. She'd have to pay attention to what Sylvia purchased.

They arrived on Fashion Street twenty minutes later. Amé admitted she was excited about their shopping day. Fashion Street was a colorful exhibition of shops ranging from magic thread to outfits designed for a night at the castle. Exotic dyes, personalized needles, and fabric that left shoppers in awe lined the street. Buttons and jewels, feathers, and ribbons burst from jars arranged on the tables of outdoor stalls. If you could dream of an outfit, Fashion Street designers could actualize it.

Sylvia towed Amé by the arm and slipped into a fabric store. A laugh escaped Amé's throat as she hurried into the first shop and looked around at the rainbow of ribbons and exquisite patterns. Sylvia shuffled around the store and peeked at the dresses on display mannequins.

A beautiful vermillion silk poncho dress with gold embroidered dragons caught Amé's interest. She stretched out her hand and slid her fingers along the seam of the billowing sleeve. The soft fabric, like down feathers, enticed her, and the red hue appeared to blaze like a firebird as she brought the pattern closer for her inspection.

"It's the newest fashion at the mortal court. They like to show off their legs and create a commotion among the more conservative members of the royal elites."

Amé turned to the sales clerk and considered buying the dress. It was so far from her usual attire, but she loved the color. "Is it for sale?"

"Oh, yes. This is one of my favorite pieces. Look at the angle of the hem. It shows off the side of the leg but drapes down, so the front is still hidden. A glimpse of seduction, I call it. The neckline is high, so it's still acceptable to wear in any social setting. With your hourglass shape, it would look marvelous."

The price would be the deciding factor. "How much is it?"

"Fifteen gold coins. The dye is made from Phoenix Orchids."

No wonder it looked like it was pulsing with fire! Phoenix Orchids were created a few hundred years ago by a witch named Scarlett Diana. She took the blood of a phoenix and mixed it with an orchid to develop petals that secreted a scented oil like charcoal. Although flammable, the orchid couldn't naturally combust like a phoenix and required an external source to set it on fire. The flower blazed for a few minutes. The smoke formed the shape of a bird with long plumage and disintegrated the flower. A new blossom grew from the ashes. The seeds had to be harvested right before the flower erupted. Part of her coveted the dress for the Phoenix Orchid's enchantment clinging to the fabric, and the saner part of her mind knew she'd have nowhere to wear the clothing. She hadn't been to the opera or to the art gallery in ages. Most of her attire got smudged in soil and plants. The strange pulse of crimson thread seduced Amé, but she decided to give it more consideration before purchasing.

"Thank you, it is beautiful, but not what I'm looking for."

"If you see anything you like, call out. I'm Natasha, the owner of the shop."

"Thank you, Natasha." Amé reserved one more admiring glance at the poncho dress and turned away. As she faced the rest of the shop, she noticed a black cloak hanging on the far wall. Four color variations were draped beside it. She called out again to Natasha. "Wait!"

Natasha hurried to Amé's side. "Yes?"

Amé pointed to the cloak and asked in a rush, "Do you know of any seamstresses or tailors that weave witch spider silk?"

Natasha's brows drew together. "I'm afraid I do not. I have not heard of witch spider silk. Why do you ask?"

Amé waved her hand in the air and replied, "Just curious. I wondered how common it was to purchase that kind of material."

Natasha nodded her head, and her features exchanged from confusion to inspiration. "There is one tailor who weaves rare magical threads. He's known as the Fashion Street King. His shop is a few buildings down from here, called the Sorcerer's Spindle. If anyone is informed about unusual enchanted clothing, it's him."

"Thank you."

Natasha drew the edges of her lips upward in a friendly gesture and said, "You're welcome."

Amé paused by the cloaks, drawn to the mental picture of the woman in her shop. Her mind niggled with the image of Xephriel in his black hooded jacket. Amé wasn't a suspicious person. If anything, she was too trusting, but she couldn't banish the uncharacteristic perception that the cloak the witch wore could be a clue to figuring out if she was connected to Xephriel's case or not.

Xephriel used witch spider silk to dull the incoming magic and emotional spectrum of people. For the longest time, she couldn't detect his indigo aura unless she was standing right in front of him. She drew a peripheral parallel to the customer with her cloak and Xephriel's mystical clothing.

What if the reason the witch woman's aura was hidden had everything to do with the cloak she wore? Could it have been a coincidence? Did that witch also use enchanted spider silk to conceal her magic identity? The possibility created a reel of conjectures in Amé's mind, and she came to a startling conclusion. If she found the tailor who made Xephriel's clothing, perhaps he could inform her about other garments he designed. Amé might find the witch if she traced the cloak's origins. It was a long shot, but since she was on Fashion Street, it was worth looking into.

Amé headed for the exit and called back to Sylvia. "I'll be outside."

Once more on the sidewalk, Amé glanced to the right and read the signboards of each shop. Five buildings down, the Sorcerer's Spindle was visible. It was in the direction of Harry & Pearls, so a quick stop wouldn't take the shopping trip off schedule. Nor would it arouse Sylvia's suspicions. Amé didn't want her friend to get involved in a murder case. It was bad enough that her seeds may have a connection.

Sylvia showed up ten minutes later with a bundle of pastel calico fabrics in her arms. "Won't these colors look amazing on the baby?" She strolled to the carriage waiting on the side of the road. "I'm going to make a few different outfits. I'll be too large to maneuver around the kitchen at the end stage. I'll need an activity while I wait for the delivery day."

"They are fabulous colors. You'll have the most fashionable baby on Soul Street."

"I'll have to dig out my sewing machine. I haven't used it since our academy days."

Amé wrinkled her nose as she remembered Sylvia dragging her to their elective costume design class. "I failed miserably at stitching a straight seam. You, on the other hand, could have started a career in outfitting the Phantasmagoria Circus."

"Food was my calling, so here we are."

"Yes, here we are."

Sylvia linked her arm around Amé's waist as they strolled down the smooth sidewalk. "Where to now? Harry & Pearls?"

"I want to make a quick stop at the Sorcerer's Spindle. I heard they sell enchanted garments there."

"Oh, I love to window shop magic fabrics. I still have no idea how the queen's shoes levitated during her last court season. She was like a heavenly being when she danced. According to the court gossip. It was in the newspapers for weeks."

Amé remembered the story. "I wonder if I could make a plant fly?"

Sylvia's answering grin was encouragement enough for Amé to try. With a mischievous wink, Sylvia instigated, "Your next project!"

"First, I have to fix the current plant dilemma."

Sylvia gave her a light squeeze, and they left the topic of enchanted vegetation. They gazed at paraphernalia as they ambled toward the Sorcerer's Spindle, trying on different accessories at a few stalls. Amé bought a pair of clip-on earrings shaped like butterflies, and Sylvia bought a new wide-rim straw hat. They filled a burlap pouch with scarves they purchased, and Amé selected a pair of lace gloves.

They arrived at the Sorcerer's Spindle. The building was reminiscent of a mansion. She and Sylvia did not frequent shops that sold enchanted clothing. Neither of their professions required magic uniforms. As Amé stared at the elegant structure of the Sorcerer's Spindle, she wondered how she had missed the magnificence during her previous shopping exertions.

Although, it had been several years since she purchased anything from Fashion Street. So caught up in her work, Amé hadn't considered a new wardrobe until Sylvia suggested it during their carriage ride. The massive building must have been built in the last six years.

Amé left Sylvia outside; a discount on shoes captured her friend's curiosity. Inside, the shop was spacious and organized by the colors of the rainbow. Amé couldn't view the entire room because it was packed with customers, but she could make out most of the layout. Fabrics were lined on shelve like books in a library. Signs hung over each section to differentiate the types of cloth. By the cash register was an antique spinning wheel with a basket of cotton beside it.

Amé dodged a mortal matron with three children clinging to her skirt. An armful of purple and blue silks jostled in her grip as she maneuvered the crowd. The odd thing about the setting, it appeared most of the clientele were women. They had a feverish mood about them as they shopped. Anticipation hung in the air as if a celebrity were lurking in a corner.

Amé turned to a sales clerk; she must have been one because she had the same uniform as three other ladies. Before she got her inquiry out, a charismatic witch entered the shopfront. Every woman in the shop turned in his direction. Amé gasped at his height. He had to be at least five inches over six feet, and his aura was radiant magenta.

Amé wasn't one to swoon over a handsome man, but this witch compelled. His gleaming caramel skin had a tinge of gold, as if the sun's beams had nestled between the layers of his skin. He reminded her of a treasure-hoarding pirate with three sapphire earrings pierced in each ear. Gold chains linked each stud. The long jacket he wore was the exact shade of his aura, trimmed in gold with emerald pants that molded to his thighs. Leather knee-high boots had dragon buckles on the sides. As he swiped a thumb over his bottom lip, Amé caught the flash of gold rings on his fingers.

Fashion Street King, indeed!

Amé shook her head and blinked as if a spell had wound its way around her head. Her instincts blared that this was the witch she sought, even without an introduction. She pushed through the sea of women. Her average height and sturdy form kept her steady on her feet as she wended toward the textile witch.

Bursting through a space between two witches, Amé stumbled and bumped into the god-like man. She let out an *oomph* and grabbed the textile witch's forearm. Amé cleared her throat, embarrassed by her position, and regained her balance.

She gazed up into a pair of fawn and moss-colored eyes and had no doubt why women flooded the shop. A little breathless, she asked, "Are you the owner of the Sorcerer's Spindle?"

He tugged down his sleeve, and his crooked grin charmed the ladies gathered around the cash register. "I am, indeed. Is there something I can help you find, Miss Witch?"

She glanced around at the clambering customers and decided a direct approach was best. "Have you ever made clothes for a customer named Xephriel Maxis?"

The witch's face lit with delight. When he responded, his accent was thick and foreign. The timbre of it was lyrical, and it rolled off his tongue like an aria. "Xephriel! Yes, he's one of my regular clients. Did he recommend me? I can make anything for you. I see in my mind the perfect dress for your exquisite shape."

"Um, no. Not particularly. I was wondering if he was the only customer who bought enchanted silk from you?"

The gleam in the witch's hazel regard dimmed, and his features were tarnished with seriousness. "I'm afraid I cannot discuss the clothes I make for specific clients."

"I want to know if you made more clothes like his."

"I don't discuss those types of garments in public. I've already said too much."

"But—"

He cut her off with a raise of his hand. "I make one-of-a-kind clothes. I won't have anyone try to steal my designs or formulas."

Amé relented and backed into the crowd. "Thank you."

The witch seemed to change his mind as she retreated. He darted his gaze around the room, and he swooped in front of her path. He leaned forward as she halted and kept his voice low. "I can tell you that no one has clothes like Xephriel, not on this island or on the continent where I came from."

Amé sighed in relief at the small consideration the witch gave to her. "Thank you."

He inclined his chin and went back to addressing the needs of his customers, all of whom chattered at once. Amé pushed through the thicket of bodies and burst onto the street. She panted as she looked to the left, where Sylvia was still debating over which pair of shoes to purchase.

She arrived at Sylvia's side and said, "Did you find anything you liked?"

"I can't decide between the green slippers or the riding boots."

"Get them both?"

Sylvia chuckled and snatched up the green slippers. "I'm not supposed to buy more shoes. I have a closet devoted to them. I'll have to sneak these in so Beaux doesn't know. He doesn't mind that I buy them, but he likes to tease me about how three years could pass before I wear every pair I own."

"You do have an affinity for shoes."

"I have a problem. If I didn't make a killing from the restaurant, it would be criminal how low I'd let my bank account get."

Amé laughed as Sylvia paid the associate at the stall. "Shall we continue our journey?"

"Yes. We have about thirty minutes left before we have to head back to the carriage."

Amé turned them toward the jeweler's district. Fashion Street had one of Libra's famous wonders, the

Arch of Amethyst. A massive purple amethyst archway separated the fabric stores from the metalwork design.

The structure was a stunning masterpiece of sparkling purple three-dimensional hexagon pyramids clustered inside a massive geode. The interior was large enough to scale the geometric crystals like a rockface. Of course, she'd get into big trouble with the imperial law enforcement if she touched the amethyst archway without permission from the kings and queens.

Beyond the archway were the shops devoted to gems and metals. Harry & Pearls sold saltwater pearls, and it was Amé's favorite jewelry shop. Harry Foster founded the jewelry store a thousand years ago, and his family inherited it. Amé had six pairs of earrings, a bracelet, and one long rope necklace from their shop.

Three feet past the Arch of Amethyst, the ivory-painted storefront with gold-plated letters heralded Amé's destination. They pushed through the diamond-paned double doors. Brilliant gaslit crystal chandeliers hung from the domed ceiling. A mural of winged people adorned the space above their heads. The walls were a creamy orange, and the polished marble floor glistened under the lights. The outer perimeter was lined with shelves of rings, bracelets, tiaras, necklaces, and brooches, all locked behind a steel-enforced cage. In the center of the main foyer was a glass encasement filled with giant oyster shells. Pink silk cushions rolled out to look like tongues. Gleaming pink pearls draped over the sides of the oyster mouths, and chocolate diamond earrings dangled from hooks.

Amé peeked through the metal bars to look at pendants while Sylvia fluttered around the central display. Harry & Pearls left most of their pearls uncut. Rumor had it that their pearl divers discovered a magical oyster species that they gifted to the witch queen.

A brooch attracted Amé's sight as she strolled along the perimeter. It was a cluster of black pearls positioned in a setting to look like a skeleton sitting cross-legged and cradling a ruby rose. It reminded her of Xephriel. A touch of a smile spread her lips as she appreciated the detailed sculpting that made up the brooch's composite.

"Did you find anything you like?" Sylvia chirped and gripped the bars to peek at the priceless jewels.

Amé pointed to the skeleton-shaped brooch. "I'm going to ask about that one."

"Oh, you and the skulls! I knew you liked your neighbor. Admit it to yourself already."

"I have no idea what you are talking about." It was the truth. She had no clue why Xephriel crept into her musings. Ever since she heard the roses singing, she felt tethered to him in a way she had not felt with anyone else. Now bones and the witch who wielded them took up undeniable mental real estate. She turned from the display and said, "I'm going to ask how much it costs."

"A fortune, like everything else on this side of Fashion Street."

Amé turned her chin over her shoulder and gave a secretive glimpse to her friend. "I have enough money to buy a set fit for the royal court."

Sylvia sucked a breath in through her teeth. "How'd you get that much money?"

Amé drew her friend closer and whispered, "A customer paid me for a flower mate yesterday."

"That doesn't mean you are swimming in gold!" Sylvia hissed back and walked with Amé toward the sales desk.

"You would be correct, except this person left a hefty tip."

"Khaos, preserve me! That was generous of your customer."

Amé paused and ushered Sylvia into a corner of the store. "To tell you the truth, I wanted to return it, but I didn't think it was a good idea."

"Why not?"

"Do you remember the odd customer I had? She left two hundred gold libras for her flower mate. I felt chasing her down to return the money might cause more conflict since she had been so aggressive during the sale."

"Some customers are like that. They become more vicious if you pursue them out of the shop. It's a territorial thing. Once they pass over your threshold, they enter their world, and it can get ugly if they aren't in a good mood. You did the right thing. It's safer to let belligerent customers go on their way and not question them. You can only control your end of the situation."

Amé pinched the bridge of her nose. "I might as well use the money."

Sylvia rubbed her arm and said, "Let's get your 'I definitely don't have a crush on my mysterious neighbor in black clothes' brooch and head home. Beaux is going to be fidgety if we're late."

"He'll be fine. We're late all the time."

"That was before he put a bun in my oven. Now, he's all, 'how many glasses of water did you drink? Do you want any gingerroot?' You'll stay for lunch at the restaurant, yes?"

Amé squeezed Sylvia's shoulders as she reached the front of the register counter. "Of course. I'm in the mood for your roast beef on rye bread."

"Our signature sandwich and the one that won my heart when Beaux made it." Sylvia fell silent as they waited in line for the next available clerk.

Once they arrived at the front of the line, Amé asked about the price of the skeleton brooch. The clerk excused herself from behind the counter and took out a brass key ring from a pouch on her toolbelt. She shuffled the metal keys until she found the one that would open the steel door that allowed her to check merchandise.

Amé watched the sales clerk select the brooch, check the price tag, secure it back on the shelf, and close the steel barrier behind her. She stopped before Amé and delivered the price. "Twelve gold libras."

"I'll take it."

"I'll be right back with your purchase." The sales clerk slipped behind the steel-enforced security bars and selected the skeleton brooch.

Amé followed the clerk to the register, Sylvia shuffled behind, and the purchase was conducted. After gift-wrapping the brooch, Amé received her shopping bag and departed Harry & Pearls. Sylvia led the way to the carriage, and they fell into amiable silence as the horses jogged toward Soul Street.

Lunch was spectacular, and Beaux brought fresh-baked brownies to their table for dessert. Sylvia had three before declaring she would change clothes and pop into the kitchen. Amé hugged her friend and thanked her for the shopping trip, then claimed her purchases and continued to Seeds of Love on foot.

At the peak of the hill, she paused and scrunched her eyebrows toward the center of her forehead. Confusion disconnected her thoughts as she observed two law enforcement officers standing in front of Seeds of Love. Xephriel and Lia were in discussion with one of the officers writing in a notebook. Amé glimpsed her door handle in the grasp of the other officer and suddenly noticed the damage to her front door. She quickened her pace as a bad feeling knotted in her stomach.

"I'm the owner of Seeds of Love. What happened?"

The imperial law enforcement officer turned to her, notebook in his hand, and informed her of their findings. "Good Afternoon. We are officers Finnigan Roberts and Henry Kief. We got a message from your neighbors that your shop had been broken into. The only damage is located on the second floor and your doors. We'd like you to take a look around and tell us what was taken."

Amé's breath caught in her throat, and a haze of gray blurred her vision. She dropped her purse on a shelf of potted ferns and charged past the officers to her staircase. Her heels clattered against the wood as she climbed two stairs at a time and rounded the second landing corner. Dashing to the right, she flung open the door to her flower mate's room.

Every jar had been emptied. A startled noise escaped her, like the sound of strangulation mixed with abject horror. Her knees buckled, sending her into a pile of tears and trembling nerves.

"Miss Floreo? Are you all right?" Officer Roberts asked as he joined her in the room.

Amé sobbed through her fingers. It would take her years to build up her supply of pre-made seeds. All that work was gone, and it left a hole in her heart.

"Miss Floreo?" Officer Roberts prodded her for an answer.

She lowered her hands and stared at Officer Roberts through her watery vision. "My flower mates. They took every seed I had."

"What is a flower mate?"

Amé wiped her face with a sleeve and stood up to face the officer. She would grieve later. Right now, she needed to help Libra's law enforcement catch the thief who stole her precious seeds. Sniffing back her sorrow, she reigned in her emotional catastrophe and said, "They are genetically bred flowers that grow into plant people. They are sentient, and I had over three hundred seeds in this room."

"Do you have a license to sell these plant people?" His skeptical tone grated against her nerves.

Amé pointed to the wall where her certificate was framed. "I do. I'm the only one allowed to sell this type of plant since I patented it with the witch council's approval."

"That will help us narrow down the search. We can rule out a rival florist as taking the seeds."

"A rival florist? Vegetation witches aren't a bunch of gang members on Blood Street! We sell flowers or work as herbal specialists on Healing Street."

Officer Roberts tapped his pen against his notebook. "I think you are being selective. Several witches and mortals practice poison as their craft. They would be very interested in creating a plant that could infect other people or create chaos in the city. Your flower mates can be turned into something dangerous if they fall into the hands of a deadly nightshade witch. The seeds could be sold anywhere now and for quadruple the price. Like it or not, your flower mates are now under investigation for counterfeit, black-market sales. Can you think of anyone who may have wanted to harm you or your business?"

She rubbed her face with her hands and tried to think around the amalgamation of emotions fogging her brain. "I have no enemies. I'm a florist, like I said. There have been upset customers in the past, but nothing that would warrant an attack on my shop."

"You never had a customer threaten you or try to steal your seeds?"

"Not threaten or steal, but—" she trailed off as the witch with the red aura came to mind. "There was a strange customer who tried to buy more than one seed yesterday. I have a strict policy of one seed per person, but she wouldn't see reason. She relented in the end, but it was difficult to convince her. She was very aggressive. It's going to sound weird, but my seeds didn't like her either."

Officer Roberts was jotting down notes, and at her last statement, he looked up. "What do you mean by that?"

"The seeds can understand language and pick up on intentions. They are sensitive to magic, and they didn't like the customer. The seeds rattled around in their jars and whispered that they did not want to leave with the witch. I couldn't find any reason why other than I had a bad impression of her."

"Was there a reason you didn't feel comfortable with this witch?"

Amé thought about the encounter, wanting to be sure she didn't misremember anything. After a minute, she said, "Her aura was wrong. It concentrated around her head, and she wore a cloak that covered her features."

"What color was her aura?"

"Red."

Officer Roberts scribbled in his notebook and queried, "Can you give us any other descriptions of the witch?"

"Not really. She was completely hidden by the cloak. As I said, the only thing odd about her was her aura. I should have been able to view the entire scope of her magic signature, but I glimpsed a small red point at her head."

"Do you think she would have stolen your seeds?"

Amé raised her palms upward in a gesture suggesting she didn't have a clear answer. "I guess anyone is capable of stealing."

Officer Roberts strolled around the room, inspecting the empty jars as he resumed his questioning. "Why couldn't she purchase more than one flower mate?"

"It's my policy. It takes a long time to make each pre-made seed from scratch. If I run out of supply, then I can't sell anything for years. It's also for the safety of my customers. The flower mates aren't real people, but the love they feel for their mortal or witch partner is. I don't want customers getting obsessed with my flower mates. I put in the contract that they can have one chance at finding their heart's desires."

Officer Roberts pocketed his notebook and turned back toward her. "Can we read the contracts? Are there names and addresses on them?"

"There are, but not for the witch with the red aura. Her handwriting wasn't legible."

"We will need the contracts as evidence regardless."

"Of course." She crossed the room and retrieved the file for the flower mate contracts.

Officer Roberts inspected the room. He turned over the benches, shuffled the boxes around, and made a general sweep of his gaze over the floor. When she handed him the file, Officer Roberts looked through the pages and then said, "Do you know which contract is the witch with the red aura?"

Amé pointed to the sheet on top. "This one. I marked it so I would remember."

After scrutinizing the page, Officer Roberts said, "If you can think of anything, please let us know. We will interview anyone surrounding the building to see if there are any viable witnesses. We'll be in touch."

Trundling after the officer, she organized her thoughts on what to address first. Amé should leave the investigation of the witch to the imperial law enforcement officers. They had greater resources and would know what to look for, but she couldn't shake the feeling that she was being targeted for some reason. Amé decided her best option for finding answers would be to go to Xephriel's friend, the private investigator. Maybe, her missing seeds and the murder case would lead to the same person.

As Officer Roberts joined his colleague across the street, Xephriel entered Seeds of Love. He crossed the storefront and stood before her, close enough that she could see every detail of his stubbled chin. "I'm so sorry, Amé. I was on my way to Market Street to go grocery shopping, and I noticed your door open. I messaged the imperial law enforcement."

"It's awful. It will take me years to build up my stock. The doorknob upstairs was broken off, too. Whoever did this clearly knew I was out of the house for a while. I'm more creeped out about someone stalking me than breaking into my building."

Xephriel reached out a hand but dropped it, clenching his fist as it fell to his side. "I wish there was more I could do to help."

"Without a witness, there's nothing that can be done. If the seeds are sold, what can I do? I'll lose money, but I still have the formula to make more flower mates. I'm going to close up my shop for a few days until I can get this mess sorted out."

Xephriel gestured to the mess. "Do you need help cleaning up?"

Amé gave a wan twitch of her lips. "I can get spare parts for the doors and fix them without a problem. I want to have a cup of tea, and afterward, we can meet with your friend. The one handling the murder case."

"Noble? Sure, we can go speak with him. I sent him a message this morning, but I haven't received his response yet. He might be at the site of the crime."

Amé ran her hands through her hair. Her fingers tangled in the knotted strands. She worked through the mess of her appearance and tried to settle her nerves and trepidation. Feeling light-headed, she mumbled, "I need to sit down and process all this."

"Do you want to come to the Humerus? I can keep you company until you are ready to leave for Justice Street."

Amé smiled at his generosity and accepted the offer with humble grace. "Thank you. I need to separate myself from the situation so I can think. I'm too caught up in my emotions to even contemplate how the murder case and the theft connect. I'm pretty sure that they do."

Xephriel shifted to the side and allowed her to depart first. "I can sense your emotions. I'm sorry for what happened. Anyone would be in chaos after losing something so precious to them."

Amé stopped at her door and turned in sudden worry. "Will you be okay around me? My emotions are unstable. I don't want to cause you harm by accidentally giving off negative energy in large doses."

He waved her concern away. "The witch spider silk is absorbing most of it, and I'll be in the Humerus. All of your feelings will be redirected with my magic into the bones. It's perfectly safe for us to interact."

"All right. Thank you again, Xephriel. I feel like a knife has been plunged into my heart. I'm so hurt."

"I don't know why your seeds were targeted, but we'll figure it out. Noble is one of the best investigators in the kingdom of Libra. He will put all the clues together and find the witch responsible."

She grabbed her purse from the shelf where she had left it and rummaged down her neckline for the skeleton key but remembered her lock had been destroyed. "Darn. I don't know how I'm going to secure my door."

"Maybe Lia can watch your shop until we get back?" Xephriel suggested.

Amé snapped her fingers. "Good idea. Let's slip over to her apothecary."

When they entered Soul Remedies, Lia was behind her counter, counting small black balls and depositing them into a glass bottle. She looked up when the bell chimed and greeted them, "Oh, Amé, I'm so sorry about your shop."

"Thank you, Lia. I have a favor to ask."

"Sure, what can I do?"

Amé glanced over her shoulder as she requested, "Could you watch Seeds of Love while I run an errand? I have some business on Justice Street, but I don't want to leave the shop unattended."

Lia swept the black balls off her counter and put the remainder in a small basket by the cash register. "I will watch your shop, no problem. Let me close up here, and then I'll be over."

"Thank you, Lia."

"Of course. I hope you can track down the thief."

Amé smiled, but she didn't feel happy. It was more of a polite response, but inside, her heart was in turbulence. "Me too."

Xephriel led Amé out of Soul Remedies, and they walked up the street to the Humerus. Amé glanced one last time at Seeds of Love before entering Xephriel's building. After her tea, she would pick up the pieces of her soul, and then she was going to fight back. She was going to find her seeds and make sure no one ever hurt her or her flower mates again.

Chapter 10

Xephriel led Amé to the Humerus, his mind a whirlwind since he discovered her shop had been vandalized. Every raw emotion that percolated under the surface of her consciousness was overflowing, and his empathy picked up on all of it. Even with the witch spider silk's protection, he felt her agony.

Her dark hair brushed his arm as she walked past him to the stairs. The scent of honeysuckle and freesia lingered in the air as he trailed behind. Xephriel ached for physical connection most of his life, but it was torturous when he was in Amé's presence. She ravished his resolve, tearing down the walls he built to keep people away, and he didn't understand why. There was a driving force obliterating his equilibrium. The compulsion to stroke her cheek when she was grieving, the gnawing demand that he hold her as she spent her sorrow, cleaved his heart in two.

The pulse of his aura was a tangible sensation. Sweet, arduous yearning suffered him to remain close to Amé. The war between retreat and advancement was a frustrating conundrum that left him in a state of chaos. He didn't hate it, but finding a remedy to absolve his empathic disorder burned in his soul, scorching his heart, and he felt branded by it. If he could remove that one aspect of his magic, he'd be able to succumb to the temptation to wrap his arms around Amé and bury his nose into the supple strands of her dark hair. He'd give anything to have the ability to comfort her with more than words.

When they entered the Humerus, Xephriel grabbed a necklace of tiger teeth hanging on a skeletal bear paw by his door. Slipping the necklace over his hood, he gripped the skeleton key of his grandfather's clavicle bone for added protection. He pursed his lips and realized one necklace wasn't going to be enough to keep Amé's ravished emotions at bay. Mostly because he didn't want to push her catastrophe away. He wanted to share her pain so she didn't have to bear the brunt of it alone. It was the first time he had that inclination, and it frightened him that he hungered to be vulnerable with another person.

He was unnerved that he would risk his life and put Amé's needs above his own.

He added two wrist cuffs made from raven bones and talons. Panicking over his reaction to Amé, Xephriel snatched a necklace of shark teeth. A sufficient level of protection shrouded him, and he felt confident he could be near Amé without incident.

Xephriel heard a whisper in the ether and closed his eyes to listen. His grandfather's spirit called to him from the bone key. Xephriel had an exceptional bond with his grandfather. He could mask his emotions to the point that Xephriel believed he was devoid of them. His grandfather loved him so much that he subdued his aura so that he could teach Xephriel how to be a bone witch. Because of that love, Xephriel's father made a skeleton key out of his grandfather's clavicle so he had a piece of their ancestry. It worked as both a talisman and a way to boost Xephriel's bone magic.

A soft breeze rustled his hood, and a numinous voice intoned near his left ear. "Do not be afraid."

"Grandfather?" Xephriel murmured through the etheric field.

"Do not be afraid." His grandfather's voice was more precise now. "You cannot grow if you do not fall. You cannot fall if you do not let go. Do not be afraid."

"What does that mean?" He opened his eyes to question his grandfather about his message, but his spirit was nowhere in sight.

"What does what mean?" Amé inquired as she stopped by his consultation table.

Xephriel resisted the urge to grumble at his grandfather for making him look like a fool in front of Amé. "Uh, I talk to spirits without realizing other people can hear me."

"Oh? What do they say?"

He stared at the ceiling and narrowed his eyes. "They are annoying and cryptic."

"Who were you talking to?" She resumed as if communicating with the dead was more natural than the weather. She traced the crow bones on his table with a finger, and the patterns flared with a grass green light.

Xephriel felt crow spirits land on his shoulders and his head. A few fluttered around the room. If she noticed how her aura affected his bones, she made no indication. He flicked his hand to shoo the messenger spirits that came through the veil and answered, "My grandfather likes to check on me."

"That's sweet of him. You must have been close." Amé responded, still oblivious to the mystical feathers falling around them like petals on a spring breeze.

Xephriel was distracted as the crow spirits landed on the table and cawed. A sheen of red from the wood cast a ripple effect over the surface, making the bones appear as if they swam in blood.

"Xephriel?"

Xephriel wasn't aware he was silent. He ignored the crows and reminisced, "He taught me bone magic, and we studied the skeletal system. Most bone witches don't go to the witch academy. We learn our trade from our families. My grandfather spent the most time with me and learned how to adapt to my empathic condition."

Amé ran her hand over the table, a shiver jerking her shoulders as she chatted. "What did he say to you?"

"Do not be afraid."

She peeked at him from under her thick lashes. "What are you afraid of?"

His mouth dried like a desert, and his gulp was audible inside the cavity of his ears. "Myself. I'm afraid to be without these clothes, to let my hood down, and open myself up to other people."

"You have every right to fear that. It's a life or death situation, and you handle it the best you can." Her gaze intensified, and he found himself falling into her kindness and frank perception of his world.

"You don't judge me for being a recluse or for being different."

"I would never judge you, Xephriel. You are compassionate, intuitive, and seek to understand others even though you are separated from them."

"I want to have connections with people. I just can't." He tensed as the mantra of his life led him to a dead end. It always did. He wanted to be different, but it wasn't meant to be. Xephriel had to live with himself and accept the fact that his overactive magic would always cause a rift between him and other people. He let out a weary sigh and murmured, "I'll go prepare the tea. Would you like to have it in the courtyard?"

Amé glanced around the room. "Is there a chair I can sit on? I'd rather stay here. The bones are comforting. It's almost like I'm in my greenhouse the way they seem to take away the troubles."

"Yes, it's against the wall over there." He pointed behind her to a cabinet of bottled bones and fragmented crystals.

"Got it!" She pulled the chair over and rested her clasped hands on her lap.

The crow spirits settled on the table, and the bones flickered a dull white glow. Xephriel listened to the whimsical spirits chatter in the ether and then turned to prepare tea for Amé. As he set about his task, Xephriel tried to dissect the reason Amé was being targeted. Both the theft and murder centered around her flower mates. By her own admission, the plants themselves could not wield any magic. Why were they so important that someone would kill and steal for them? He tried to put it in perspective of his rare bones.

Bone collectors would risk diving to the bottom of the ocean if it meant they could scavenge a whole mermaid skeleton. Enthusiasts for dragon bones braved enchanted lairs that more than giant beasts called home. It was not out of the realm of magical thinking to imply that plant aficionados would covet Amé's flower mates. That made sense for the theft, anyway. But the murder? Amé was more likely to be killed for her craft if there was a fanatic involved. A rival florist wouldn't kill random people. They would know what to do with the seeds or at least figure out a way to mutate the magic to their will.

The kettle whistled, and he filled the teapot with steaming water. He returned to his consultation room. Amé idly ran her hand over the surface of the table. The crow spirits cawed at her, not in warning but in encouragement for her to listen. Witches had specific designations, and their magic was limited to whatever they were predestined to be at birth. No matter how loud the crows sounded to Xephriel's ears, Amé was deaf to the spirit world.

He set the tea tray down and leaned over to whisper to the crow spirits. "She can't hear you, my friends. Is there something you wish to relay to her?"

Amé jolted in surprise and searched the room for ghosts. "Are there spirits here?"

Xephriel held his palm out to indicate the murder of crows flapping on the table. "Crows. They want to give you a message."

"Me?"

Xephriel listened to the sound waves, the different intonations, and frequencies of the crow spirits' caws and interpreted, "There is a good omen surrounding you. Your heart is pure, and your mind is in tune with the hearts of others. You are guided by love, and so you embody positive energy."

If Xephriel had any residual doubts about Amé's innocence, they were obliterated. The dead were the epitome
of truth. The feelings that stirred for her, the deep-rooted
uncertain vibrations that started to bond between their
auras, began to crawl out of the grave he dug in his soul.
He would have buried the memory of their spark, but the
crows' blessing halted the metaphorical shovel, and he
was left to stare in trepidation as his heart beat for her.

He was going to be tormented forever.

Xephriel would have to reject her no matter what he
felt. For both their sakes, he'd have to shut himself inside
the Humerus and never speak to her again. It was absolute
anguish to understand he could never touch Amé, that
she would always be a mirage he clung to like a desperate
survivor. Xephriel would live with the knowledge that
the woman he cared for was a mere building away, and he
couldn't have her. He didn't think he'd be strong enough
to endure that kind of life, so a deep sickening part of him
wished that Amé didn't call him more than a friend.

Her voice ripped through the analysis of his feelings,
and the satin alto of it made the hairs on the back of his
neck rise. She hummed a pleasant "ah" and said, "That
sounds pleasant. Thank you, um, spirits."

Xephriel gulped around the tightness in his throat and managed to reply, "I call them the Corvus." At the mention of their summoning name, the crows bowed and took flight. Their message was relayed, and the spirits returned through the veil and fluttered into the etheric plane.

Amé rubbed her arms. "Are the Corvus still here? It feels cold in the room for some reason."

He shook his head no, and his hood flopped with the motion. "No, they are gone now. They felt a strong allure to your aura. That's why they came through the veil. Your connection to life may have drawn them. Most spirits long to reconnect to the physical plane. Your magic is like a homing beacon to anything wishing to return to the living. In the case of the Corvus, they had an undeniable desire to impart their blessing."

Amé shivered, but not from fear. She smiled as she looked up at the ceiling, and the candlelight made her tresses appear smooth like water. She turned back to him, her expression alive with wonder. "It sounds romantic when you explain it like that."

"You are one of the few people outside the bone witch community to describe an encounter with spirits as anything other than creepy or sorrowful."

"I'm not like other people."

That was a fact Xephriel was coming to appreciate.

"May I have some tea?" She asked and nodded toward the teapot.

"Yes, of course." He rolled his shoulders and blinked as if broken from a trance. Xephriel poured the reddish liquid into her cup.

"Rooibos." Her nose twitched as she sniffed the tea. "This is exotic." She took a sip and sighed, "And expensive."

He answered with a grin and poured tea for himself. "You looked like you needed the good stuff."

Amé stared across the room, her tone lowering as she said, "I feel worn down. I need to find out why the murder and theft happened."

"You really have no ideas?"

She shook her head no. "I wish I did, but I keep coming back to the strange customer. She can't do anything with the seed other than plant it. It could be mutated, but I'd know if another vegetation witch was in my shop, and she wasn't one. Once the seed is planted, again, she can't do anything to the flower mate. If she harmed it, the flower mate would wither and die. At the end of the day, it is a plant. A resilient and magical plant, but it isn't flesh and blood with bone structure. They are designed to court, not to do terrible deeds. Going against its nature would cause the magic to collapse, and the flower mate can't survive without that component. Another vegetation witch can undo the code I've created within each plant cell or change it. Since she's taken all my seeds, I have to consider that she may have found another witch to manipulate my flower mates. But why? I don't understand any of this."

"Maybe Noble will have an idea."

Amé perked up at the mention of his friend. "Oh, yes! Let's finish the tea and go see him."

Xephriel grabbed a chair from the side of the room and slid it over to the table. He drank his tea in silence, letting the bones absorb the cauldron of emotions spewing from Amé. It pained him to feel her suffering, but not in the usual sense. There was no physical reaction to her negative projections, no cringing audio feedback. Bewildered and anxious, he pushed his own feelings into the sanctuary of his home and searched for clarity and balance. They had a case to solve, and emotions would clog the way.

After they cleaned up the dishes, they set out for Noble's building. When they got to the mews, Xephriel hired a carriage that took them to Justice Street. Xephriel sat on the opposite side of the carriage, afraid of the proximity to Amé. As they traveled down the road, Xephriel still didn't have any adverse reactions to her emotions.

His mind was full of confusion as he peeked over at Amé. How could she not cause emotional friction? How was it possible her magic didn't clash with his empathy? Did he believe in the heart song like a fool, or did he remain cloistered and safe? His life was tragic and poetic in its solitude, but shaking the inclination to open his world to Amé was harder to ignore the more entangled they became.

He opened his mouth to catch Amé's attention, to articulate what, he didn't know. As he produced sound, the carriage came to a halt. Amé stuck her head out the window to inspect their location, none the wiser. Xephriel's moment to delve into the strange connection with Amé faded, and he shut his mouth, clenching his jaw from further examination.

Xephriel paid the driver and turned toward Noble's building. Amé gaped at the condition, and her reaction was comical. A laugh burst from him, and Xephriel bent over in hysterics. Her mouth was shaped in a large "o," and her hands grasped her head as if to keep her mind from exploding. He caught his breath, coughing as he tried to explain Noble and his eccentric nature.

"I'm sorry. He's impossible, and I always forget to warn people. To be honest, the state of his building doesn't register as unnatural after seeing it like this for over ten years."

Amé dropped her arms but kept her astonished stare fixed on the front door. "How in the name of Khaos is this thing still standing? Is it being held together by magic?"

"I have no idea. Noble is an omni-grim or Pale One in some dialects. If anything is holding up his home, it's an army of ghosts, but there aren't any, so I would guess it probably looks worse than it is."

"I don't know if I should be impressed or horrified."

"Both?"

Amé lifted her foot to the first stair but paused and turned halfway. "Did you say omni-grim?"

Xephriel cleared his throat. "Um, yes."

Her tone was near reverential, but he caught a whiff of fear as she murmured, "I've never met one of the Pale Ones."

"Noble is the only one in Aequitas. He isn't dangerous. Most people have silly superstitions against omni-grims and hold extreme prejudice. He's been an outcast from society, like me, since we were children. He's my best friend and one of the greatest protectors of this city."

Amé seemed caught in a haze of apprehension. "Do the omni-grims really have no limitations when it comes to death?"

Xephriel hoped explaining Noble's powers would put her at ease. Most mortals didn't know what Pale Ones could do, but witches didn't even utter their names for fear of their magic. "Yes. They can kill anything. Even an aura or a soul. They can manipulate an entire corpse, not just the bones, and prevent death, too. They are practically a god, which is why most people fear them."

Amé stared at him as he described his friend as a lesser version of Khaos. Her voice wobbled as she said, "I'm envisioning this ancient witch surrounded by black candles and chanting spells from the first witches."

Xephriel waved his hand to dismiss the misconception of his friend. "No, he's the same age as me. He doesn't use candles to summon spirits. They pop out of the ether and find him without encouragement."

"Well, this should be an interesting meeting, for sure."

Xephriel agreed with a bob of his chin. "He's the kindest, most honest man I know. Eccentric but loyal and has a keen sense of justice. You are completely safe with him, and I would not put you in danger."

Her voice was more serious than he had ever heard it. "I'm about to walk into the domain of a Pale One. I do not have the magic to defend against a being that could separate my soul from my body. I may look composed on the outside, but on the inside, I feel like everything I've known about myself has been shredded. I trust you, maybe more than I trust myself right now."

Xephriel looked at her, really surveyed her, and understood the front she had been putting up. He hid in darkness so that his insecurities would not be on display. He was quiet and distant so that he couldn't be harmed by the dissonance that turned his magic against him. Amé's defense, her way of keeping in control, was to appear as if everything was fine. She didn't snarl and complain, didn't wash her troubles away with tears, but it didn't mean she wasn't in emotional catastrophe. Despite the tremor of fear he sensed, there was courage overshadowing it all. She took the world in stride and forged a path through the darkness so she could embrace the light.

Amé deserved reassurance that her trust had not been misplaced. Xephriel diminished his magic guard and let his aura seep past the witch spider silk's barriers. Indigo glowed around them, filling the space that divided them from the sidewalk to the stairs. He stood still as her aura reached out to understand what kind of witch and man he was and let that spark between them fizzle over his body.

Down to their atoms, beyond their souls, they became an orchestration of sound waves, spiritual compatibility, and inescapable colliding passions. Their auras meshed into a unified phenomenon, and it felt more intimate than a mere touch.

Her grassy green aura burst. Their magic was tangible, dancing together in a tangle of destiny. Xephriel shut his eyes and reeled himself back into hiding, refusing to go further into the psychic bond. Amé's breaths were short and shallow as her aura flickered like a lightning bug. She put a hand to her chest and stared. Just stared at him as if she couldn't quite name what happened but realized that the profound exchange had changed them.

The front door crashed open, and Noble stumbled over his threshold. "For Khaos' sake, Xephriel! I thought there was a witch raid out here. Turns out it's you and— hell-ooooo. I did not expect to meet your lady love on my doorstep."

"Lady love?" Xephriel was tossed out of his stormy entanglement with Amé and thrown into confusion by Noble's choice of words.

"Oh, don't tell me." Noble paused and glanced between them as if he didn't believe his own eyes. "You two don't know." He exploded in hysterics and doubled over, grabbing the doorframe for support. "Oh, god. I never thought I'd see the day when two oblivious people showed up on my doorstep and had no idea their souls were the stuff of legends. Xephriel, shame on you. I can't believe that empathic sensitivity of yours didn't pick up on it. Well, come on, come on. I'm headed to the crime scene. Everyone might as well tag along and tell me why they're here." Noble rattled off his sentences as if he shook them from his mind, and they tumbled out of his mouth without a filter. He grabbed his hat decorated in bones and joined them on the sidewalk.

Xephriel pinched the bridge of his nose. "What are you talking about?"

"Never mind that now, we have a case to solve! There will be plenty of time for you two to figure out what I mean later. Hurry up!"

Xephriel chased after Noble, and Amé rushed after him.

Xephriel shouted at Noble to slow down. "Why are you running?"

Noble evened his pace and returned over his shoulder, "I have three auras rattling my brain every second of the day, and it behooves me to dash up and down streets like a wild animal. Do keep up, and tell me why you sought me out."

Amé caught up to them and panted, "Are we going to walk to the crime scene?"

"It's only on Entertainment Street," came Noble's reply.

"That's four roads over!" Amé complained and sped up.

"You'll have plenty of time to chat," Noble stated and didn't look the least bit concerned with their jaunt across the city.

Xephriel groaned and did the one thing he hated. He grabbed Noble by the elbow. He let go as soon as he dragged his friend to a stop and winced as a sharp pain stabbed him in the middle of his forehead. He faced Noble and raised his voice. "Stop. We can walk over to Entertainment Street, but you will contain your overactive personality for the duration. Once we get to the crime scene, you can scurry about all you want."

Noble widened his green gaze and said in surprise, "I don't think you've ever used that tone of voice with me before."

Xephriel passed a glance toward Amé. "She's been through a lot. Please, can we walk slowly and have a discussion about why we came to you?"

Noble blinked in astonishment. "Of course." He turned to Amé and gave her a humble bow. "Nobeleace Dracaena at your service. Who may I have the pleasure of addressing?"

Amé glanced between Noble and Xephriel, unsure of how to respond, but eventually murmured, "Amé Floreo. I'm the witch who made the magic seeds."

That perked Noble up, and he straightened with a devil-may-care grin. "Miss Floreo! How wonderful to meet you. What can you tell me about your seeds?"

Amé slid her gaze to Xephriel before returning her attention to Noble. "I made a magic plant called a flower mate that emulates the true love of whoever sows the seed."

Noble strolled down the cobblestone lane and asked, "True love, you say? How did you come up with that concept?"

Amé fell into step beside Noble but kept a bit of space between them and replied, "I wanted people to learn about the deep secrets in their hearts and find the meaning of love. The flower mates can walk and talk like a mortal and witch, but they do not transform into real people."

"Interesting. Why do you think someone had your seed?"

Amé delivered her information without hesitation. "Either I sold my seed to the woman who committed the murder or the person I sold the seed to give it to the killer. I am not sure which of those options is true."

Noble sauntered along, appearing to count his steps, and considered her words before asking, "Why would someone need another person to plant your seed?"

"Intention. The seeds will not grow unless love is present. The more they are cared for, the stronger the magic. The plants rot as soon as they sense malcontent. A caretaker would need another person to sow the seed because they were unable to convey their purpose to the flower mate."

Noble moved his head from side to side. "We can conjecture that the woman who had the seed wanted it to grow, or there would be no point in getting someone else to plant it. We have a statement from Mr. Rendell. The killer insisted that he plant the magic seed in the Mosaic garden. That leads me to believe she tried to plant one of your seeds before and failed. She knew what was going to happen, so she selected a person she was confident could accomplish the task. Love is the greatest magic and emotion of all. Envy, hate, desire, obsession, and panic, so many things come from the complexity of love. Those are a few triggers for murder. Why do you believe she needed your flower mate, Miss Floreo?"

"I have a few guesses. There have also been a number of odd purchases over a few months. I've been trying to discover why a person would disguise themselves to collect more than one seed, and I have no idea what anyone would want with three hundred. I have no idea why the witch in your investigation needed my flower mate, and I do not know why my supply was stolen."

Noble cracked his knuckles. "Let's start with the theft. Why do you think that person could be connected to the case?"

Amé recounted the incident with the law enforcement officers, then said, "I can't prove the witch murdered anyone, but my seeds sensed her intentions were not good."

"Has she ever been in your store before?"

"No, but that's the thing I keep puzzling over. She wasn't in before, but there were other customers that behaved similarly."

"How did they behave?"

Amé's features were mucked with emotion as she recalled the details. "There was a witch with a yellow aura. She wore a mask and overpaid for a seed. She was twitchy when I spoke to her and left with the completely wrong seed for her personality. A blue aura witch came in wearing a cloak, and it was the same scenario. All of the witches had different auras, but they all acted like they needed to bolt from my shop as soon as they entered it. They all chose the wrong type of seed and didn't wait for me to deliver the price. They tossed the money on the counter and ran for the exit."

Noble glanced out the side of his eye and asked, "How do you determine what seed personalities mesh well with each customer?"

Amé waved her hand in the air. "I engage with the customers, get to know them. Then the seeds help with the rest. If a seed feels a connection with a customer, it will kind of purr and glow. If they don't have an affinity for the client, then they will resist. The seed will shake or whimper. I can tell which seed is compatible and which is not. Like I would with any other plant."

"You are positive that you sold three different seeds that were not compatible with their sower?"

Amé blushed deeply, and her embarrassment was tangible to Xephriel. She coughed and stated, "I did."

Noble tapped a finger on his lips and hissed out a breath. "I sense the thief and the killer are the same person, too. How did she change her aura? That is impossible."

"As impossible as having three auras?"

Noble's lips spread into a saccharine smile. "Oh, you have spunk, Miss Floreo. I like that. Yes, as impossible as having more than one aura. I have not met or heard of anyone who can change their aura color. Let alone hide it. Even Xephriel can't completely hide his aura behind those clothes he wears."

"I did wonder if her clothes were hiding the aura, but Xephriel's tailor didn't think so."

Xephriel frowned at her words. How did she know Rael? He asked, "How did you find my tailor?"

Amé's face was red as an apple. "I asked a seamstress on Fashion Street when I was out shopping earlier. She said the tailor at the Sorcerer's Spindle was famous for rare garments. I thought I'd ask if he made any magic cloaks with the same witch spider silk that you wear."

Xephriel felt a twinge of anger at her poking around his private life. "You could have asked me. I would have given you Rael's name, and we could have gone together."

"It was a spur-of-the-moment decision. I looked at a cloak, remembered it took me years to sense your aura, and connected the dots to the significance of your clothing. I will involve you from now on, but the tailor said that your clothes are one of a kind. I don't think the witch hid her aura by using a magic cloak."

Noble interrupted their flow of dialogue. "Unless," He paused and looked up at the sky. "Unless it's the Taxidermist's magic."

Xephriel's breath hitched, and he wheezed out, "The Taxidermist?"

Noble steepled his fingers and brought them to his pursed mouth. After a palpable minute, he resumed his line of supposition. "The Taxidermist has a particular talent for sewing skins. It would not be out of the question to suggest that whatever aura the skin possessed could transfer to the wearer. The problem is that we do not know who the person is beneath the skin. I also do not know if the aura overshadows the original aura, blends with it, or none of the above. If the person is mortal, it might give them an aura for as long as they wear the skin. I could investigate if any witches have gone missing, but it would take ages to comb through which skins the Taxidermist sold to our killer, and I don't think it would shed light on the case. It would draw attention to the Taxidermist, and I have no inclination to mess with that horrible witch."

Amé gasped and put a hand over her mouth. "Why would the Taxidermist involve himself with my flower mates?"

Noble lowered his chin and stared across the road, his features stony. His voice was frigid and frightening when he said, "The Taxidermist does not care why people come to him, only that they pay his price. Sometimes he wants gold, sometimes he wants a body, and sometimes he takes a soul. If he gave the woman the ability to become a skin walker, then we would have difficulties profiling the killer. Her appearance would have been different for every victim. The toxicity of the Taxidermist's magic will have spiraled her mind into insanity with each skin she wore. Her personality would have changed with each killing as well. We're looking at an impossible solution, but I have never backed down from a challenge. We must find the bones of the victims, interview their spirits, and try to find a connection. With any luck, one of the victims will be willing to lead us to their fingerbone that was collected by the killer. There are still questions we have not answered. What is the time frame between each murder? Was it important that she wait, or was it a coincidence? Why did she keep the finger bone? Why did she send the bone to Mrs. Rendell? Are you ready to find out the truth, Miss Floreo?"

Xephriel watched Amé's profile. She was stark white and trembling, but she said with all the bravery of a queen, "I am." She looked right at Noble and added, "I think I know why she waited between each victim. If her intention was to grow the seed into a mature flower mate, then she had to wait for the full moon. The flower mates are grown during the three days the moon wanes to full and then waxes toward the gibbous. It has to draw down the most power it can from the moon in order to transform."

"That means she had at least a month to select each person." Noble resumed his walk toward the Mosaic garden. He met Xephriel's gaze and said, "Are you ready, my friend?"

"I am."

Noble clapped his hands together and rubbed them in anticipation. "The chase is about to begin. Oh, and Xephriel?"

Xephriel raised his brows. "Yes?"

"I think you ought to stay close to Miss Floreo. She's in grave danger. Whoever is masterminding this operation might do her harm. I think you are the best person to be around if she needs back-up."

Xephriel sputtered. "Back-up for what? Stay close, how?"

"Oh, come now, Xephriel. Stay in her home, do not leave her side, and be her shadow. In the event, the thief turns out to be the killer, and she comes after Amé, you can send a message for help or add your magic to Amé's and fight off trouble."

Xephriel turned to Amé and struggled for words. "Is— is that—I mean, if you're okay with it—do you mind if I stay with you?"

She did not respond right away as they rounded the corner and entered the center circle of Aequitas. Amé tugged at her bottom lip and said, "I suppose I can move my valuables up to my apartment, and you could stay on the couch if you needed to sleep there. I hadn't worked out what I was going to do at night with an unlocked shop anyway."

Xephriel felt the blood drain from his face, his palms sweat, and his heart palpitated. "You're really okay with me staying with you? Sleeping in your apartment?"

Amé tilted her head, her aura glowing around her like an emerald shroud. "I don't have anyone else to call. My parents live outside the city, and my best friend is pregnant. You have proven to be reliable. I agree with Mr. Dracaena. I'd like to have you by my side for security and assistance."

Xephriel fumbled in his pocket and gripped his grandfather's clavicle bone. He heard the whispers of his ancestors from the etheric plane and used their presence to anchor his rising panic. He wanted to help Amé, but he was afraid of what their constant nearness would do to his magic stability. He had Noble to buffer between them right now, but if he was alone with her--Noble thought he could handle it, so Xephriel wouldn't argue. In the back of his mind, he wondered what would happen if Amé needed to rescue *him*. "I'll–I'll do what I can."

Noble had a secret grin, as if he'd orchestrated the entire conversation for some sneaky purpose, and said, "Make sure you invite me to the wedding."

"Noble!"

"What?"

Amé hid her face behind her hands, but he heard a muffled giggle. Xephriel groaned in frustration and followed Noble toward Entertainment Street. He had a distinct impression that he'd been hoodwinked, but Xephriel couldn't decide if he liked the stealthy play by his friend or if he would live to regret it.

Chapter 11

Amé liked organization and being in control. Without order, Amé didn't know how to function. Her entire peace of mind centered around the fact that she understood how everything fit into her life. The risks she took were calculated and planned. Her current state of affairs led her into a labyrinth of stress and chaos that she did not comprehend how to escape.

Occupying herself with analyzing why her seeds were stolen helped to ground her anxiety and discombobulated state of being. She set about picking her way through the events that led up to the theft, and that calmed her down.

Amé needed to trust Xephriel because there was no other lifeline. She had an enemy, and the word pounded against her consciousness like a gong. *Enemy*. Amé couldn't tell Sylvia about her predicament because she was pregnant, and bringing trouble to her doorstep was a terrible idea. Her parents were too far away. When she turned to Xephriel, it was in earnest and in desperation. In their rising tide of magic, an ineffable symphony replaced all the worries.

Her world tilted sideways when she met Nobeleace Dracaena. His trifecta of auras zinged against her own, and the feeling was indescribable. Something about him was comforting, despite the bizarreness of his personality. Other than that, she couldn't make heads or tails of Xephriel's friend. Noble fired questions at lightning speed. Some answers she gave without conscious engagement, the words were automatic and repetitive.

Amé did narrow on one question. The finger bone. Why did the suspect require a bone when that was unnecessary to grow a flower mate? The bizarreness of that ritualistic behavior rolled around her mind until it became adjacent to every aspect of the investigation. Amé picked apart the question like an experiment, trying to decipher why that one element was important.

Her seeds blossomed no matter if a mortal or witch did the planting. That had no bearing on how the magic worked. Amé dissected her flower mate makeup in her mind, the picture like lab notes spread out across the

214 • MARY E JUNG

imaginary workstation. She tried to figure out what triggered the witch to seek outside assistance.

Amé's blood was the ingredient she used to animate the flower mates and make them sentient. Vegetation magic flowed through her veins. No other magic should have impeded the growth of the flower mate unless it was death magic. That was her opposite, and it would make sense that the seed refused to grow every time if the witch applied that kind of power. The conjecture didn't line up because the witch was trying to grow the seed. The problem must have been the desire inside the witch's heart. As Noble said, love was powerful, but it could branch into different forms that were poisonous.

Amé picked at the mystery. Scratching away at the scab of evidence. Her mind whirled around possibilities.

Envy and obsession were the two feelings Amé cautioned her customers against. If there was a witch buying multiple seeds, it was likely she became obsessed with having a permanent flower mate. Why choose different personality types? Why not stick with the one that didn't grow and try to make it work? Why not ask for a custom-made seed?

If envy was the issue, then the witch might be using the seeds to get a lover to pay attention. The reason for different personality types maybe was experimentation to see which seed would draw the awareness of the person she was trying to seduce.

As Amé worked through the problem, they arrived at the Kaleidoscope Art Gallery on Entertainment Street. Noble asked them to wait outside while he informed the gallery owner that they were going to dig out the bones and investigate the Mosaic garden. Xephriel tucked his hands in his pockets and leaned against the stone wall that surrounded the building.

"Thank you for agreeing to stay with me. I didn't even think about what would happen when I went home tonight."

"No problem. I'll do my best to make sure you aren't uncomfortable with me."

Amé waved her hands in front of her to disperse his concerns. "No, no. I'm perfectly fine with you being in the apartment with me. I'm worried all this time together might aggravate your empathic dissonance."

His mouth softened; it was the only thing she could view under the hood. "I'll be all right. I have the bones I'm wearing and the witch spider silk to keep me safe. If I need a break, I can go downstairs for a bit. It'll be fine."

Amé's shoulders sagged in relief. "Good." She fidgeted at the reminder of his clothes, and her words rushed forth. "I didn't think it would harm anyone if I asked about the type of clothes the Sorcerer's Spindle sold. The tailor seemed pretty upset about me probing, too."

Xephriel's shoulders hunched as he exhaled. "Rael and I have an agreement that we don't share information about the witch spider silk with other customers. It's because of how dangerous it is to collect. I went to him specifically to ask if he would spin the silk into cloth. He happens to be an expert in magic threads. His specialty is in Scythean brown spider silk. I researched everything in order to find a way to protect myself from other people's emotions. No one had ever tried weaving spider silk before, let alone disturbing the ancient witch spiders in the Arachnid Mountains. Rael agreed to go to the witch spiders and gather the silk to try to make my clothes. He almost lost his life. One of the witch spiders turned on him and bit his calf. He didn't give me details of how he survived. Half of his lower leg is severely scarred and crudely braced because of the after-effects of the encounter. We both try really hard to forget the ordeal. I cannot damage my clothes because if I need more silk, someone is going to have to brave gathering it again."

Amé took an involuntary step forward, her hand outstretched, but she didn't touch Xephriel. She ached to give him comfort, and that gnawing realization made her heartbroken for him.

Her voice was rife with remorse and sympathy. "I'm so sorry. That sounds awful for both of you. Had I known the situation was delicate, I would have come to you first."

Xephriel lifted his hands from his pocket and let them dangle at his sides. "You didn't cause any harm. I might have overreacted. It's good we can cross off the enchanted clothes factor in this situation."
"Thank you."

Noble scurried up to them and chattered in his way. "Bad news. We can't go into the Mosaic garden. The imperial detectives are scanning the area because of the multiple homicides, and I'm not allowed in there. Officer Terrance and I don't get along, and the owner of the gallery isn't available. I'll stay and see if I can reason with the imperial detectives to let me in, but they sure as hell aren't letting you two near the crime scene. Sticklers for rules the lot of them. I'll message you both tomorrow."

Xephriel gave a nod of acknowledgment while Amé said, "Thank you, Mr. Dracaena. You can send the message to Seeds of Love on Soul Street."

"Noble is fine to use, and I'll send the message as soon as I can get the detectives to budge."

"You can call me, Amé, too."

Amé felt a tingle at Noble's charming grin. "It would be my pleasure."

Xephriel moved away from the wall and said to Noble, "We'll let you handle this. Keep us posted."

Noble gave a little bow with a mischievous wink. "Will do."

Amé shook her head at the quirky witch and turned away. Noble whistled and strolled around the block to the Mosaic garden while Xephriel steered them to a public stable so they could hire a carriage.

They arrived at Seeds of Love, and Amé was exhausted. She thanked Lia for watching her store and sent her off with a magic plant called Gilded Marigolds. Lia hugged Amé and returned to the apothecary. Xephriel and Amé climbed the stairs to her apartment. Amé directed Xephriel to her small living area off to the right.

Amé put a kettle on for lavender and chamomile tea, then busied herself in the kitchen by checking the soil saturation for the herbs on her window sill. One of the potted flowers caught her interest as she tended to the plants. It was a weed called cosmosia, but she liked the shape and fragrance, which is why she grew it in her home. The unique property of the flower was that it bloomed in the light of the full moon. The shuffle of Xephriel's boots across her carpet shook her out of her musings on plants.

Nervousness fluttered in her stomach at having Xephriel in her apartment. She had not had a man in her home before, and a current of endorphins pumped through her veins. Her blood felt warm and thick, making her muscles luxurious and heavy. Moving at a lethargic pace, she set out cups for tea and tried not to think about her heart fluttering.

The memory of their auras twining together overtook her mind. Xephriel's magic had summoned her own like a conductor. The unexpected wave of his midnight blue aura captivated her, and from the ether, she heard a low hum. As her green aura poured into the atmosphere, Amé listened to the ancient beat of drums that heralded a connection she didn't believe possible.

The heart song.

A thrum of an incoming musical tempest had trembled her soul. All she had wanted to do was wrap herself in Xephriel's aura and fall into the new magic of their combined making.

Noble had interrupted the connection, and like a derailed train, their mystical magnetism scattered. She once more belonged to herself, but that mellifluous thread lingered.

Now, she was faced with what to do about it.

Xephriel couldn't have physical contact. That was how the bond set into place, how it grew until they unified their auras and souls. If she couldn't touch him, couldn't feed that maddening song with her magic, she'd go insane.

Heart songs didn't necessarily mean that two people were in love. It marked the couple as soul mates, but it could happen with anyone. Amé could have a heart song with Lia, her cousin Violet, or the milkman and not be in love. It often grew into love because the intensity of the bond absorbed half of each soul of the couple, transferring it into the other person so that they became whole in every viable way. The final ritual was often sexual. Amé wasn't clear on the details because the phenomenon was passed down by word of mouth, but most people, especially witches, associated the heart song with finding their one true love, their predestined mate.

How this impossible, wonderful experience was going to happen with Xephriel, she didn't know. Maybe, there was a way to do the ritual without touching? It would require research, but they might be able to form the heart song bond and not worry about making skin-to-skin contact. After that? Maybe, Xephriel would be open to courtship, or maybe it would push him further into his reclusive nature. Amé might even lose him forever. After the heart song was entwined, the couple wouldn't feel the insane need to bond. They could go back to their normal lives, but they would always know they belonged together.

She didn't even know if the bond would kill Xephriel. That amount of emotional connection might cause his empathic condition to explode. It was a hopeless, horrible situation. Something that should have been the most beautiful moment of their lives was a disaster in the making.

First, they had to acknowledge they were heart songs. Amé got the impression that bringing it up would be as difficult as completing the ritual.

She glanced at the witch she suspected was fated to be hers and didn't know what to do.

Xephriel was perusing her mini library. Most of the information was on plants, but she had a few fictional novels she purchased from the bookstores on Soul Street. She watched Xephriel pick up a textbook titled *How to*

Make Medicinal Tonics. The flipping pages sounded like birds taking flight as he skimmed through the contents. He slid the book on the shelf and turned as if sensing her gaze upon him.

"I have mostly plant books." She didn't know what to do with her hands and wound up grabbing a sprig of dried lavender off the counter.

Xephriel strolled into the kitchen. His height almost reached the top of the entryway as he ducked under the frame. His lean build folded into one of her chairs, and the tops of his knees banged the table. *If only she could view what lay beyond his hood*--Clearing her throat, Amé turned to the dried chamomile hanging above her head and brought down a cluster to prepare the tea. It was busy work to keep her mind off the heart song dilemma.

"Thank you for staying. I'm not the socializing type, so I don't have much to entertain guests. I'm more comfortable in my lab." She was rambling, but the nervous tingling in her chest increased from his nearness.

"I think you may have figured out I'm not a socializer, either. This is a comfortable apartment, and your books look interesting. I also have a library of bone magic volumes and skeleton drawings."

"What kinds of books do you have on bone magic?" Her interest was piqued, and her nerves began to settle as their conversation progressed.

"Many kinds, but I like to read about the scientific findings on bones. The whole story of a person stays in their bones. You can tell age, whether the person had a terminal disease, or what part of the world they were from based on the patterns on their surface or in the marrow. It's more than magic. There's a whole process to understanding biology, too."

Amé crushed the chamomile and lavender in a marble bowl with a pestle. "Wow, all that from bones!"

"Bones are my life. It sounds a little funny saying it like that, but I feel it in my soul." He placed a hand over his heart and tapped twice.

Amé shook the crushed herbs into a nylon pouch and settled it into the teapot. "Can you read bones inside a living person?"

"It's more difficult to do it while people are alive. Flesh and blood create a barrier around the bones, and they don't respond to a bone witch's magic as well as a dead person."

"I get a little wigged out when I see a full skeleton. It's like there's a piece of the person still in their bones."

Her back muscles spasmed, jerking her shoulders as she imagined the drawings of corpses in her science classes at the witch academy.

Xephriel supported his elbows on the table. "An imprint remains on the bones. I can read the soul's aura even if the person has been dead for twenty years. So long as there is even a sliver of bone left, I can detect their energy signature. Once I establish a connection through the bone, I can form a bridge between my psyche and the person's soul."

"What's the most interesting bone you've found or been given?" She poured hot water into the teapot, then gripped the porcelain handle and carried it to the table.

Xephriel wiggled a little in his seat and confessed, "The dragon scales are my favorite. I purchased those in an auction. It cost me sixty gold libras."

"Sixty gold libras?" She repeated in shock. "I had no idea bone reading was such an expensive business."

A rumbling chuckle echoed from his throat, deep and alluring. His lips parted to reveal a broad smile, and it caused a tickle in her stomach.

Xephriel turned his empty tea cup around on his saucer as he said, "I inherited my grandfather's wealth. It was to help me set up the Humerus and hopefully find a cure for my empathic condition."

Amé poured the chamomile and lavender tea into Xephriel's cup and then her own. "What's it like to speak to your family in the spirit world?"

"You could, too, if I helped you bridge the communication gap." He picked up his teacup and blew across the surface.

Amé never considered speaking to her ancestors. She tilted her head to the side and mused, "I suppose. They won't be mad I disturbed them from their peace, will they?"

"Most people don't mind visiting their family members. The problem comes when they are kept on the physical plane against their will. Ghosts are souls forced to remain half in our world and half in theirs. The dead like all their pieces together. A ghost protects their body or covets what they have in life. If anything scatters, it causes unrest. Curses can keep a soul trapped as well."

It was so easy to chat with Xephriel. The tea helped with the nerves, too. She forgot about the trembling of her hands, the fuzziness of her uncertainty in his company. "I didn't realize there were so many aspects to death. How would I speak to my grandparents?"

Xephriel took a sip of tea, his angular jaw moving as he swallowed. "Ideally, you would need one of their bones, but I can persuade spirits to visit if they have a strong affinity with the living person that summons them."

"I can't dig up my grandparents' bones to say hello."

He cleared his throat and fell into the rhythm of their dialogue. "No, that's not really how I operate, either. If you have an item belonging to your ancestors, I can use other bones as a conduit to encourage them from the spirit world."

"I have my grandmother's books."

"I remember you said she was a muse witch. Their auras can imprint on their work as well as their bones."

Amé's eyes glistened with moisture as she recollected the wonderful memories of her grandmother. "I swear I can still feel her every time I read one of her books."

Xephriel placed his empty cup on the saucer and ran a pointer finger over the rim. "That connection might be enough to ask your grandmother to visit for a short time."

"I'll keep that in mind. Thank you, Xephriel."

His lips curved into a radiant smile as he said, "I'm at your service."

The way he conveyed his words pooled warmth in the base of her belly.

She listened to her fingernail tap against the table and drifted into silence. Once again, her mind wandered toward the probability of them being heart songs. She wondered why his empathy reacted like a curse. Amé stood from her seat and glided toward her bookshelves. Her fingers brushed the book spines as she pondered a combination of plants that might help Xephriel's empathic condition.

"What are you looking for?"

Amé wiggled a book called *Magical Remedies From the Bog of Illaria* from its spot and brought it to her oak table next to her ivory chaise lounge. "I'm wondering if there's a magic plant that targets empathy. I know you said you tried everything, but I'm curious what the doctors may have given you to help dull the effects of your dissonance."

Xephriel scratched at his stubble as he asked, "Why are you suddenly so curious about my empathy?"

Amé peeked around the bookshelf. "Call it the scientist in me wanting answers to the impossible. As your friend, I'd like to know more about you. I can't imagine being forced to live alone, never interacting with people beyond pleasantries and business."

Xephriel rose from his seat and said, "There's not much else to learn. I wish things were different, but magic isn't something that's easily changed or eliminated. The medela witches don't have the technology or ability to study divergences inside the mind. In my case, it's my magic and body that are different. It's unclear which is the main cause. Most people would consider themselves blessed to be born a witch, and I do, but I wish the part of me I loved the most wasn't a detriment."

Amé didn't feel pity, not in the least, but she had a tenderness toward Xephriel. He joined her in the living room, and his voice was so quiet when he asked her if he could help that she almost didn't hear it.

She pointed to the other side of the room. "Of course, you can help. Select any book that has to do with magic plants. I think we need to study herbs unique to witches. If you note anything familiar in the books, maybe that can help me understand what the doctors used to treat you."

Xephriel didn't move right away and rubbed a thumb over his palm. He continued in that quiet voice, his words warm in the atmosphere. "I'm sorry about your seeds."

Amé leaned against the bookcase. "I want people to be happy. This experience has taught me that people are unpredictable, and it's best to get to know them better before assuming anything. If I truly want to help people, I need to do more consultations with them. Give them a chance to really understand what they are purchasing. It will give me a chance to understand whether my flower mates are right for them."

"Still, it hurts when someone takes what you love and destroys it. I would know. I feel like my empathy does that to me every day. I've grown used to the idea that I'll never have the true love you speak of. I'll never have intimacy with anyone."

She cleared her throat and decided to take a leap of faith. "I've wanted to get close to you for a while."

Xephriel looked like he would take a step toward her, but at the last minute, he turned and walked to the other side of the room. "I'm glad you gave me the rose bushes."

Amé smiled, unsure if that was an admission of his feelings or if he simply wanted to change the topic. She didn't mind either way and replied, "Me too."

Amé turned back to her perusal and selected a leather-bound book. The book title read: *Gems and Their Healing*. She opened a page to rose quartz, the stone for universal love. Her finger trailed over the page, her reflections wandering into a strange dreamy fog. She may not know a way to overcome the obstacles between her and Xephriel, but Amé had hope. That small glimmer was all she needed to turn to the stars and wish for Khaos to dismantle the impossible.

Chapter 12

Xephriel sat on the lounge with Amé, reading through books on magical botanicals. The temptation to stroke her hair behind an ear or hold her hand overwhelmed his cautionary personality. His grandfather's words, "do not be afraid," tumbled around his mind like a melody he couldn't get out of his head. With each page turned, the resolve to keep his hood up, to block out the world, collapsed.

"I haven't recognized anything in the books to indicate a specific target to empathy," Amé's voice cut through his musings, and he peered at the page she was reading.

"My condition is complex. Empathic witches processes the emotions of others so that they share their experiences. The magical components inside our minds are necessary to connect to people, both alive and dead.

The emotional link is a form of divination. Bone witches have an additional sensitivity to touch. The layer of the epidermis that conducts magic is thicker. Both conditions help bone witches to divine and communicate with the dead and their remains. The healing witches at the hospital have not yet discovered why my magic is more intense than other witches."

She set the book aside and scooted so she faced him. "I've been growing a weed that is called 'cosmosia.' It's a magical plant that blooms on a full moon and emits fluorescent pollen. It happens to be one of the flowers I crossbred to create my flower mates. The nectar from the cosmosia increases as it draws down the moon and absorbs moonbeams. In my opinion, your empathy is doing the same thing. I conjecture that your mind is signaling the magic to draw in emotions and then increase the potency of your empathic nature. I was wondering if I studied the cosmosia plant if it would give me clues to what your body does when you absorb too much of another person's emotions. If I could find a way to mutate the plant to push energy out instead of drawing it in, there might be a way to reverse your empathic dissonance. I could bring my research to a medela witch on Healing Street and see what they think."

Xephriel gripped the teeth necklaces around his neck, and shame colored his tone as he said, "I'd be grateful for even a glimmer of help. The anxiety from my dissonance is debilitating most days. When I'm overwhelmed by my empathy, I feel my heart pump harder, my pulse races, and my veins thicken as the blood rushes. I get dizzy, hot, and my breaths are rapid. A headache usually forms, and I have to stay in a dark place to ease the pain. The longer I remain in contact with a person, the more images fill my head because of the magic absorbing emotions through my skin. That part causes nosebleeds and nausea. This is all with the witch spider silk I wear. If it's direct skin contact, my mind feels like it's been hit with electricity, and I inevitably have a seizure."

She clutched her fingers tightly in her lap, her knuckles turning white. He wondered what she was trying to hold back. Her emotions came in garbled as if she felt too many things at once. Amé swallowed and wondered out loud. "The empathy has become a weed to your magic because it's mutated to the point that it overshadows everything else."

Desperation gnawed at Xephriel to have direct contact. She cared so much about his condition, and it was a far cry from the pity he received from others. Pity or fear.

Witches had a tendency to flee when they knew their feelings were on display. Amé didn't complain or close off their budding friendship because he could decipher every nuance of her emotions. She wore her feelings like a badge of honor. All he wanted was to feel normal, and there was a chance with Amé. Instead, he scooted farther away and turned from her yearning brown gaze.

"Do you think there's a cure?"

"Everything has balance. There may not be a plant that works for you, and that's why the healers couldn't find a way to manage your dissonance. The mind is a complex place. The cosmosia plant jogged a thought on how it's important to know why magic behaves a certain way. When a plant is diseased, I have to be careful and study genetics, environment, and possible pests to cure it. If the plant dies, then I discover a way to form resistance for the next generation. Analyzing cells takes time, and there are times when the answer isn't evident. That doesn't mean a cure doesn't exist. The answer has yet to be revealed." She closed the books on the table and glanced at the clock on her wall. "I can't believe it's dinner time. We've been looking through books for hours!"

"I didn't mind." His indigo aura flared like it did when they were in front of Noble's building. His face warmed at the embarrassing reaction his magic had to Amé.

Oblivious to the increase of dark blue aura filling up the room, Amé said, "I didn't either, but I think my stomach might object if I make it wait any longer. I'll go to the kitchen and see what I have stocked in the ice box."

Xephriel watched her head to the kitchen. A faint beat like a drum sounded from the etheric field, and a low bass tone resonated against a silky alto frequency. It was too atonal to be apparent if the two vibrating strings generated a heart song, but a distinctive bond existed between him and Amé. The sound waves caused a ripple effect from his fingers to his wrist and traveled up his arm.

An image formed in his mind as he listened to the stirrings of legend made real. Vines wrapped around a skeletal rib cage as leaves blossomed through the bone gaps and produced vegetative skin. A rose burst open in the center of the chest, crimson like blood and glistening as if it held a soul. A divine voice whispered in his ear, "rebirth."

What he felt with Amé was sumptuous, like his soul was being caressed. Tranquil and blissful, she was a haven of quiet that demolished the tautness of the discordance that caused him agony.

He stood up and entered the kitchen as Amé situated a basket of vegetables on the counter. An undeniable compulsion to run his hands along her forearms seized his being. He wanted their mellifluous connection, to ride the current of their souls growing and blossoming into the extraordinary. For too long, he dwelt in solitude, hiding from the world. Amé gave him a glimpse of normalcy, of what it felt like to be like everyone else, and he desired more.

"I found a slab of smoked pork, cheese, and of course, I have vegetables. I'm thinking of pan-frying peppers, onions, asparagus, and lemongrass."

He shuddered from his diaphragm, and a rasp escaped his throat. Her voice knocked him out of whatever trance made him lose all sense of reason, and he tripped backward. Grabbing the back of the chair, he panted as he realized how close he came to stroking a strand of her hair. Xephriel inched away, fitting into the corner of her kitchen and catching his breath. He had to be losing his mind; that was the only explanation for disregarding the fact that one touch from her would send him to the hospital.

Xephriel distracted himself by peering at the white star buds she had positioned on her window sill. "Is this the cosmosia?"

"Yes, I like the scent and the composition of the blossoms. I harvest the nectar for perfume."

A crash from downstairs had them both jumping. Xephriel moved first. The door banged against the wall as he hastened out of Amé's apartment and down her stairs. Without a skeleton or pieces of bone, he had no weapon. All that mattered was making sure whoever broke in didn't get any farther than the first floor.

Amé was right behind him, her footsteps echoing off the stairs as they dashed to catch the intruder. Xephriel whipped around the corner at the bottom landing and searched for the cause of the commotion.

Nothing. The shop was empty and shrouded in twilight.

Amé stopped beside him and let out a gasp. "Look!"

A piece of paper lay on the floor of her shopfront; the front window smashed in the middle. Picking up the note, Amé read the message to him. "Come to Blood Street if you want your seeds returned."

"What is this?" Xephriel leaned over her shoulder, re-reading the sloppy script.

"It must be the same person who broke into my store. Why do they want me to come to Blood Street? What have I done to this person? I don't understand why I'm being targeted."

"Are you sure there isn't a grudge you don't know about?"

"No! I certainly haven't gotten into a disagreement that would lead to being harmed."

Xephriel squinted against the darkening world outside her shop. The street was quiet. He turned to Amé and said, "I think we need some security in this place."

She raised her brows at his suggestion. "I'm all ears."

"I could set up an alarm system with a skeleton guard."

"Pardon?"

Xephriel waved in a placating manner. "Not a human skeleton. A wolf spirit can howl and warn us if there's an attempted break-in. Plus, I doubt a thief will come near a building with a dead wolf growling at them."

"Good point." She scraped her nails over her scalp, her frustration and fear heavy in the air. He felt it weigh down on him, but again the pain did not follow.

Xephriel gestured toward the door with his chin. "Do you want to go now?"

"Yes," She pleaded and dropped her arms to her side.

Xephriel guided Amé into the Humerus. They wended through a maze of halls on his first floor to a set of double doors. He opened the storage space to reveal whole skeletons positioned around the room. They almost looked alive. He passed a squirrel, a cat, and a murder of crows above his head. Eagles appeared to swoop down from the ceiling, wolves crouched around foxes, and a bear stood on its hind legs in the back. Amé yelped, and Xephriel turned around to watch her disentangle her gown from a lion's open maw.

"Are you all right?"

She shuddered from the unexpected snare, but she said, "I'm fine. I wasn't watching where I was going. Everything caught my attention at once, and I couldn't tear my eyes away from all the different species. I don't even know half the names of the creatures in here."

"They are part of my collection. I don't travel often, but I will venture out to an auction or outside the city if I'm notified about a particular set of bones. My father keeps me in the bone witch community loop."

She inched toward him and gripped the edge of his jacket. There was no connection to his body, but Xephriel swore he felt her touch all over his skin. He cleared his throat and kept walking. Her hands fell to her sides as if she realized what she'd done and shifted away.

"How are they maintaining a shape? Shouldn't they be lying flat?"

Xephriel looked over his shoulder. "At the risk of sounding cheesy, it's magic."

Amé huffed out a laugh and arched her neck to gaze at the birds dangling from the ceiling. "Magic indeed."

Xephriel crouched down so he was even with a wolf skeleton. "Wolves make excellent guardians."

"I'm getting 'back off' vibes, and it's not even animated yet."

"He won't harm you. Wolves are loyal, and I've been caring for these bones for almost fifteen years now. It's like having a pet."

"A pet without fur."

He laughed and patted the wolf on the head. "She'll come around, Arkon."

"You named it?" She clasped a hand to her mouth as if regretting that she doubted the wolf's identifier. "Can it hear me?"

He stood up and adjusted the teeth and claw necklaces around his neck. "Not yet. Of course, he has a name. How else would I call his spirit back from the etheric field?"

She crossed her arms and thought for a moment. "I don't know. Maybe you wave a bone for it to fetch."

"The vegetation witch has a sense of humor."

She let out another huff of amusement. "All right. Show me how it's done."

He took off his gloves and placed them in his pocket. "Animals are a little harder to call back from the spirit world than humans. They don't have as great a desire to roam our plane after they leave it."

He closed his eyes and placed his hands on both sides of the wolf's head. He called Arkon's name, and the air began to buzz with static electricity. Arkon was called three more times before a howl was heard in the ether. Arkon's skeleton animated and delivered a loud bark. The skeleton wolf toppled Xephriel backward and made to lick his face.

"I'm happy to see you too." He pushed Arkon off and scratched the wolf's skull.

"It's moving!"

He arched his neck to look at her from the floor. "What did you think was going to happen?"

"I didn't expect the wolf to be so real."

Xephriel stood up and replaced his gloves. "Arkon's spirit is connected to his body now. Of course, he will be alive in a way."

She inched forward, extending her hand to touch the wolf. "Can I touch him?"

"Of course. He recognizes me as the alpha, so anyone I say is in my pack he will treat as family."

Amé stroked the head of the wolf. "It's smooth but a little jagged too."

Arkon yipped and wagged his tail. Xephriel whistled and led Arkon out of the Humerus. "I have a job for you, my friend."

Arkon's head angled to the side.

"I need you to watch Amé's shop for us while we sleep. Don't let anyone near the front door. Bite anyone who tries to enter and howl to warn us." Xephriel pointed to Seeds of Love, and Arkon yowled, settling on his haunches in front of the door.

"I pity any fool who tries to rob me now."

Xephriel's pride swelled through his chest, and he grinned broadly. "They will definitely regret getting anywhere near your shop." He rubbed the back of his neck as he peered around her shopfront. "We can eat, then clean up down here."

Amé pulled the note from her gown pocket and studied the script, then glanced outside at Soul Street. "You know. I'm thinking."

Trepidation pooled in his gut. "About what?"

"Noble mentioned the Taxidermist."

"Yes?"

She pursed her lips together before suggesting, "I think we should pay him a visit. Surely, he must know to whom he sells his skins. Maybe, we can bargain to get him to tell us who is stalking me and vandalizing my shop. The note indicated I should meet the thief on Blood Street. Maybe we can kill two birds with one stone."

"Have you lost your mind? If we make any deal with the Taxidermist, we might very well end up dead or worse."

Her features were fixed in determination. "It's worth a shot. I want to catch this witch who thinks she can bully me. We still have no idea if the theft and the murder are connected, but I'd like to cross one of those variables off the list."

Xephriel tried to reason with her, keeping his tone calm and quiet. "Amé, we can't go to Blood Street."

Nothing about his tone placated her in the least. In fact, this time, it did the opposite. She seethed and declared, "Okay. You stay here and watch my shop. I'll go ask him and see if I can dig up a name on the criminal."

He flinched as each of her words impacted like a blow. "You've really lost it. I know you have. Otherwise, you would not even humor the notion of meeting the Taxidermist."

Amé planted her hands on her hips, the paper crinkling as she tightened her fist. "I can't sit by and watch someone take over my life. I will not wait while my fate is decided by a maniac. I'm being threatened, my shop vandalized, and my work impeded. The Taxidermist might have a list of people he sells his wares. I say we check it out. If it's a dead-end, then we can say we tried and go home. At the very least, I can scope out the person who wrote this note."

He shook his head in the negative, refusing to budge to her will. "We will regret this."

She was adamant and didn't retreat, either. "Xephriel. You're a bone witch. You command the dead. Noble trusted your skills to help me if I needed assistance. I need you now. I'm not going to be talked out of this. Not to mention, I can purchase a poisonous weed. We are witches, and we have magic. We can protect ourselves."

"You say that, and yet the Taxidermist is the most powerful witch in Libra. More so than those who rule the witch council."

"If he tries anything, I'll send a viper vine after him. He's flesh and blood, and poison will stop him if he tries to harm us. You can conjure up a skeleton to bash his brains in."

Xephriel's mouth hung open, and his tongue moved, but no words formed. His voice finally figured out how to work again, and he said, "My god. Where did this blood-thirsty witch come from? Where's sweet, lovely Amé who prunes roses?"

Amé stuffed the paper in her pocket, flipped her hair over a shoulder, and returned with, "She's on vacation. She decided that there was too much insanity happening and left her alter ego in charge. That witch is saying, 'Bye, Xephriel. I'm headed to Blood Street'."

She walked right out the front door. Xephriel had no other choice but to follow.

Chapter 13

Blood Street was a place of evil. It contained all the terrible people and magic in Aequitas. It was a cataclysmic monstrosity that shouldn't exist, and yet the kings and queens of Libra did nothing about it. The Court of Harmony had their imperial law enforcement officers planted in every crevice of the street, making sure the secretion of ill-doings didn't leak into other parts of the city. To attempt to quell the malice of Blood Street, the Court of Harmony would need to arrest the Taxidermist, and no one had ever gone against the witch. Even with the king of sin out of the way, there was no telling what other miscreant would rise up to take his place. Blood Street was a permanent thorn in Aequitas, buried so deep that it was better to leave it alone than dig it out.

Amé had no business near the cesspit of horrors, but she needed to talk with the Taxidermist. That note kept running a loop in her mind, and her vision slid side-to-side as she passed every crooked shop and filthy dealer. Possessed or enslaved by the sudden change of events in her life, she flipped her reservation on its head and was now hell-bent on obtaining answers. Poisoned by the fact that the next move of the thief and vandalizer could be her death, Amé embraced the adrenaline and the determination and charged toward the contemptuous and famous red road.

Red glass had been sealed over the dirt from the front of the street that connected the inner circle of Aequitas to the end. Grooves were chiseled into the surface, along with a strange magic that glamoured the walkway so that her feet didn't slip. The texture doubled as a mirage, and the road appeared as if it flowed like a river of blood. The road was designed so it was easy to wash off the remnants of fights, murder, and mayhem while hiding the splotches that couldn't be erased.

A black wall of cooled lava, metallic mystery, and black stone blocked Blood Street from the rest of the world. Dead End. That was the literal name of the far reaches of the horrifying lane.

Xephriel had used every excuse to get her to turn back. He tried bribing her with the food they left at her apartment, but she snagged some street cuisine at the center circle. He persuaded her by pointing out Noble could join their quest, but she had no time to pick up another crew member. He even tried pleading, begging her to see reason, but Amé went temporarily deaf. Tarnished and weary, Amé surrendered to the wild thing inside her mind that upturned the puzzle table, blew up the order, and let whatever inner mad witch take the reins.

Now they were here, her feet tapping on the crimson glass as she searched for a deadly nightshade witch.

Waste, fetid and coagulated debris, heaped from metal trash bins. The stench was so pungent that Amé had to tear off a piece of her gown and tie it around her nose and mouth. An arm, maybe still attached to a body, maybe not, lay visible from an alley, gloomy and foreboding. Unlike Soul Street, there were gaps between the buildings where Khaos knew what happened in the darkness. Xephriel, despite his grumbling about their destination, remained at her side. He had slipped off a bone key from his brass ring and now held it like a talisman. Every so often, he'd grab his head, and a tiny pang of guilt filtered into her mind as she waited for him to bend over from the rotten emotions sure to be gushing out of Blood Streets' residents.

Out of the corner of her vision, Amé spotted a deadly nightshade witch selling her wares. Her fingernails were cracked and blackened from touching poisons all day. Her hands were gnarled and permanently disfigured. That's what the darker side of vegetation magic did to the body. It twisted it into a constant state of fighting off the pain. The poison remained a steadfast presence that gnawed so incrementally that the person lived in blissful hell until it hit the body all at once. The agony of a poison episode was indescribable and left the victim hallucinating and disconnected from reality. That was the type of magic Amé needed to wield if she was going to meet with the Taxidermist.

She shifted and sneaked under the awning of the tent. An array of dried herbs clustered in little boxes. Amé didn't want half-dead plants. She wanted fresh vegetation that she could manipulate with her magic. She leaned toward the deadly nightshade witch, the reek of her yellow teeth and coffee breath mingled in the air.

"I need a viper vine seed." The seed would be enough to carry in her pocket, and if she had to fight, her magic would make it burst into a vicious carnivorous plant.

"Don't carry the live stuff," The other witch sneered, but the light in her pale blue gaze let Amé know she sensed the power of vegetation magic in her presence.

Amé pulled out five gold libras from her purse and held them out. "How about now?"

The witch flicked her gaze behind Amé's shoulder. "I'll get into trouble with the imperials and be hauled off to the Court of Harmony if I give you a fresh seed."

Amé put two more gold libras on the pile, her palm cupping the glittering and tempting metal. "This is well above the asking price, and you know it. Viper vine is common on this street. Any deadly nightshade witch worth her magic has at least one seed. There are far worse dealings on this street. The officers don't have time for minor transactions. Don't you think?"

The witch took the coins, her grubby fingers leaving a sappy residue on Amé's skin as she said, "One seed, and don't be telling nobody I have them."

Amé used her other hand to pretend she was zipping her mouth shut. "Not a word."

After a few minutes of rustling and cursing from inside her shop, the deadly nightshade witch returned with a tiny leather pouch. She passed it to Amé with a wink and said, "I'd be careful with that. They tend to eat their masters since they like the vitality of flesh."

Amé didn't reply and turned away from the other witch, slipping the pouch into her gown pocket. She was discreet as she wiped her other hand down the side of her gown. Xephriel hissed out a breath and placed a hand on his forehead. She slipped into the shadows of a nearby alley and addressed Xephriel. "Are you all right?"

"No, I'm not all right!" He all but growled. "My empathy is clashing like a violin out of tune, and it's causing my ears to ring and giving me a headache."

"I could buy some herbs to help with the headache," She offered and searched for a shop that might be considered an apothecary in this place.

"I'll be fine. I'm wearing extra bones, and my grandfather is keeping away the wandering spirits. Let's get this done so we can leave this god-forsaken part of town."

"Your grandfather?"

Xephriel revealed the key-shaped bone in his hand. "This is from his clavicle. He's protecting me from the majority of the spirits, ghouls, and evil fog."

Amé's face heated. They were on this train wreck now, and she had to see it through. She inspected the seed to make sure the witch hadn't tricked her and, satisfied it was the correct product, Amé hustled down the glassy lane.

"Do you even know where you are going?"

Amé didn't, but she heard rumors about how to contact the Taxidermist. "He frequents the gambling halls. I figured that was a good place to start."

"We're on a wild goose chase! Wait a second."

She heeded his command and waited. Xephriel muttered something under his breath, and his aura swallowed the light around them. As the midnight blue shrank back into his body, he said louder, "He's in the gambling den called Rosey Rump. Let's go."

She blinked in surprise. "How did you know?"

"The dead. They refuse to leave until they've had their revenge on him. He's so powerful they can't do anything but wait, watch, and pray he dies."

Amé shivered at what Xephriel described and picked up her pace. They weaved through crowds of drunken, drugged, and plain delirious people until they came to their destination. The Ruby Rump's doorway looked like it puked customers as a riot of people clogged the entrance. Amé was slammed into a wall as a pair of fighters tussled in the street. Xephriel grunted as he dodged the brawlers, and the grim line of his mouth was white around the edges. He was staring in the direction of the gambling den, rooted to the spot.

"I can't go in there."

Amé had two options. She could abandon her attempt at heroics, or she could leave Xephriel on the street. Since her heart was kind and the raging adrenaline had worn off, Amé chose Xephriel. They'd come this far, but she knew if he tried to go through the crowd, it would be too much for him, even with the protection of the bones and the witch spider silk. Amé could go in alone, but that was all kinds of stupid. It was one thing to meet with the Taxidermist, and it was another to fight off a slew of miscreants that were drugged and drunk off Khaos knew what.

"Since we can't get in to contact the Taxidermist, let's walk some more and see if we can find the person who sent the note."

His shoulders sagged. He rubbed his face with his black-gloved hands. When he dropped them, his tone was exasperated. "We'll walk to Dead End. If we don't find anyone holding a suspicious sack of seeds, let's go home, okay?"

"That description matches a lot of the occupants of this street, but okay. I'll march right back to the center circle if we get to the end of the road and nothing happens."

His tone sounded relieved as he whispered, "Thank you."

She didn't want to give up, but at least he agreed to keep looking for the culprit. As Amé stretched her leg out to walk, another rambunctious brawler pushed her right into Xephriel. He caught her as she pitched forward and tugged her flush with his chest. They twisted as their balance tipped, and Xephriel's back collided with a wall. She half stood, half lay against his body, her legs tangled in his, and she stared in panic at his three-day stubbled chin.

She waited for his pain to kick in, for the first sign of his empathy turning against him at their contact. She was stuck, and the warmth of his body, the clove and nutmeg scent of him, wrapped her in a mystical cocoon. Amé tore off the cloth around her mouth, the sudden hitch in her throat making it difficult to breathe.

The air felt vacuumed from the space, and the cacophony of Blood Street deafened. Amé was aware of her aura seeking Xephriel's like a spiritual caress. Beyond the veil of the physical plane, supernatural drums beat. Loudly. So forceful was the tempo that it blared in her ears and burst past her psychic senses. Trumpets and flutes, cellos, and French horns orchestrated together. She swallowed, her mouth dry, and her heart hammered with the intensity of the music.

Heart songs.

Undeniable and unrestrained, their harmonious aura strings vibrated in magical chords.

Amé wiggled, desperate to free herself before Xephriel collapsed. She was overcome by the magnitude of her discovery, but if she caused Xephriel to be hospitalized, Amé would not forgive herself. His arms tightened as if he recognized their bond, but then he pushed her onto her feet. Scrambling away, he leaned a hand against the wall. His panting was the only thing she could hear beyond the majestic music. He turned his chin toward her, and that bowed mouth captivated her.

Amé knew, right then, she was ruined forever.

No other man would have her heart or soul because she cast it out in entirety to Xephriel. If she was heart-broken forever because he rejected her, then so be it. She belonged to him, and he belonged to her, and nothing in the world would change that pure, unadulterated fact. A courageous anthem was sung to her soul, and Amé did not falter from the heart song.

Amé, point-blank, asked him, "Xephriel, do you believe in heart songs?"

He was so still she thought he became petrified by what had occurred. That blasted hood. She was desperate to view her heart song's features. His mouth worked around a gulp, and his throat bobbed. She feared his incoming rejection. Steeling herself for the worst, for the blow to her heart, she waited. His lips parted, air rushing between the curves. Then his voice filled the silence, and she nearly died from the shock.

"How could I not believe in a magic I'm feeling to the core of my being?"

Droplets fell from her eyes as she blinked. Her tongue felt glued down, and she couldn't respond, so he continued in the same cathartic tone. He said, "I should be bent over with a migraine or near incapacitated, but your aura is like a remedy. I've never once touched another person and felt reverence instead of pain."

Her voice unclogged from her shock, and she asked, "You really aren't hurt?"

"No," He pushed off the wall, strode toward her, and slipped his gloved hand into the strands of her hair. His thumb brushed over the soft spot next to her ear, and he leaned in to whisper, "I have never felt better in my entire life."

She may have sobbed or extolled her joy. The sounds leaving her mouth were indistinguishable as she gripped his hand. Leaning her cheek into his touch. All she could articulate was, "My heart song."

He gave one nod and dropped his hand, so he could lace his fingers with hers as they strode back to the road. Heart song or no, they had an investigation to resume, and Amé was more determined than ever to find her answers. They had walked three paces when a sinister witch peeled out of the etheric field. Blood Street emptied, people scurrying like rats before a great flood, and the most nefarious place in Aequitas became silent. Abject terror, more potent than the grave, spread over the area. Xephriel and Amé froze to their spots.

"I have not had a display of magic like that on this street," The wicked voice drawled. "I think that's a first for me, sensing a heart song initiation."

Amé didn't need an introduction. The sheer power of the witch before her made his identity clear. The Taxidermist's black hair was slicked back from his forehead, a braid tossed over his shoulder and dangling down to his waist. His eyes were narrow and shaped like half-moons. Eyes the color of florescent rainbows glowed with unholy light from the irises. His nose was pushed inward like those from the empire of Han. His tanned lips were thin and twisted in a terrifying grin. The Taxidermist wore a long red silk coat with a wide hood and black slacks. His boots shone under the gas lamps lining the street. Sitting on his shoulder was a marionette, and it was alive. The strings were broken, and it clicked its wooden sticks together as if it were knitting. It turned its beautiful black bobbed head toward Amé and smiled. Amé nearly wet herself at the insidious thing that stared at her with skin, hair, and eyes that must have been real, but she was too terrified to contemplate asking.

"You're looking for me." It was a statement, and one that revealed his magic had an aspect of telepathy or prophecy.

Amé's teeth chattered, she was shaking so hard, but she managed to utter, "I want to know if you have any records of the skins you sold. I was looking for someone and wondered if you could help."

Insane, she was insane for addressing the Taxidermist like that, but the intensity of her adrenaline started feeding into her system again. Even with her skin pebbled from fear and the muscles around her spine cringing, Amé still wanted her answers.

The Taxidermist's look was rife with pity, and his lips turned down as he responded, "I'd never give you that information. Not even if you were Khaos himself."

Amé watched as multicolored strings wove around the Taxidermist, his aura so complex and layered. She'd never seen anything like it. There must have been more than ten colors present, and they danced around him like serpents ready to strike. The little puppet on his shoulder gave a giggle, and her strings danced on a supernatural breeze. Amé knew they couldn't fight a witch like that, but she clutched her gown where the viper seed was concealed. "We'll be on our way then."

The Taxidermist wagged a finger. "Not so fast. I'm intrigued by the two of you."

That couldn't be good.

Xephriel must have decided it was time to run because he whistled, and out of numerous passageways, a howling wind blew into the main road. The Taxidermist's florescent rainbow gaze widened, and he spun around as the wailing gale attacked him. Xephriel gripped Amé's hand to the point of crushing, and they charged for the center of Aequitas. Whether they made an enemy of the Taxidermist, she didn't know, but she was too intent on fleeing to care.

They ran until Industrial Street and hurried to a nearby stable to hire a carriage. When they reached her front porch, it was pitch black. Arkon leaped from his guard post and rubbed against Xephriel's legs. They were both gasping, bending over as they calmed down from their mad dash across the city.

When they could move again, Amé preceded Xephriel into her shop and led them up the stairs. Her heart was pounding from their escape from the Taxidermist. Her mind reeled from Xephriel admitting they were heart songs. Amé was in shock, in complete disarray from the ordeal, and she wanted the order of her life returned. Her brain was on overload, and she longed for familiarity, for a safe haven where she was in control. If she went upstairs now, she wouldn't fall asleep. She needed to do something to relax, and her lab seemed to answer that call.

"Do you want to see my lab?" She gestured toward the room on her left.

Xephriel leaned on the wall; his tone was low and roughened from sprinting. "I think I've had my fill of excitement for the day."

"I'm terrified and exhilarated all at the same time. I won't calm down if I go up to the apartment in this state."

Xephriel crossed his arms. "We wouldn't have been in that situation if you had listened to me. You had no plan, no understanding of what the Taxidermist would do. We were lucky to escape. The ghosts caught the Taxidermist by surprise. We drew his attention when our heart song triggered, and I don't think that's a good thing."

"I couldn't stand by and watch one more thing go wrong in my life. It was a promising idea at the time."

Xephriel bristled. "We didn't discover who wrote the note, the Taxidermist didn't give us any information, and you still have a poisonous plant in your pocket. What exactly are you going to do about the viper vine?"

Amé narrowed her gaze and patted the seed. "I'll put it in my lab. You never know when a killer plant will come in handy."

He pinched the bridge of his nose, or at least she assumed that was what he was doing since the bottom half of his face was visible. "I don't want to argue about the plant. I'm sure you know what to do with it. I'm worried about the unnecessary risk you took tonight. You were trying to do what you felt was right, but it wasn't thought through. From now on, we need to plan before we take action."

"I wanted to get this over with before anything else bad happened."

Xephriel unfolded his arms and inched toward her. "We don't want to add to our problems. Please, next time, let's talk about our options before we make any decisions. We should definitely involve Noble. He will know what to do. It's his job to handle dangerous situations."

She stared up at his hooded countenance, his body close enough that she could sense the heat. After a considerable pause, she said, "I promise to be more cautionary."

"All right, then," He conceded and followed her toward the door. "I could use a moment to come back from that craziness, too."

Amé lit a few gaslights to illuminate the space. An orange glow from the flames cast an inviting ambiance over the shelves of bottles and leather-bound books. The lab had a fragrant air of heterogeneous floral nectars and pungent earth with a hint of alcohol. A long marble worktable covered in beakers, a microscope, clay pots, and a small cauldron over a gas burner took up the center of the room. A cabinet of dried flowers and herbs was opened to the right. Small wooden bowls of dirt were lined and labeled for pedological research beneath the bottom shelf of rosemary, sage, thyme, and peppermint. Another microscope was to the left of the bowls. Ten small bar-rels of dried flowers were arranged under the window. Hanging on the left wall, she had a leather apron. Leather gloves and safety goggles lay on a shelf next to a stack of notebooks and a box of pens. A rack of books shielded half the window. Another wooden worktable was visible under three scales, a portable gas burner, tongs, and droppers. Perfume bottles from the oils she cultivated were alphabetically organized by the word's first letter.

"This is where the magic happens?" Xephriel leaned over the worktable and inspected a beaker of rose-mary extract.

She spun in a circle with her arms outstretched, pride for her work coating her tone. "Yes. I cooked up all my flower mates right here."

He looked around the room, studying the beakers and sifting through her books. "I feel honored you shared this part of your world with me."

"Of course. We can learn from each other. Right now, I want to fiddle and get the nerves out of my system."

He seemed to understand her desperation to banish the events of the night, so he inquired, "Tell me what you learned at the witch academy."

Amé gestured at the whole room. "This. Lots of research and experiments. For the first three years, we have lectures and exams. The instructors teach us languages, show us magical artifacts, drill us on Libra history, and lead us through about ten other subjects. Then we start concentrating on our specific magic gifts. For me, it was vegetation. I spent a lot of time in the royal gardens or in the lab. The castle laboratory is huge, and it takes up half a floor."

"I have not been inside the castle. It sounds amazing."

She crossed the room and took out an empty jar, placing the viper vine inside. "I was on the academy floor. I have not met any of the courtiers or royals."

Xephriel leaned against the work table. "I'd like to go."

"I could take you to the academy. We can peek in on Hennley."

Xephriel chuckled and crossed his arms. "You'll embarrass the poor girl."

Amé laughed as she imagined Hennley's face when she caught her spying. "Oh, most definitely. We'll have to go in the afternoon when all the classes are finished." She swiped her hand along the surface of the table and asked, "How about I make a lotion you can use when you get headaches?"

He answered with a hint of pride. "I'm intrigued. Show me your skills, my vegetation witch."

Avoidance was the name of their game, but they both needed space before they brought up the heart song. Xephriel hadn't complained, but he kept rubbing his head. She wanted to give him time to get his empathy under control before broaching the subject.

Amé looked for lavender, rosemary, chamomile, and St. John's wort. She grabbed a basket and gathered the other supplies as her mind began to work out a recipe for a topical ointment for Xephriel. Once she had her base ingredients, Amé prepped herself and her station. She bent over to fill a beaker with distilled water. A leather apron kept her dress clean from any splashed materials. Leather gloves protected her hands as she lined up the beakers and moved her pots of dirt out of the way.

Balancing a beaker of distilled water over a small gas burner, she lit the fuse so the base of the glass heated. In a jar to her right was an ointment of honey, lavender, beeswax, and olive and Theobroma oil, or the common name 'cocoa butter.'

As the contents of the beaker began to boil, she added twelve drops of lavender oil, twelve drops of chamomile oil, twelve of rosemary, three drops of St. John's wort oil, and the skin of a ginkgo seed. She used a six-inch glass stick to stir the mixture. When the beaker cooled, she drained the liquid into a clean jar. The base ointment was added to the oils, and she mixed them until the creamy substance coagulated.

Amé took off her gloves and set them on the table. Taking the glass stick, she smeared a hefty amount of ointment on her hand. She rubbed it into her skin and waited. Her nostrils flared at the musky bottom notes of the infusion, the middle floral notes, and a final sugary detection at the top notes. A pleasant euphoria worked through her senses as the blended lotion into her skin.

After a time, she removed her goggles and beckoned Xephriel to a stool. "I'm not showing any skin reactions, so I think it is safe. Every person is different, so we should first apply it to our hands. That is the safest place to check for an adverse allergic reaction."

Xephriel, trusting and confident in her work, removed his gloves. He had beautiful hands, long and boney, large, and his fingernails were well manicured. Flexing his fingers, he extended his arm so it lay flat on the table. Amé dropped a dollop. He rubbed the mixture into his skin and held his hands up for her to inspect.

Amé squinted; she couldn't quite tell if anything had occurred. "Put your hand near the gaslight, so I can watch for any rash or blisters to form."

"How long do I have to wait for a reaction?"

"It happens within the first fifteen minutes of application. You might also feel like your throat is closing up. If that happens, we'll have to go to the hospital."

Xephriel clenched his jaw at her mention of dying from asphyxiation. "That doesn't sound pleasant."

She elucidated on the concoction she spread over his skin. "It doesn't happen often. My concern is the ginkgo skin I used. That's not a common plant, and used over a long time can act like a poison."

After about fifteen minutes without any ill effect, Xephriel slipped on his gloves. "Now, what do we do?"

"That's the grand finale. I'm out of ideas."

She screwed a lid on the jar of ointment and handed it to Xephriel to use when he needed to calm down the headaches. Amé moved to clean up her workstation, but Xephriel gripped her wrist to stall her motion. Her brows raised, but she waited. His fingers unfurled, and he drew back, the motion slow and gradual.

He cleared his throat and lifted his hands to his hood. He fingered the edges as he said, "I want to show my face."

Her heart pounded like a hammer against an anvil. "Xephriel—" she began to protest, wondering if it was too soon to be letting all their truths come to the surface, but it was too late.

Amé suspected he was rugged and handsome from the bottom half of his face, but she was unprepared for his overall allure. He had sharp cheekbones, sculpting a defined, narrow countenance that squared off at his jaw. His aquiline nose separated a thick brow that had a soft arch at the ends. Never in all her life had she seen eyes that looked like Khaos crafted them himself. Midnight blue with a burst of azure around the pupils, they evoked an image of a celestial eclipse. His thick, curled lashes blinked, and the world felt like it tipped forward and rocked her foundations. She took in Xephriel's smooth broad forehead and feather-soft umber strands. He parted his hair to the side, and the close-cropped style swept behind his ears. At the apex of his hairline, the fringe made a smooth arc.

She knocked into the table as she stared, unable to think as his blue gaze transfixed her to the spot. Her mouth may have hung open, but she was too surprised, too enthralled to school her features.

They stood facing each other, neither moving, and Amé heard a diatonic chord vibrate in the distance. Her soul felt plucked as if she became a mandolin being tuned to Xephriel's deep and mysterious aura.

Her heart battered against her rib cage. Her fingers trembled, not from fear but from the realization she could never come back from this moment. They were locked into a tango of uncertainty and divine fate that they could neither break nor diminish.

At last, she found her voice. "Your eyes remind me of a star bursting."

"A gift from my mother." Every adoring truth revealed itself on his face. She could view everything. The crinkles around the corner of his eyes, the vulnerability, it was all laid bare.

"She must be lovely."

Xephriel swallowed, the knob in his throat bobbing as he worked his jaw to speak. "I love my mother. She's very devoted to her bone magic and to me. I wish I could visit her more often."

Amé gulped around her tight throat and decided to dive back into the heart song conversation. "About earlier. Not the Taxidermist part, but when we—we—collided."

"The heart song? It's been eating me alive. All I want is to touch you again."

"You do?"

He closed the distance and brushed his hands down her arms, the silk of his gloves softer than feathers. "When we were planting the roses, and our hands grazed, I sensed it. I was frightened I'd never be able to fulfill that bond, that the dissonance would hurt to the point I'd want to die. Then I was afraid I'd break your heart and break mine as a result of rejecting the bond. I've been avoiding bringing it up because I didn't want to be disappointed. I wasn't sure you were interested in me other than a friend. Then things changed," His words faltered, and she watched as a multitude of emotions passed over his features. He took a deep breath and confessed, "Amé, I've noticed you for seven years. Do you understand what I'm saying? I've wanted you for years, and because of the heart song, I can consider making a courtship offer to you."

Her arms tingled from where he rubbed his hands up and down as if savoring the miracle of his empathic liberation. As if she were the cure he searched for, and he was going to soak her up until his soul drowned. Shocked and thrilled, Amé said, "You never hinted."

"I wouldn't have been able to give you what you deserved. Not until the heart song, which apparently overrides the empathic dissonance. It makes sense. Heart songs are about eternal harmony. You are the only person I can ever be normal with, the only person I can touch. You're my salvation."

Amé placed her hands on his chest, sensing the thump of his rapid heartbeat. He didn't retreat, and he let her run her palms over the hard plane. She paused and peered up, taking in his extraordinary features, and said, "You wouldn't be opposed to a courtship?"

"Is that what you want?" His question was whispered as if he was afraid she had asked it only to reject the notion.

Amé slid her hands down and linked her fingers around his waist as she replied, "Yes, a courtship and to see where the heart song leads us."

His grip tightened, and a glorious smile transformed his countenance. "It would be my honor to go on that journey with you."

She didn't let go of Xephriel. "Thank you for joining me here. It's my safe place. Thank you for removing the hood. I know that must have been terrifying."

"I wanted to do it for you. *You* are my safe place."

They stayed facing each other, letting their auras mingle in the dim setting of the lab. When the time was right, they headed upstairs and slept, their skeletal wolf guarding them through the night.

Chapter 14

Amé opened her eyes to the streams of sunbeams filtering through her goldenrod embroidered curtains. A peaceful night's rest had passed, and she sat up in bed feeling refreshed after her fiasco from the previous day. All her emotional upheaval disintegrated when she rolled out of bed, padded through her bedroom doorway, and discovered Xephriel preparing breakfast without his hood.

She retracted into her bedroom to make sure she wasn't hallucinating. Rubbing her eyes, she resumed her course to the kitchen. Xephriel was not wearing his hood; that was a fact.

Thoughtfulness drew his brows together as he used his hand to fan steam toward his face. Savoring the aroma of what appeared to be an egg souffle, he then diverted his attention to a pile of strawberries.

"Good morning, Xephriel. How did you sleep?" She greeted him and picked up the ripe red fruit.

He slid his celestial gaze to her, and she almost melted at the smile that stretched his lips. As he cut the strawberry tops, he said, "Good morning, Amé." He left off the part about how he slept, and she winced. The couch was comfy but not meant for a man of Xephriel's height.

"How's your empathic condition? Is it okay to be without your hood?"

"I can feel the scope of your emotions, but it isn't harming me. I'm still wearing the bones and witch spider silk, so most of your emotional output is muted anyway. The heart song harmonization stands as true today as it did last night."

She gave his hand a squeeze and settled into a chair. He set the bowl of strawberries on the table and the ramekin of egg soufflé in front of her. She inhaled deeply and said, "Thank you for breakfast." She dipped her spoon into the cuisine and savored the creamy texture.

"I used the leftover bread and cheese from last night. How does it taste?"

"Like there's a party of flavors in my mouth! Khaos! That's delicious." Amé took another bite and luxuriated in the yeasty, rich fluff of eggs, cheese, and bread coating her tastebuds.

His lips lifted, and his cheeks became rosy with his delight. "I'm glad you are enjoying it."

As she lifted her spoon for another bite, she heard a growl and bark from below. She slammed the spoon down, and they dashed down the stairs to investigate what trouble awaited. Every time she had a moment of peace, a new chaotic event transpired to shake her world apart. Xephriel put up a hand to indicate she should stay back. They had cleaned up the glass from the night before, but she had no desire to confront trouble wearing her night shift.

The wolf barked, creating a scene in front of the other shops, and owners opened their doors to watch the commotion. Xephriel came back inside, bringing Arkon. Blood stained the skeleton wolf's maw. The look Xephriel gave her was grim. He held out his hand to reveal a black velvet box glistening with blood and dented from Arkon's canines.

"What is that?"

He put his hood up and said, "This is one of the bones missing from the other victims in the well."

Xephriel pursed his lips and opened the box. Inside lay a pristine ivory finger bone. Amé recoiled and dropped to the stair. He lifted it out, his deep blue aura shrouding him as he fell silent. Arkon yapped and jumped around the shop as Amé waited. And wait—the time stretched, palpable and unnerving, but Xephriel did not move or make a sound.

His voice shook. "Another mortal. The spirit is foul and restless. I can't get an accurate reading from the bone."

Amé leaned over her knees and tried to breathe through her panic. "We have to go to that well today. We have to find the killer and discover if it's the same witch harassing me. I can't take one more day of not knowing the truth."

Xephriel set the bone in the box and pocketed it. "Let's finish breakfast, you can get dressed, and then we'll go find Noble. We can trace the bone with the spirits once we make contact with the bodies."

"Miss Floreo?" She looked out her front door to see a pair of law enforcement officers.

"Yes?" She frowned in confusion at their appearance.

"Do you remember us from your theft investigation? We'd like to ask you more questions, please." Officer Kief addressed her as she rose from her perch.

Her day was getting more bizarre by the minute. "Yes, of course."

Arkon growled, and the officers retreated out of Seeds of Love. Xephriel placed a hand on Arkon's head and said, "Rest." The bones clattered to the floor in an ivory heap. The officers entered the shop but made sure to stay clear of the wolf skeleton.

Officer Roberts pulled out a notepad and pen. "We found some of your seeds."

Amé jerked back in response to their disclosure. "Where?"

The officers looked at each other, and then Officer Kief said, "There was a body found this morning on Blood Street. Your seeds were scattered around it. We matched the descriptions you gave us when we investigated your theft, but the seeds had shriveled up. The colors were still fortunately visible."

"I don't understand. Why were my seeds scattered around a-a-body?" Amé didn't like the way this discussion was headed.

Xephriel looked from one officer to the other. "Why is she being questioned? She reported her seeds missing. The thief is causing trouble, not Amé."

Officer Roberts indicated Amé with his pen. "We are trying to connect the dots. Any information that you can give us would be appreciated."

Amé didn't know what to think about the murder. "This is getting more ridiculous by the minute. Blood Street isn't exactly a quiet place. How did a body wind up displayed for all to see?"

Officer Roberts pocketed his notebook and addressed her. "We do not have an answer for that either. Homicide is common in that area of the city, but this was purposeful. The seeds were dotted around the body in a heart shape, and all the fingers were cut off and taken. The cause of death appeared to have been a stab to the heart after the victim was poisoned."

Amé threw up her hands in frustration. "First the theft, then the letter, and now a body. What in Khaos' name is going on?"

Officer Roberts pinned her with a narrowed stare. "You've been getting threats?"

Amé felt old, like she'd aged a hundred years in the last ten minutes. She let out a weary sigh. "I was going to report the note, but you showed up before I could get the message to the Court of Harmony."

Officer Kief stepped forward. "What kind of threats?"

"I got a letter that said, 'Come to Blood Street if you want your seeds returned.'"

"Did you follow those orders?"

Amé hated that she had to admit what happened, especially since it put her in an awkward position with the body being found. She wasn't a liar or a coward. "I did. We didn't find the person who wrote the letter."

Officer Roberts pointed to the bones on the floor. "Where did that blood come from?"

"I don't know. The wolf sensed a presence he didn't like and, I assume, took his guard duties seriously."

Officer Roberts knelt down with a handkerchief and wiped some of the blood off the wolf's bones. "We'll take the sample to one of our blood witches and see what they say."

Officer Kief narrowed his gaze at Amé. "Can you tell us when you arrived home last night? The time of death on the body was seven hours ago. Right at midnight."

Amé rubbed her arms and swallowed. "We were here. Asleep."

"Can anyone confirm that?" Officer Roberts intoned as if he asked these questions multiple times a day, and it was routine for him to articulate them.

"Xephriel and I were here together. There's not going to be anyone around at midnight to confirm we're asleep in our beds, now is there?"

Officer Kief turned and gave his partner a strange look, then turned back to her and said, "Until we know more about the investigation, please stay here in Seeds of Love. We may need to ask more questions as the investigation proceeds. Do you have a friend who can stay with you? Since you are getting threats, it might not be a good idea to be alone."

"I'll stay with her." Xephriel volunteered and clasped her hand.

The protective touch let her know how serious he was, and it warmed her heart. "What am I supposed to do about my busted shop? I can't leave my door like that. It isn't safe. I'll need to go to Industrial Street to get supplies."

Officer Roberts gestured for his colleague to follow him off to the side for a moment. When they had finished their discussion, he turned to Amé and said, "You may leave, but stay with someone at all times. If we need you, we will leave a message here. Respond once you read it."

"Will do," She intoned.

"We'll be in touch." Officer Kief headed out of Seeds of Love first, with Officer Roberts close behind.

Amé turned to Xephriel. "I'm going back upstairs, eating breakfast, and getting dressed. Then we are going to find Noble. I don't know what's going on here, but it's clear to me that all signs point to my seeds and a psychopath obsessed with them. I'm not ruling out the Taxidermist's involvement now, either. He might have set that body up to lead the imperial detectives to me. Last night wasn't exactly a casual exit from his territory. Is the killer working alone, or did we rope in the most dangerous witch in Aequitas? We need to get to those bones in the well, and we need to get answers fast."

"I'll clean up and return Arkon to the Humerus while you get ready."

"I'll be ready in twenty minutes."

Chapter 15

Xephriel pounded the bone knocker against Noble's door. After ten minutes with no response, Xephriel climbed back inside the carriage with Amé and gave the driver instructions to Entertainment Street.

The Kaleidoscope Art Gallery was a complex geometric composition of stained glass squares and triangles. The overall appearance gave off a dream-like quality as the sun dispersed rainbow colors against the sidewalk. Three triangular branches of the building ascended toward the sky like mountains, and the central rectangular entryway stood sentinel between them. Behind the enormous conglomerate of architectural artwork was the Mosaic garden.

Gold roses arched over iron trellises to create a metallic tunnel that led to verdant blossoms and shrubs.

Xephriel and Amé hustled through the ivy hanging through the gaps of the arches. Xephriel spied the gazebo from Mr. Rendell's memories and steered Amé around a bend of hedges. There, near the stone well, was Noble, and he wasn't alone.

Agitated and rife with mystical energy, Noble shouted at one of the uniformed imperial detectives from the Court of Harmony. "Damn you, fools! I need to summon the bones out of the well. It will be faster. Can you move out of the way so I can do my job and interview my witnesses?"

Xephriel hurried to Noble, wheezing as he came to a halt. "Noble! What can we do to help?"

Noble's curly brown hair flopped into his eyes as he spied Xephriel. He let out a relieved breath and drawled, "I'm about to break every rule in the justice book and call the bones from the well without the imperial detectives' permission. Officer Terrance is impeding my investigation as usual."

Xephriel watched the imperial detectives inspecting the ground near the well. "Should we help them?"

Noble groaned and rubbed his face. "I have been trying to do that all morning. They don't like my methods."

"How much trouble will we get into if we call the bodies out of the well?"

Noble dropped his arms, and the grin he gave Xephriel was feline. "None at all. It will piss them off to no end, though."

Xephriel felt his lips twist in response, but he said, "Let me go reason with them. Maybe they can interview Amé while we work on getting to the remains."

"Good idea, my friend! Distract them so they can't object to zombies crawling out of the world egg."

Xephriel shook his head at his friend's idiosyncratic line of thinking. Most bone witches had a care for those outside their community, but Noble charged right through all sensibilities and did what he pleased. Slipping away to try and negotiate with the imperial detectives, although Xephriel doubted it would have any effect, he signaled for Amé to join him. She scurried over to the well and waited for him to give her instructions.

Xephriel said to the imperial detectives, "It would be a lot faster if you let Noble encourage the bodies out of the well."

One of the imperial detectives rose from her examination of a stone, her red aura blaring like a horn. "We need to gather the evidence around the well first so that the bodies that come out of it do not disturb anything. Mr. Dracaena is being impatient."

Xephriel winced against the onslaught of the officer's aura. "How long have you been looking around the well?"

The officer sniffed and said, "Since yesterday afternoon."

"Officer—" He paused to allow her to introduce herself.

"Officer Terrance," came her terse reply.

"Officer Terrance, there can be no further reason to keep searching for clues. Let us have the bones, and you can continue to gather evidence."

"We did a magic sweep. Now, we are doing a methodical search of the grounds. You can have your bones when we have completed the interviews at the art gallery."

"When will that be?"

Officer Terrance widened her stance and placed her hands on her hips. "Tomorrow or the day after."

Xephriel was patient as he reasoned with Officer Terrance. "We can do several things at once. A detective can interview Miss Floreo, Noble can assemble the victims, and the rest can search the grounds as you see fit."

"It's not procedure."

Xephriel watched her aura glow apple red as her irritation grew. It pained him to be in her presence, but he forged through the adversity. "I'm a bone consultant brought in to help Noble. Miss Floreo created the seeds that are part of the evidence and witness statement. It's perfectly fine to let us work with you. Time is not a luxury, is it?"

After a pause of consideration, Officer Terrance conceded. "All right. I'll interview Miss Floreo. Tell Noble not to make a scene or a mess."

"Thank you."

"I mean it. The last time we worked together on a case, he demonstrated his magic by standing on a bar in the middle of the peak hour and knocked on the ceiling until a skeleton fell through the mortar."

Xephriel tried to hide his laughter behind a cough. "I understand. No dramatic flair. We'll remove the bones and do the consultations. That's it."

Officer Terrance narrowed her dark chocolate gaze. "See that you do."

Xephriel watched Amé wander to the gazebo with Officer Terrance, and he returned to Noble. The glee on his friend's face was almost diabolical when Xephriel informed him they had permission to animate the bodies. Xephriel reminded him not to stir up too much trouble with the imperial detectives. Noble waved off his concern and strolled to the well, hands outstretched, auras glowing like white beacons as he commanded the dead to rise.

The ground trembled, and the moisture in the air became dense as it grew colder. A stench of festering flesh permeated Xephriel's nostrils, and a yawn from the etheric field echoed in his ears. The imperial detectives fled from the well, and he caught Amé's umber stare from across the garden. Apprehension creased her brow as the well vibrated and sent a jolt through the ground.

From the well, a howling wind stirred, and the scratching, grunting, and clattering of the dead rose out of the depth. The bones jostled as they tumbled from the well and assembled. The sound was akin to a marimba, and body parts linked and fused together. Noble conducted his magic, so their souls used the animated bodies as a conduit to communicate. Four revenants stood erect in the garden.

Half-decayed corpses, bits of flesh and cloth hanging onto their bones, swayed as Noble's magic coursed through their remains. Gray and speckled with black rot, a couple were more skeleton than zombie. The undead stood in a line like soldiers awaiting orders. Noble clapped his hands and slid to the front of the line. He counted the bones, inspected each joint and crevice with a magnifying glass, then moved to the next. Down the line, he scuttled like a crab, dipping and spinning around each revived carcass until he came to the last.

"Two more finger bones missing. All the same finger. The middle phalanx. Odd. There's no magical correlation with that finger. Perhaps, the killer had a fetish? There are scratches, fractures, and trauma to the bones, but that's to be expected. The fleshy bits all make sense with the time frame of decay and the water log from the well. The first death was eight months ago. Hello, Mr. Rendell! Moving on. Nothing remarkable, no imprint of the killer. I'll need to take a closer look as we interview each one." Noble turned to the passel of imperial detectives and pointed. "Take notes, don't just stand there! For Khaos' sake, do your jobs." He clapped his hands and swung his attention to the revenants. "Interview time, people! Let's start with you, shall we? Name."

Xephriel swore he heard Officer Terrance grouch from her side of the garden.

Unlike Noble, Xephriel had to have direct contact with the bones to communicate with the spirits. The finger bone in his pocket vibrated, and Xephriel recognized the connection from that morning. He grasped the scapula of a female corpse.

His mind spun in a whirlpool until a gray mist puffed in his psychic vision. He hovered as an astral projection in the center of dreams and spiritualism. The soul of a girl, no older than sixteen, he would guess, floated in the obsidian realm. Her sunken eyes, as if her sockets had been vacuumed into her skull, stared at him from her mournful place.

"Hello, I'm here to help you." Xephriel kept his distance as a gray haze outlined the ghost. The spirit was in a state of unrest, in a vortex of unholy emotions that sucked at Xephriel's empathy instead of invading it. She was draining, and he was apprehensive about where the interview would lead.

"She should die. Die like us. She should die." The girl moaned, and her haunting words rolled into the realm. Thunderclouds formed around the spirit; lightning clashed in successive patterns as she searched for a way to escape her prison of eternal grief.

Xephriel hovered in the space, arms held up in a cross to protect his psychic form as the storm threatened to ravish him down to his atoms. Dying in the spirit world meant nothing would exist on the physical plane or this one, not even his soul. His body would crumble to dust and float away. He had to get control over the situation.

Xephriel summoned a shield of bones to surround him in a floating circle. The etheric plane allowed him to have contact with his ancestors without it causing his empathy to implode into chaos. They lent their power to him through their spirits. The bones surrounding him were not the ones lying in the catacombs of his family's estate but the raw magic bestowed on all those in control of death. The ghost's hatred, her vindictive cry, bounced off the protective barrier. Xephriel, despite the danger, kept his voice calm so the spirit would recognize he was a friend and not a foe.

"I'm here to help you rest in peace. No one will harm you again. We are gathering evidence to find the person who did this to you. Can I ask you a few questions?"

The girl's mouth twisted to the side, her agony and despair a mask as she regarded him. "Peace. She dies, and I'll have peace."

He watched her through the levitated bones of his ancestors. "I cannot take a life."

"Die. She deserves to die." The spirit swayed in a trance, lost in a relentless void of her last memories of life.

Xephriel put more space between the ghost and his astral projection. "I understand you are in pain. Let me help. What is your name?"

"Eve. Eve Morgan."

"Eve." He let her name linger in the air, so she could hear his sincerity. "I'm going to take your bones to your family. Do you know where they reside?"

"I lived on Market Street with my parents. One bone is missing. The one in your pocket." Her message came in clearer, and her features were less distorted. The storm was less violent.

Xephriel gave a nod of encouragement. "Good, you remember your family." He patted his pocket, though the real bone was still on the physical plane. "I have your bone safe with me. I'm going to connect it with the rest of your body so you can rest in peace. After we reunite your bones, you will be taken to your family. Before I do that, I need you to tell me, who buried you in the well?"

"A witch. A horrible witch. Witch. Witch. Witch. Her skin smelled like garbage. She wouldn't let me go home. She followed me around the garden. She deserves to die."

He did not put any inflection in his tone and did not dare provoke Eve. The clouds and lightning dispersed, and he pressed, "Do you know her name? What does she look like?"

"No. Cloaked in darkness. Her voice was deep. So deep. Deep like the well she dropped me into."

Xephriel kept the torrent of bones surrounding his body, protecting him from the girl's emotions. "Can you tell me what happened? What she wanted?"

Eve floated, the cascade of her despair an overtone in their speck of the realm. "I stepped into the garden to view the roses. She asked me to help her. She wanted to plant a seed. I didn't want to get my clothes dirty. She said it would take but a minute, but twilight was approaching. I heard—I heard a whisper. I don't know what was said. Whispers were all around, and I grew frightened. I tried to leave, but she forced me near the well. I can't remember. I can't remember. Just pain. Pain. Pain. Down. I fell into the darkness."

Eve roared, and her hair fanned out around her as a supernatural hurricane stormed. Xephriel remained safe in his bubble of bones and magic. He held up his hands and shouted over the torment of the girl. "It's all right now. I'm going to guide you to your family. Breathe. You are safe. Let the pain go and breathe."

"Die. Die. She deserves to die."

Xephriel respired calm and collected, even though his heart thundered from the peril. "I cannot kill her, but she will receive justice. We are going to find her, I promise."

The wind gusted with the force of the girl's wail for judgment. She sobbed and said, "It was cold. So cold where I was lost."

"I know. We found you now. You'll be safe."

Eve began to fade, the link to her bones growing faint from the energy she spent. In the ether, her voice whispered, "I heard her say the name 'Elias.'"

Xephriel felt Eve recede from his vision. Opening his sight to the physical world, he brought his awareness back. Amé stood beside him, holding back tears, nausea, and anger all at once. He felt everything she projected as she stared at Eve's bones.

"Rest," Xephriel murmured to Eve, and the bones clattered to the ground. He drew the black box from his pocket and opened it to return the phalanx. A bit of bone magic had the piece fitted where it belonged.

He murmured to Amé, "I can't keep her connected to the physical plane. She's a danger to herself and to others. If we animate her bones, she might tear this world apart in her quest for vengeance. The other victims are our hope in tracing their missing finger bones and finding the killer's residence."

Amé's eyes misted. "That was awful. All I could hear were her words. I can't imagine what it was like for you to feel her in that much pain. We have to find the killer."

Xephriel took her hand. The heart song vibrated between them, and he heard the complex chromatic lines of music harmonize together. The bond between them was getting stronger. Two days ago, he was frightened of the legend come to life, but now he couldn't imagine a day without it. It felt so euphoric. His very soul extolled from the luxury of his empathy. Had they not braved Blood Street together, Xephriel doubted he would have made the leap and activated the heart song. That would have been the greatest loss because Amé gave him the sanctity of a touch. Even if she was his entire world, Xephriel could live in peace.

He twisted halfway so he could inspect the next set of bones. "I've got another spirit to interview."

Amé let go of his hand and sat on the edge of the well. "I'm going to stay in case they give away anything that jogs my memory about a seed sale."

"I can't hear you until I come back to the physical plane, so if you discover something, bring it to my attention at that time." He moved in front of the next animated body.

The woman had an outline of pink around the bones peeking between her festering flesh. Her hair hung in lank blonde curls down her rotting shoulders. He grimaced at the patchwork of decay that exposed her bones and knew he'd get a shock from her emotions. Animation of a body was more magic than the reinstatement of life. Noble hadn't fused the soul and bones together, so it wasn't true necromancy. Xephriel's current reluctance formed because this body was more recently dead than the others. The emotions and the memories would be more pervasive. He steeled himself for the discord that would occur and placed his hand on the radius of her arm between the folds of her decomposing muscle.

A ripple of anxiety and confusion hit Xephriel like a cannon blast. He almost let go but breathed through his nose and let the magic glide through his body. Stuffing down the initial shock wave, he forced his jaw to unclench, his shoulders to cease squirming, and drifted into the etheric field. A nosebleed would greet him on the way back to the physical plane, but Xephriel couldn't do anything about it until his consciousness returned.

He faced the next spirit. This time there was no storm. Potent despair clouded their part of the etheric field, and

Xephriel tensed against the feeling as he said, "May I have your name, please?"

She whimpered, "Miriam. Miriam Parker."

Her depressed resignation broke his heart. Her awareness of the spiritual plane was tangible, and he softened his tone in sympathy. "Miriam, I'm Xephriel Maxis, and I'm a bone witch. I'm here to help you. I have a few questions about what happened the day you left the physical plane. Can you describe your attacker?"

Again, she let out a sigh of resignation, that bleak understanding that she was no longer living seeped from her spirit. "A woman. She had on a mask. Couldn't see. Couldn't see."

Xephriel nodded and fisted his hands as a dose of fear radiated off Miriam's spirit. "Can you tell me what she said to you?"

"I didn't want to go into the garden. I wanted to go home—my kids. My kids were with the nanny. Late. I was so late." The pink of her aura dulled, and gray misted over her spirit.

"Don't worry. We'll reunite you with your family. Your kids will know you are safe."

Miriam's brows frowned in confusion, and she said, "I think she had a deep voice. Low, almost like a man. She smelled horrid. Like rotten eggs."

"Thank you, Miriam. You are doing great. Can you tell me anything else?"

Miriam's features pinched as if she were concentrating with all her might. "She asked me if I was ever in love. She forced me to take a seed. I fell with it clutched in my hand. I was pushed. Pushed and hit over the head. My hand was thrust into the dirt, and then she kicked me. I screamed and screamed and screamed. I don't remember anymore. Just darkness. So much darkness."

"Thank you for telling me your story. I know you are in pain right now, but we are going to gather your bones and take you to your family. You will get to say goodbye, and then you will have peace here."

"I want my children."

Xephriel couldn't cry in the spirit realm, not real tears anyway, but that feeling drenched his soul. "I know. I wish I could give that to you, but a better life awaits you here. I commune with the dead a lot, and most people are happy when they move beyond the veil of the living. You can find peace too."

"The woman. She–she said–" Miriam struggled, and then her words croaked out, "She knew me. Spoke my name when I was in the garden. I went there every Tuesday after work. The Mosaic garden is the most beautiful."

That got Xephriel's attention. "She knew you?"

"Yes. She knew my name. Said Miriam Parker. I couldn't see her face, but she knew me."

Xephriel snatched at the clue, a kernel of hope blooming in his chest. "Thank you, Miriam. It will be okay. I promise. Do you think you could find your fingerbone for us?"

Miriam shook her head no. "I want to stay in the garden, where I feel safe. I don't want to see that woman ever again."

"It's all right. You can stay here until we reunite your bones."

"Thank you."

Xephriel faded from his astral projection and felt his nose dripping with blood. Miriam twitched, her arm hanging off its socket as he said, "Rest." Her body slumped to the ground.

Amé fished in her pocket for a handkerchief and rushed to hold it over his bleeding nose. "You look pale. I don't think you should do any more interviews."

He shook his hooded head and denied her request. "I'm fine. I know when I'm at my limit. Miriam was too close to the living, and it caused a stronger bond between us."

Amé had discreetly picked a bunch of lavender flowers that she inhaled before replying, "Yes, the gooier ones are starting to get to me."

Xephriel pinched his nose, and he sounded nasal when he said, "Did Noble interview the others?"

She slid her gaze to the right. "Yes. He said to let you talk to everyone in case they say anything different."

"All right. Hold on for a little bit more. Once we get through the line, we can start piecing things together." He moved to the next victim, separating his conscious and subconscious, and asked, "Will you tell me your name?"

"I'm Harris Donavan."

Xephriel sat down on a chaise of bones, and the weariness from transferring his essence in and out of his body started to catch up. Even in the spirit world, Xephriel's energy drained. He asked Harris, "Do you know who put you in the well?"

Harris' reply was immediate. "A woman. She said I needed to plant a seed. Plant it for her Elias."

"Who is Elias?" That was the second time he heard the name.

The man scratched his head. "Don't know. Elias, she said. For her, Elias."

"Can you tell me anything else? Why she wanted you to plant the seed?"

"She—She said—" Harris paused and stared into the dark space of the etheric field. His voice came in garbled as he recited, "She said I could make it grow. I had the power to make it grow. All I needed to do was think about who I loved most."

"Did you plant the seed for her?"

"Yes. Like she asked. I tried to leave. She screamed at me. I did it right. I did what she said, but she yelled that I had done it wrong. I shouted back and turned to leave the garden. She stabbed me. She stabbed me in the gut." His features contorted into a rage, and his aura flared red.

Xephriel rose from his perch, preparing for another spiritual storm. "I know you remember your death, but we are working on granting you peace and justice. We'll take your bones to your family."

Harris dropped to his knees and gripped his head in agony. "They'll never see me again."

Xephriel knelt in front of Harris, sensing his anger was not as tempestuous as Eve's. "With death comes loss, especially one that fate did not decree, but there is also hope. Hope that your family can still have a connection with you. Hope they will see you again. The planes of the spirit realm are endless. Don't spend eternity waiting for them, locked in your misery until it becomes a cage. Find your peace here and know that the one who did you harm is being brought to justice."

Harris looked up and pleaded, "Will I be able to tell my kids and my wife goodbye?"

"We will make sure you get all the time you need with your family before helping to bury your bones."

Xephriel made to drag his astral projection through the etheric field, but Harris stopped him by declaring, "I remember she looked familiar."

"Familiar how?" Xephriel asked and hovered in the obsidian space.

Harris frowned and stared at a point behind Xephriel. His face sagged in disappointment. "I'm sorry. I don't know. It was a flash of a memory and then gone. I thought I may have seen her before."

"That's all right. One more thing before I go. Can you sense your finger bone?"

"Yes. Yes, I know where it is."

Xephriel began to fade but asked before the link was severed, "Can you take us to the bone?"

"Yes."

"Thank you, Harris."

His vision opened to the physical plane, and Xephriel instructed Harris' bones to rest. A sharp pain pierced Xephriel's occipital lobe. Amé took his hand, bringing his attention to her worried expression. He entwined his fingers with hers and pulled the cloth away from his nose to show the nosebleed had stopped. Unfortunately, his condition worsened, and his head ached.

"I'm all right. I need a little rest and maybe some lavender."

She past her lavender bunch to him, and he inhaled deeply, hoping the headache would recede enough so he could continue the investigation. Xephriel moved away from the bones and carrion. Noble joined him by a wooden bench, and they sat down to discuss what to do next.

Noble kept considerable distance between himself and Xephriel on the bench. "Are you all right? You look pale and not in the sense that gives us bone witches' power."

Xephriel kept the lavender near his nose and grouched, "I'll be fine. My head hurts, but nothing that won't resolve itself. I need to rest."

Noble looked dubious but said, "All the victims were mortal. That's interesting. We can scratch magical sacrifice off the list. As for the rest of the motivation, it's still a mystery. I can trace the bones. I think you've done enough today. I'll go with the officers and follow the trail to the killer. I need to control the bodies anyway. You and Amé can stay here and guard the well."

Xephriel set the lavender in his lap. "Let us know what you find. Harris is the only spirit I'd clear to leave the garden. He's the most in control. Miriam wants to protect her body, and Eve is a danger to herself and others. She needs to be taken to her family first after we close this case."

"Will do." Noble then leaned over and said to Amé, "Take care of him for me?"

Her answering grin was like a slice of paradise. "Always."

Xephriel watched Noble spring up from his seat and swagger over to the imperial detectives. He swiveled on the bench, so he faced Amé, "You heard the spirits?"

"They were talking on the physical plane, too. There's a man named Elias that the witch loved. One of the spirits recognized her. The witch recognized one of the spirits. She has to be someone these poor people came in contact with a lot. She had to live on Entertainment Street or work nearby. It would make sense if she chose this place as her hunting ground. What's odd is that the art gallery didn't report anything amiss to the Court of Harmony. Surely, a well of dead bodies must have smelled. There must have been complaints."

Xephriel stroked his chin. The stubble he hadn't shaved prickled against the silk of his glove. "Maybe we can figure out the clues while Noble is trailing the phalanges."

"None of the victims mentioned the Taxidermist, so unless we can get to the newest body, we have to assume he isn't involved. I don't want to provoke him further. This all has to connect. I'm certain of it. I don't know how or why." She chewed her nail as she finished her conjectures.

Xephriel rubbed a thumb over his palm and said, "The complications continue to weave through this case."

Amé twisted her gown and bit her lip. "You know, now that I think about it." She leaned her head back and stared up at the cloudless sky. All her thoughts came out at once. "I know I sold a flower mate seed to a man named Elias. It's starting to come back to me. Elias Browning. It's rare for men to ask me for a flower mate. That's why I remember his name so clearly. He bought a custom-made seed and was very happy with it. He came back and told me it opened his heart to a world of possibilities, and he was going to ask a woman if she was interested in courtship.

His face was so full of joy. He was a mortal who worked at the—omg—at the Kaleidoscope Gallery! Xephriel! He worked here."

Xephriel jerked to a stance and ran over to Noble, who had reassembled Harris' corpse in order to trace the killer. He rattled off the information Amé gave him and pointed to the gallery over the stone wall. Noble's green gaze gleamed, and he jumped, clicking his heels together in excitement. Gathering the detectives, Noble dispatched two toward the gallery, and the other three followed him and Harris.

Noble glanced over to Amé. She was pacing beside the bench. He instructed, "You two stay here and guard the well. We're close to catching our criminal. I can feel it."

"Shouldn't one of the imperial detectives stay with us?"

Noble spun in a circle, thrilled at the turn of events. "No need. Order is happening. The picture is coming together! I fear our killer might flee here if we don't catch up with her. You are both on guard duty. Don't let anything happen to those bodies. You are both more than a match for her if she comes here looking to eliminate the evidence."

Xephriel trusted Noble. If his friend believed they would catch the killer, then Xephriel would stay put and wait. He gave one last "good luck" to Noble and returned to Amé's side.

"Noble wants us to wait here."

Amé ran her fingers through her sable hair. "I'll try to think of more details while we wait. I can't believe I didn't think of Elias sooner."

"You were distracted by the theft and the note. Now the question remains, if Elias worked at the Kaleidoscope Art Gallery, did that mean the killer did, too?"

Amé pounded a fist against her palm. "Maybe. We are close. I know we are close to figuring this out."

Xephriel's lips broadened into a smile. "You sound like Noble."

"I should switch my career and become a detective," She teased, but a light sparked in her soil-brown gaze. Xephriel sensed she loved the chase, the puzzle, as much as Noble, and she would not rest until all the pieces of the case fit together.

Xephriel watched Noble sling his jacket over Harris so they could take the animated corpse through the streets of Aequitas with minimal detection. The small group of detectives followed Noble and the revenant out of the garden toward the lair of the killer. Xephriel reached down and instructed the bones of Miriam, Eve, and Mr.

Rendell to rise. He hid them in the corner of the garden. They deserved some peace while they waited for justice. Xephriel led Amé to the well, where they sat and waited for the ordeal to be over.

Chapter 16

Amé didn't have any more information to add to her earlier revelation. Elias had seemed so happy. The flower mate had worked for him and led his heart to find love in a real person. She didn't understand how he was involved with the killer. Unless it went back to envy. If the killer loved Elias and he chose another woman, then perhaps the killer wanted to try to win him back or replace him with a flower mate. The woman Elias wanted to court might have been the killer, but then why would she kill her lover?

She let out her exasperation. "I don't know what else to think at this point. It's all tragic. Noble will find the other finger bones, and then we will have our answers."

Xephriel had abandoned the lavender, claiming his headache was better, and replied, "Are you all right with all the bodies? It's not what you're used to, and I didn't think to ask if it bothered you."

Amé waved a hand to dispense his concern. "I'm fine. It's certainly outside my area of expertise, but I didn't stare at the bodies. The ones that were more–more–skeletal were not that bad. I was more bothered by the fact that the corpses were *speaking*. When I heard their stories, it broke my heart."

Xephriel asked, "Do you want to brainstorm on who might be behind the killings?"

Amé looked down at her shoes. "I believe the witch with the strange red aura is the same witch who buried all these people in the well."

"Why did she leave the other body out in the open?"

Amé wiggled her toes and considered her answer. "True. That doesn't fit, but the note wanted me to come to Blood Street to retrieve the seeds. What if she was leading me there to either kill me or suggest I killed that person? Maybe, she couldn't use the well anymore because the imperial detectives were inspecting the area. I could have been victim number five lined up, except she didn't get the chance to make contact."

Xephriel leaned his head back, his throat bobbing as he mused, "It makes more sense that she was luring you out to be a victim than it does for her to set you up as the suspect. What is her goal with the seeds? With the bodies? Stealing the seeds and killing people doesn't seem to connect."

"There must be a piece of this puzzle we are missing."

Xephriel crossed his arms. "Supposing this all links, why did the witch start threatening you after she killed four people? Why not steal the seeds first?"

"Good questions. I think she was honestly trying to grow the seeds and believed she could if she picked the right one. I was her supplier, if you will. I don't think she initially planned the murders or to target me. She tried four times to get the seed to grow. One seed she must have bought herself, and the other three she purchased under disguises. I find it hard to believe she gave up so easily after one failed attempt and started killing people. Hennley doesn't handle flower mate purchases, but I didn't expressly tell her not to. If she sold seeds to this woman, it is possible that the woman obtained more than the four we know about before the killings. Repeated failures might have started her down a path of obsession. A need to make the flower mate grow no matter what she had to do to accomplish the task."

Xephriel kept rocking as if the motion helped him dissect the problem. "She decided to steal all of them and keep trying until something worked?"

They turned to face each other at the same time. Amé said, "I think so. At that point, she didn't need me to give her seeds. She had them for herself. That must have been when she decided the seeds weren't the problem but my guiding her to the wrong personality type. She probably blames me for selling her dysfunctional seeds. Most disgruntled customers do. She stole them to give herself complete control over the process from start to finish. Why try to lure me to Blood Street?"

"You brought this on yourself, you know." A rich feminine voice, alluring in its almost tenor timbre, droned in the quiet garden.

Amé and Xephriel jumped to their feet and watched as a cloaked woman glided through the hedges. Tendrils of black and gray smoke twined around her like serpents, and a hissing sound from the inky aura further depicted the imagery. "Amé Floreo. Arrogant, foolish. Your seeds took everything from me, and now I will do the same to you."

Amé quailed at the way the witch's magic signature clung to her psychic senses like tar. "Who are you?"

The witch prowled closer, the air ominous and fetid with malicious intent. A stench of death crept from behind the dark clothes she wore, even from a yard away. The witch almost slithered as she moved, like a ghoul trespassing over a graveyard. Her voice was rattling and hoarse as she coughed up a glop of phlegm. "Hah! Do you think I'd reveal that kind of information?"

Amé had to keep her talking and get her to reveal her identity. This was her chance to catch the witch responsible for using her seeds in such a dastardly way.

She watched Xephriel out of the corner of her eye, his body taut as he tracked the witch's movements. Amé coaxed the witch, applying her honeyed customer service voice to glean information. "You can tell me your name. You spent a lot of time trying to get my attention. Surely, you want us to be better acquainted."

A clicking of the woman's tongue signaled she was patronizing Amé's bravado. "I don't think so. I want you to suffer as I have suffered. Elias was everything to me. We were friends for years. I waited and waited for him to ask me to enter into a courtship. I pined for him and loved him better than anyone, even when he didn't acknowledge those feelings. I knew it would take time to break him down, but I was patient and worked tirelessly to show my love. Making his lunch every day, sitting in this garden talking about everything we could think of, and staying late at the gallery. Then one day, he walked into work and asked Beatrice, the secretary, if he could court her. It felt like my heart cleaved in two. I had to listen as he told me, his 'best friend,' how he had purchased a flower mate seed, discovered his heart's desire, and realized Beatrice had been the one for him all along. I nearly choked to death on my lunch."

Amé moved closer to the plants in case she needed to use her magic in defense. The witch stopped at the other side of the well and sneered. Amé said, "It sounds as if you didn't express to him how you felt. Courtship is a way to learn if two people are compatible. At any time, you could have told him about your love and let him decide. Even before then, you could have been blunt and asked him to a court. None of that gives you the right to come after my flower mates and me."

The witch hissed and spat. "You are the one who sold him the flower mate! Your flower mate convinced him to choose Beatrice! He would have been mine if not for you. Whatever witch magic you used placed a love spell on him."

"My flower mates can't do anything except become a temporary companion to the person who nourishes them. There's no spell, no love magic involved. I don't sell anything that takes over a person's mind. The decision he made was already something he must have been thinking about, or the flower mate would have led him to you."

"I don't want to hear your self-important babble! I watched them swoon over each other for months. Finally, I decided to make him jealous, so he'd realize what he was missing and break it off with Beatrice. I purchased my own flower mate and brought it to work. Do you know what Elias said?"

"I haven't the foggiest."

The witch roared, "Good for you. Good for you, he said. He was happy I'd found a way to realize my heart's desires. He didn't notice that the flower mate was a near copy of him. It was clear he had no interest in courting me and never would. I was rejected after years of pining and cultivating a relationship. I was always going to be the best friend."

Amé gripped the oak sapling, ready to launch her magic if the witch so much as twitched wrong. Xephriel had pulled out his grandfather's bone key and appeared wary. Amé pleaded with the witch, "What's wrong with being a friend? There are many kinds of love. You could have cared for him even though you weren't in a romantic relationship. I would have helped you understand the flower mate's purpose if you had explained your situation. We could have found a way to solve your heartache together. Perhaps, you were looking in the wrong place inside your heart." Amé hoped the detectives would return soon, so she kept the flow of dialogue going for as long as possible. "My flower mates can't bring you real love. They aren't real people. It's not possible to change a plant into flesh and blood. I can't make a permanent presence."

"How exactly were you going to help? You and your one seed per person bull shit. I had to go through that little assistant to get another. I stole six seeds that day, and they all failed to measure up. I tried to make Elias grow from my desire, but the flower mate ended up looking like some mutated version. It was never perfect, and I won't settle for anything less than that. After all the seeds failed to grow properly, I got the idea to get other people to plant the seeds for me. I gave different friends money to buy a seed, and they did their best, but the flower mate didn't come out quite right. That's when I took to disguising myself. You didn't even notice I was the same person."

"How did you fool me?" Amé was shaking from the horrible aura rubbing against her own, but she had to know more about the witch in order to save other people from dying. To save herself.

A decaying smell wafted in the air like a gas leak as the woman spat on the ground. The glob of black goo from her mouth oozed over the grassy path like a slug. The acrid density of her magic spewed outward, and she snarled, "The Taxidermist. His skins gave me a new appearance every time."

"No wonder your aura keeps changing. You're a skin walker."

That sickening voice from the woman said, "It all worked out so nicely until that gardener failed me. I thought someone who had knowledge of plants would surely be able to grow one the way I envisioned it. The flower mate died the same as the others, and since he failed me like everyone else, I decided to do something about it. I cut off a finger. The green touch. Isn't that what they say about people blessed with plant skills? I intended to bury the finger and the seed together. I'd tried everything else. Maybe I needed a little magic of my own. I started collecting fingers and studying plant and bone magic. The same thing happened. Nothing. The seeds withered and died."

Amé curled her lip in disdain. "You thought of everything, didn't you."

The woman's hand, gray and gnarled like a monster, crept from beyond the folds of the cloak. A chunk was missing, and dark blood had coagulated around the wound. Amé stared at the jagged outline and deduced Arkon was the reason for her injury. The witch pointed a spindly digit at Amé. "I was going to steal your seeds and make you cry your eyes out. Let you wallow in the same agony as I did every time I watched Elias and Beatrice together. Then I'd use every last seed until my perfect Elias was created. No matter how many people I had to convince to plant it, I was willing to try. Elias started asking me questions. Why didn't I have lunch with him anymore? Why didn't I return any of the messages he sent to my house? Where were Jessie, Margot, and Patricia? They hadn't been to work in ages. Why? Why Why? On the night I killed that whiney girl, he came to my house. I was washing up the finger I'd collected when he let himself in. I'd given him a key long ago to come whenever he pleased, and he noted the blood trail on the floor. He smelled the decay of the skins in the closet. He watched as I peeled the latest image off my body. He demanded to know what I was doing, and so I told him I was trying to grow true love so he would realize how perfect we were together. He hadn't gotten the hint and was still courting Beatrice, so maybe seeing it firsthand would enlighten him. He called me insane and said he would get the imperial detectives. Something broke inside of me. Something that shattered my soul, and before I knew what I was doing, I grabbed the knife and stabbed him. Clarity and insanity warred as he dropped to the floor, begging me to take him to Healing Street. I was in a haze. I killed him. I killed my love. Who was to blame for all of this? You, Amé Floreo. The Taxidermist gave me one last chance to get my revenge. He summoned me last night. I was on Blood Street, watching you. The Taxidermist knows everything that happens on his street. He said if I did him a favor, he'd reward me by getting rid of you for good. All I had to do, was take one more life and scatter your seeds around the body, so it drew the imperial detectives' attention and made you a murder suspect."

Amé's heart almost stopped. The final body was the Taxidermist getting his revenge. A symbol that he controlled Blood Street and all the dealings in his jurisdiction. He hadn't succeeded, and neither would the witch in front of her. "Any minute, the imperial detectives will return from the gallery, and they will arrest you."

The witch cackled and drew a sack from under her cloak with her other hand. "I don't think so. I've got nothing left to lose. When I watched you deal with that witch on Blood Street, I came up with my final plan. Dump the seeds, destroy every memory of Elias, and run. While the detectives were busy arresting you, I'd leave Libra. You ended up here, and I think it's fitting you see what I have planned for your flower mates in person."

All the blood drained from Amé's face, and black dots fuzzed her vision. "What are you going to do with my seeds?"

"You'll see."

"You're no witch. You're a monster," Amé cried and felt her knees tremble.

"You think I'm a witch? You should eat your words."

Amé staggered at the confession. "You're mortal? How is it possible to have all those auras if you have no magic?"

The woman paused, the sack of seeds hovering over the well, and ran her other hand down her side. "Witch skins. I gave four of my employees to the Taxidermist as payment. The skins won't give me magic, but they will give me an aura. The last dreg of life left from the witches who were harvested. Even other witches can't tell the difference." The woman drew a bottle from her pocket and wiggled it so the purple liquid sloshed inside. "I bought this on Blood Street from a potion witch. It will amplify a plant's growth tenfold. It's supposed to make poisons more potent, but it will do the trick for what I have in mind."

Amé decided to abandon her plan of defense and lunged for the enchanted mortal. She was terrified of what would happen if hundreds of flower mates grew at one time. "Stop!" She shouted, but the witch hacked a laugh and dropped the sack and bottle into the well.

Amé shrieked and watched as the seeds fell into the darkness. She was petrified, her mind commanding her to run for the woman, but her feet remained rooted to the spot. Decisions warred within her, go after the criminal who was fleeing the garden or find a way to stop the inevitable magic churning in the well.

The ground vibrated, the intensity cracking the dirt. Amé was knocked over and crawled to the well to gain her footing. Massive roots sprung out and drilled through the garden. An enormous stalk shot out of the well and speared toward the sky. The petals unfurled, the species a combination of every flower mate she ever created, and inside the pistil, six eyes blinked from the anthers. Teeth snarled from the stigma, and the ovary yawned open like a beast's maw.

The carnivorous flower bent its head and sniffed the air for its prey. It swooped down with a clawed leaf, jaws open, and snapped at the woman. Amé dove away from the slapping leaves that attempted to squash anything that moved. The stigma of the flower reared back and shot seeds at the fleeing mortal. Seeds the size of Amé's fist rolled across the garden.

Xephriel covered her from the spitting flower. "What do we do?"

"I don't know! If I use any magic on the plant, it will become stronger. We need–" She stopped and gripped the front of Xephriel's jacket. In desperation, she said, "We need death magic. I need you to kill it."

His mouth hung open, and he garbled for words. "I–I don't know–Amé, that thing is twenty feet in height!"

"Please. I'll distract it and keep it in place while you wield your magic. If you mix your blood into the flower mate, it'll die. I need you to do this, Xephriel."

He clenched his jaw. "I don't think I can. It'll kill me from empathic overload. It's sentient."

"You can do it. I know you can. Your magic is the opposite of mine. It's my blood that makes it come alive. It's your blood and magic that will kill it."

"How much blood do I need?"

"I used a drop when I constructed each seed, but you might need more."

Xephriel stared at the giant plant. "I'm going to have to touch it."

"Retreat if it's too much. I'm sure the detectives have already dispatched a message to the fire company and the Court of Harmony. They must have seen the flower mate from the gallery. I can't guarantee that, and we can stop it faster. I might be able to strangle it with other plants, but that potion is going to work against me. It will mutate the flower mate to the point my magic won't be enough to quell it. A bit of death is all I need."

He debated, his lips pressing together and then softening. After what felt like forever, he said, "All right. I'll do it. If I feel like I'm going to pass out, then I'll fall back."

"Thank you. Try to get enough magic into its system so I can suffocate it or bind it until the fire witches can burn it to ash. I'm going after that mortal, and I'll try to contain her until the detectives get here to arrest her."

Before she slipped away, he pulled her into his arms. Xephriel buried his nose into her hair and said, "Be careful."

She pressed a soft kiss to his jaw. "I will. I believe in you. I know you can help me stop this."

Amé ducked out of his embrace and charged for the woman. The flower mate snarled and snapped at her, but she was wedged behind a fountain. Amé summoned her magic, the peridot aura glowing brighter than it ever had in her life. She was a beacon to all the plants in the garden, including the monster born of ill intent and potion magic.

Sticking out her hand, Amé gripped one of the invasive roots and pushed her magic into the plant. Flowers and vines, grass, and weeds sprouted. Lichen and vines crept over the spider web of roots, and the flower mate turned its attention toward Amé. She gritted her teeth as she sewed vines around the base of the flower mate, holding it in place until she got the mortal to safety. She dashed to another section of the flower mate and did the same thing. Mushrooms popped up, and moss and crocuses made a carpet wherever her feet landed.

The flower mate brought its head down to inspect the bobbing green light that was Amé. More magic flowed from her hands, her aura so bright she could view it three feet out from her body. The flower mate swayed as if in a trance, watching Amé as if unsure whether to lunge or curl up. Amé took the momentary lull in attack to scurry for the woman shivering by the fountain.

"Come on! It's scented your intent and knows you're the enemy. I don't know how long we have until it turns on me, too."

The woman's cloak hood had fallen back, and Amé viewed the twisted features of a skin walker. She knew the madness that infested its host after using the Taxidermist's magic for too long. She had been witness to it in the hospital when she volunteered as a medical herb dispenser. Some skins adhered to the point the doctors had to cut them off, like a dead animal carcass being sheared for its hide. The screams were unbearable, but the insanity of the magic was far worse.

Amé witnessed that infection firsthand now. The woman's skin was thin and gray, splotched with black pox that ate away at her. A black aura pulsed at the center of her forehead. A mystical hole had formed where the psychic vision of a witch would normally be. The smokey texture of the Taxidermist's invasive magic wafted. The woman was gaunt, so thin and pathetic that she wasn't even the semblance of a mortal anymore. Her pale gaze sunk deep into her sockets. Purple and blue-green tinged bags swelled under her eyes. Her nose dripped as if she no longer had the brain function to control her body's hygiene. Her hair hung in sweaty clumps. Tufts of it clung to her scalp as if to prove she was once more than this fishy scab of a being.

The woman's mouth widened, and a silent scream strangled her throat. Her eyes darted back and forth. She clawed at her face, and the skin over the top of her original appearance peeled away.

Amé spied the flower mate, still entranced by her green light, and reached for the woman's cloak. She hauled her out of her hiding spot and then charged across the garden for the safety of the Kaleidoscope Art Gallery. The woman struggled in her grasp, trying to free herself, but Amé held tight.

"I can leave you to that thing, but I'm not that cold-hearted. It hasn't figured out that I'm trying to subdue it. Now move."

The woman dug in her heels and halted their progress. "Let me go!"

Amé watched as the flower mate caught on to their escape. Its dangling eyes blinked in their direction. She

326 • MARY E JUNG

hissed at the woman and yanked her toward the gold rose arches leading toward salvation. "Come on!"

"No!"

"Do you really want to be eaten alive by a plant?"

The woman bit her arm and twisted out of Amé's fist. "I'd rather do anything so long as I don't have to go with you."

Amé sucked a breath through her teeth as pain throbbed where she was bitten. "Are you out of your mind?"

The flower mate roared. How it produced sound, Amé had no idea, but she watched in horror as it mutated. The roots receded and formed legs. It broke the hold on the vines and snarled as the stalk became the shape of a torso. The leaves became arms. All the while, the flower mate's fangs glinted in the afternoon sun.

"Khaos save us," Amé gasped out, and she charged after the woman once more.

Chapter 17

Xephriel had no idea if he'd survive the ordeal of attempting to stop the monstrous flower mate. He didn't have time to contemplate his death as he pulled off his glove and used a jagged stone on the well to cut open his palm. The wound ached as blood bloomed over his skin. Racing for the root of the flower mate, he commanded the bone magic to surge.

The midnight blue of his aura pooled into the atmosphere, shrouding his vision as he reached the flower mate and poured everything he had into the root. "Die," He conveyed his intention.

Nothing happened. The flower mate kept growing. The roots sucked up his blood and slurped down his magic as if it were a nuisance and not a death command. There was too much life, too much power being drawn from the world egg for Xephriel's bone magic to have any effect. It would take an omni-grim or a team of bone witches to kill the flower mate.

He tried again because he wanted to help Amé and because he didn't want to die at the hands of a flesh-eating plant.

Xephriel gathered more of his magic from the depth of his soul. He could hear his grandfather shouting from the ether, but the roar of the flower mate drowned it out. He commanded again, "Die."

Still, nothing, and now the roots were shrinking back and transforming into legs. The flower mate took a determined stride toward the Kaleidoscope Art Gallery. Xephriel glanced behind and spied Amé, racing after the woman who created this mess.

Amé punched her fist into the ground, her aura a blaze of green light as it shot out of her body and into the surrounding plants. Roots, vines, and twigs glowed with vegetation magic and crawled from the garden bed to capture the fleeing criminal. Amé shouted her intentions. The leaves and branches obeyed as her hands directed the plants. She formed a prison of vegetation around the mortal woman. After securing the mortal, she went after the flower mate.

Xephriel felt his mouth drop in awe as Amé used her magic to summon vines and capture the legs of the giant flower mate. She held it immobile. Her face contorted in rage and determination. Roots from the surrounding trees jutted upward and speared the flower mate in the middle. Branches twisted around its arms, holding it captive.

She was sweating, and her face grimaced with the effort it took to keep her magic steady. Xephriel tore off the other glove and bled that hand too. He closed his eyes and drifted into the etheric field. He drew on his ancestral bloodline, calling his magic and family to his aid.

The etheric field vibrated, the strings of the universe plucking to Khaos' tune. A mist settled around Xephriel's feet. Thousands of spirits filled his psychic vision, all from his bloodline, but one separated from the rest. His grandfather. Xephriel listened as the words of his grandfather boomed through the spirit realm. "Let go."

"I can't. If I lose contact with the flower mate, I won't be able to channel the death magic."

"Let go of yourself."

"What does that mean?" Xephriel shouted, and for once, he despised the cryptic nature of souls.

His grandfather was patient and held up a bone. It was the key that was fashioned from his clavicle. "Let go and take off that damn hood. Empathy is a two-way street."

Blinding light overtook the vision, and Xephriel felt pain beyond comprehension. His knees buckled as he came back to the physical plane, and he tore off his hood. He screamed and swore his blood was near-boiling. The skin on his back burned and felt shredded like a current of lightning traveled up his spine. Agony that cut deeper than any knife carved out his soul. He flung his head back as he felt everything at once. Every emotion from the flower mate, the raw intensity of life flowing from the world egg.

His ancestors surrounded him like an army of the dead. His voice roared, his throat raw as he was consumed by scorching pain. Blood gushed from his nose, his vision blinded from a migraine, and nausea rolled inside his stomach as if he were tossed about at sea.

Then everything stopped.

The empathic dissonance.

The pain.

The burning.

It all stopped, and he heard the chant of Amé's magic anchoring him from across the garden. A triad of notes plucked through the etheric field, elongating into a charismatic mellifluous chord. The crescendo of lush music suspended in a majestic fermata. For once, Xephriel didn't mind being devoured by the feeling. Rapturous, the song elaborated until a crescendo of instrumentation permeated his spirit. Shades of blue and green entwined in his psychic vision as alto and tenor voices exalted their duet.

Empathy is a two-way street.

He let the emotions of the heart song, the power of his feelings for Amé, push through the pain, and he directed his bone magic once more. "Die."

The flower mate shrieked this time and began to rot. Black and brown disease ate away at the plant as it curled in on itself. It was all Amé needed. She screamed, sending tentacles of branches to wrap around the flower mate, roll it to the ground, and suffocate it until the vegetation rotted and flaked away. She collapsed, depleted of energy. Xephriel ran toward her, panic overriding the exhaustion creeping through his senses.

He fell to his knees and scooped her into his arms. He buried his face into her mahogany strands and breathed in the earthy scent that always clung to her like a permanent perfume. Mist blurred his vision as her breathing rattled from her open lips. She coughed a harsh, barking sound and wrapped her arms around his neck.

"I knew you could do it."

"Me?" Xephriel wiped his saturated nose on a sleeve and stared into her spectacular brown eyes. "You were like a warrior."

Amé smiled, her teeth showing as she said, "I was really pissed off." She tried to laugh, but it came out as a hack. She sat up and peered over his shoulder. "I'm going to get into so much trouble from the witch council for this."

"It wasn't your fault."

"No, but I bet they suspend my license to grow more flower mates."

Xephriel slipped his fingers along her jaw and bent over so their foreheads touched. "If that happens, I'll go with you to try and rescind the order. You worked too hard to have your work disappear. We'll convince them together."

Amé placed her hands, blistered and soiled, over his pounding heart. "We'll do everything together." She pulled away and rubbed her face, a streak of mud slathering over her flushed skin. She pointed to the woman in the cage of vegetation. "What do we do about her?"

Xephriel looked at the carnage of the garden, and his features grew thunderous. "I don't know about you, but I want answers."

Amé rose to her feet, stumbling as she balanced. He made to rise to help her, but his headache, which he'd been trying to ignore, seared him to the point of delirium. Xephriel fell back, his breathing shallow as he vomited. He gripped his head, and his eyes watered. The pain was so intense.

Amé wobbled on her feet and shouted at him not to move. Through the white haze, the blurring vision, he watched her search the weeds and ruins of flowers. She ripped a plant out of the ground and dashed to his side.

"Eat this."

Xephriel couldn't lift his hands, so he opened his mouth. She fed him the bitter herbs, peppermint, from the taste of it. He swallowed the pungent herbs and lay back, gasping. Amé placed her hand over his forehead, and her aura was so luminous it blocked his vision from the sun above. His pain began to ease, the headache and nausea subsiding, and once again, he could view the world with clarity.

"I can heal through the herbs if they are recently ingested. It doesn't work if it's topical," She explained and cupped his jaw between her hands. "Are you all right?"

He breathed out a spicy breath and nodded. "I am. It still feels like I'm being clawed from the inside out, but I can see, and the headache is going away. Thank you."

Her smile was so beautiful his chest constricted. She leaned forward and brushed her lips over his, and murmured against his mouth. "I'm glad you are better. Can you stand?"

"I think so." He rolled up and felt a wave of dizziness, but it receded, and he managed to rise on his feet.

Amé glared at the imprisoned woman. "I'm getting my answers. Even if I have to beat her with a stick, I'll get her to talk."

"There's the bloodthirsty alter ego I missed so much."

Amé narrowed her gaze, and he wisely made a motion that his lips were sealed. They leaned into each other and made their way to the prison of plants. Placing a hand over the leaves and twigs, Amé parted the space until the woman was visible.

"Who are you?" Amé had a no-nonsense tone, and even Xephriel didn't interfere.

The woman inside the bundle of branches snarled. "I'm never going to tell you."

"She's Rebecca Devonshire, the owner of the Kaleidoscope Art Gallery." The imperial detectives finally arrived, and they had three other people with them.

Amé stared at the woman enclosed in plants and flowers. "Oh, my god."

Xephriel slipped his hood back up and said, "We know how she was able to get away with stalking people. She runs this entire section of Entertainment Street. She had all the resources available to buy as many seeds as she wanted. People trusted her. That's how she was able to hide the bodies and get others to plant the seeds without questioning her motives."

Officer Terrance jerked her chin toward Rebecca. "Beatrice reported to Rebecca that her boyfriend, Elias Manning, went missing four months ago. Rebecca said she would message the Court of Harmony with a missing person's report. When Beatrice didn't hear anything, she went to the Court of Harmony to inquire about the investigation. No paperwork was ever filed, and no records showed a message was sent. Beatrice was too afraid to confront her boss, so she kept quiet. Her coworkers started going missing, and she contacted the Court of

Harmony to put in a missing person's report. Beatrice let us into Rebecca's office, and we found all the evidence we needed to arrest her. Including the location of Elias Manning's body. It was all graphically described in her personal journal."

Rebecca's howl of laughter shook Xephriel to the bones. It was the sound one made when one had no soul. Whatever was left of her, the Taxidermist must have taken. She was a husk, a shell of a being, and death was the only kindness she could receive now.

"We'll take it from here, Miss Floreo, Mr. Maxis." Officer Terrance unclipped a set of thin stone manacles from her belt.

Amé peeled back the branches with her magic, and Rebecca tumbled forward. Xephriel said to the officers, "Do we have permission to take the bones to their family members?"

Officer Terrance gave her consent. Xephriel glanced over to Amé. She looked relieved, as if a world of troubles had lifted from her heart. Sliding his fingers through hers, he brought her hand to his mouth and placed a soft kiss on her knuckles. She peeked up through her lashes and smiled.

"The bones scattered when the flower mate tore up the ground. I'm going to have to collect each piece and put everyone back together."

Amé gave a nod. "Let me know when you are finished."

Xephriel laughed and swung their clasped hands. "Making me do all the grunt work."

The brown in her eyes gleamed as she said, "I recall holding a giant flower mate captive. My arms are killing me."

"You did wrestle a twenty-foot plant into submission, my brave vegetation witch."

She made a fist and lifted her arm to show her rounded bicep. "These arms aren't just for digging up posies." His answering smile felt like it lit up his soul. "Remind me not to get on your bad side."

She leaned into him and rested her head against his arm. "You could never get on my bad side."

As they strolled across the chaos of plants, bones, and mortar, Xephriel believed to the core of his soul that he couldn't either.

Chapter 18

Three months later

The seven members of the witch council stared down at Amé. Their identical calculating expressions caused a tremor through her being, zinging through her bones and frazzling her nerves. Ancient wards written in the language of the first witches glowed in gold and silver around the antechamber. Although the wooden panels and bamboo flooring created an agreeable atmosphere, the iridescence of magic and penetrating auras of the seven most powerful witches in Libra diminished Amé's enjoyment. Even the stunning mural on the domed ceiling, depicting Khaos and the creation of the world egg, did nothing to ease the tension of the meeting.

Amé was summoned to the palace to hear the verdict on her flower mates. Her license had been revoked after the incident with Rebecca. The Court of Harmony sent divination witches into her shop to investigate every nook and cranny. The witch council sent their agents, Amé still had nightmares about them, to sweep her building for illegal magic. When she was deemed safe and of good intentions, the witch council put her on probation until all the cases involving her seeds were closed.

"We invited you here today to inform you of the findings in the recent investigation of Rebecca Devonshire and her misuse of magic." Artaria Veritas, the High Witch of the council, leaned forward. Her dazzling white hair glowed like starlight.

Amé gulped as her aura was brushed by the power of pure white magic. Artaria's pearlescent aura marked her as a descendant of one of the first witch twins crafted by Khaos. Even at ninety years of age, Artaria was beautiful, and her appearance was still youthful. Her midnight blue lashes blinked as she waited for Amé to utter words.

"Thank you for the opportunity to join this meeting." Amé regarded each witch with a healthy amount of respect.

Artaria's lips twitched, and she folded her hands before her in a sage and patient way. "We find you innocent of any involvement in the investigation and your seeds to be deemed a scientific and magic marvel. We wish to grant you a license to recreate the flower mates. Rebecca purchased the seeds of her own free will, she stole them of her own volition, and her obsession was not a direct cause of the seeds or magic. We have found several supporting claims that your seeds changed lives, and love was truly found as a result. Please, accept your new license, and we wish you luck."

Amé almost burst with enthusiasm, but she managed a professional remark. "Thank you. I appreciate the second chance."

"You are an asset to our community. We look forward to your progress and production."

Hesiod Meridian, a miracle witch with a bright blue aura, said, "You will need to read over the procedure we outlined for how you will sell them. We feel a better vetting system will help you discover a wider customer demographic and a healthier one."

Amé stepped forward and received the folder that contained her license and the new practices. She gave a low bow at the waist to the council at large and said, "I look forward to working with you."

"Khaos, go with you, Amé Floreo."

She turned on her heel and departed the chamber of witches. Outside the room, Amé let out a relieved breath. She flipped through the pages in the folder. After a perusal of the stipulations on her flower mates, she headed home. Xephriel was waiting in the Humerus for her news.

Amé burst through the Humerus in a flurry of delight. "The witch council approved my flower mates again!"

Xephriel was assembling a squirrel skeleton while she made her exuberant declaration. He set aside the bones and tweezers and said, "That's great news. I know you were worried they wouldn't issue another license."

Amé plopped down in a chair and drummed her palms on the table. "I'm so excited! They said the investigation with Rebecca was complete and handed over a new certificate. I have to send in a written proposal of the contract, and every customer has to be preapproved by the witch council before purchasing a flower mate."

"That will help take some of the pressure off you. The witch council can vet customers, and you can do your own interviews to help clients select an appropriate seed. Noble hasn't stopped complaining about the smell of Rebecca's house. He said he can still taste the evil of the Taxidermist's magic."

Amé shivered and made a small squeak. "She was foul, but it wasn't entirely her fault. She wore too many skins, and the insanity ate away at her. I'm not in the least bit upset that the witch council stepped in to help. They said the flower mates are a positive contribution to our kingdom, and their initial purpose can work with the right guidance."

"We need more positive energy in this city. According to the report, Noble loves to analyze cases even after they are complete. Rebecca's choice of witch skins is what caused her to lose her mind faster. A mortal skin doesn't contain magic, so the victim hears the voice of the dead. With witches, the magic decays with the skin, so it isn't just the voice of the victim. It's the unraveling of the witch's matrix too."

"I've never encountered a case as bad as hers. Most of the people I dispensed medicine to had a fighting chance at redemption. I wonder what else the Taxidermist did to her."

Xephriel felt a creeping sensation up his spine. "I don't want to find out. I'm surprised he hasn't come after us."

"He sent a pretty strong message to Rebecca and her final victim. Maybe, he believes that's sufficient enough to keep us in line?"

"You never know with the Taxidermist."

Amé leaned against the back of her chair. "No. We don't. We are small fish compared to the sharks he controls on Blood Street. I doubt he's going to enact a new plot for revenge."

Xephriel picked up the tweezers and pinched the ends together. "I hope so. I don't want to get tangled up with the Taxidermist ever again. What else did the witch council say?"

"They said the bodies were all accounted for and buried in their family cemeteries. Mortals were easier to manipulate than witches. That's how she chose the sowers. The skins were a different matter. She even had a journal, although most of it was illegible. The Court of Harmony corroborated that the theft, the murder on Blood Street, and the murders in the well were all done by the same person. The families were given a special ceremony in the castle, and the royal court commissioned a memorial in the Mosaic garden."

"Back to our normal routine?"

She threw back her head and laughed. "Normal. You and I will never be normal, Xephriel."

"Well, you come closer than I do."

She wiggled her eyebrows and said, "I like my witch men weird and unpredictable."

His cheeks warmed, and he was certain the color of his skin had changed to apple red. "From anyone else, I'm not sure that would be a compliment."

Amé leaned forward and slid her hands across the table so she could grasp his forearm. "I love everything about you."

"Bones and all?"

"Bones and all." She glanced at the time and exclaimed, "Oh, no. I've got to relieve Hennley. She's been watching the shop all day."

"I'll go with you."

Amé slid off the seat and said, "I'll be in the greenhouse. I have a few deliveries to wrap up."

"That's all right. I need a break. I can help with the packaging."

They left the Humerus and relieved Hennley, then entered the backroom. Xephriel loved the floral-infused air of the greenhouse. It was larger now, with plants from all over the world. After their ordeal with Rebecca, Amé decided to take a break and renovate her shop.

They knocked out the wall separating the backrooms of their buildings. Xephriel helped expand the greenhouse for more plants and installed the solar panels for the winter season. They designed their interior space as a salon to meet during the day and unwind at night. They moved all their books so that a small library edged the perimeter of the living area, and Amé set up a window arrangement of lavender and sage.

Like all heart songs, their bond grew as they interacted and touched. It was gradual, building on the complexity of their auras and souls until it became an ineffable orchestration every time they were near. It was time to complete the bonding ritual.

Xephriel wanted to ask Amé in a romantic way. They hadn't declared their love yet, but in his soul, it felt right to merge their auras and magic.

After he finished packaging the plants for Amé, Xephriel returned to the Humerus to prepare his surprise. He slid out a box that he had stashed and began his master plan.

He placed silver candle holders in the shape of dragons on the side tables. Purple candles with the scent of lilacs and honeysuckles fit into the sconces, and the tails of the dragons wrapped around the stick. Next, he took out polished turtle dove bones and hung them from the gas-lit crystal chandelier. He set two flute glasses and a bottle of red wine on the coffee table. Across the bookshelves, he sprinkled red rose petals and placed amethyst and rose quartz in between. He even went to Industrial Street for witch lights that glowed from solar power. Those he strung around the furniture. Then he took the black and white roses from the bush outside the Humerus and arranged them in vases.

Once the scene was set, he waited for Amé to find him.

After thirty minutes, she slipped into the room. Amé lifted her hands to her mouth, her overjoyed exclamation flitting through the air and warming his heart.

"When did you do this?"

He rubbed the back of his neck. The hood remained off in her presence since their encounter with Rebecca. "I wanted to surprise you."

"Is there a special occasion? I love the roses."

Xephriel revealed a pink velvet box from his jacket pocket and strolled to where she stood. He cleared his throat, opening the lid to offer his gift. Inside the box lay a bracelet made of alternating dove vertebrae and rose quartz beads. A representation of his love. He lifted the bracelet and presented it to Amé.

"Xephriel, I don't know what to say." Her words came out breathlessly as she touched the delicate bones and gemstone beads.

"It's a symbol to show I'm devoted to you and to convey how I value the love growing between us."

Her chocolate-brown gaze was misted. "Did you make it?"

"I did." He reached for her wrist, which she extended gracefully, and clasped the bracelet. "Will you answer the call of the heart song and bond with me?"

Amé's joy burst across her features like a sunrise on a summer day. "Of course, I will bond with you. I love you."

His heart bloomed with magic that had nothing to do with their witch powers. "I love you, too."

He leaned forward, his hands slipping up her neck until he cupped her jaw. Xephriel lowered his lips and pressed a kiss to her parted mouth. Amé sighed into his embrace and wrapped her arms around his neck. She ran her fingers through his hair and breathed him in. Xephriel never felt more consumed, and he pulled her closer. Amé purred into his mouth as he deepened the kiss, her pleasure vibrating down his tongue and unraveling his senses.

The air filled with static, their energies combining to create a concerto of life and death. He never imagined his world would open up to so many possibilities that he would be able to know the touch of another person. There among the dry bones and enchanted blossoms, he never felt more alive.

Acknowledgments

It takes a team to run a village, and the same is true for bringing a book to readers. I want to thank my entire team for their dedication and amazing work on Blossom and Bone. My editor helped guide me when I waved the white flag for my manuscript. My sister beta reads my work and keeps my author feet planted in the right direction. My formatter makes everything look so pretty. My cover designer makes visual magic. But there are other people in this equation, too. My children are only six and three, but they are so patient when Mommy goes into the black hole of writing. They wait for me to come back out and are happy when space invasions happen again. They have a vivid imagination, and that's a gift I can't replace or replicate. My dear, sweet husband takes on the minions when I'm writing and wields the power of fatherhood. I can't do any of this without his support. My family is very supportive, and I am thrilled to have that cheering squad in my corner.

As always, thank you to my readers who are steadfast in their fandom. I am so excited to go on this journey through my witchverse with you. May the words in each book give you the message you need and the love that blooms in your hearts.

<u>Libra Coin System and Politics</u>

One Gold Libra is equal to $20.00 US dollars

One Silver Libra is equal to $5.00 US dollars

One Copper Libra is equal to $1.00 US dollar

There is no paper money

* * *

Two Queens and Two Kings. Two Mortals and
Two Witches

Court of Mortals and Court of Witches

The Witch's Council: All witches answer to the witch's
council, even the king, queen, and their court.

The Academy of Witches

The Court of Harmony

The Witch Council Agents

The Imperial Agents

The Dungeon Masters

The Taxidermist

* * *

Libra is a mix of a democracy and a monarchy.
It is balanced in all ways.
Good and evil,
people and power,
and justice and judgment

Made in the USA
Middletown, DE
05 August 2023

36155427R00203